CW01456294

PRINCE

OF THE

UNDYING

KAREN KINCY

Prince of the Undying – copyright © 2024 – Karen Kincy

All Rights Reserved

No part of this book may be reproduced without written permission from the author.

This is a work of fiction. Names, characters, places, and incidents either are products of the author's imagination or are used fictitiously. Any resemblance to actual persons, living or dead (or any other form), business establishments, events, or locales is entirely coincidental.

ISBN-13: 978-1-7379251-6-3

Editor: Laura Apgar

Dust jacket artwork: Saint Jupiter Graphic

Hardcover case artwork: Dark Imaginarium Art

Interior illustrations: Just Venture Arts

Page edges: Painted Wings Publishing Services

❀ Created with Vellum

I

I cursed under my breath when I found him, because I
was almost too late.

A man knelt in the bloodstained snow, his head
bowed, his face hidden by his long black hair. His ragged
breaths fogged the air. He clutched his arm with pale fingers,
though that did little to slow the crimson soaking his clothes.

He had to be the necromancer.

I had hunted him down at last. In this snow-blanketed
forest, there was no one else but the dead.

He looked too elegant for the battlefield, with its mud and
broken bodies. With shaking hands, he unbuttoned his black
coat of wool and wolverine fur, which was much too fine for a
soldier or rebel. It belonged in a wealthy gentleman's
wardrobe. He tossed aside the coat and gripped his arm tighter.
Red trickled between his knuckles.

When snow crunched under my boots, every muscle in his body tensed.

He staggered to his feet. "I'm unarmed."

He had a honey-gravel voice that made his words both smooth and rough, and he spoke German without any trace of an accent.

Where was he from?

"Don't move," I commanded, also in German.

His hair still obscured his expression. My fingers tightened around the hilt of Chun Yi, my sword. Its familiar sharkskin was a comfort.

When the wind blew his hair from his face, I forgot everything but him.

Starkly handsome, he had cheekbones so sharp you could cut yourself on them. Dark stubble shadowed his jaw. His lips curved into a smirk, as if he knew exactly why I was staring at him. His stunning eyes glinted a pale, absinthe green.

Looking into his eyes was a mistake.

They were haunted—the eyes of a man who had seen too much, done too much. The emotions in his gaze ran so deep that it was impossible not to drown in them. Worse, he stared at me with what could only be longing.

Tension thickened the air between us. My heartbeat was hammering in my throat.

He kept smirking. "How are you going to kill me?"

"I haven't decided yet," I lied. Lying seemed safest.

"I would prefer your dagger. It looks sharp."

"Sword."

"Ah. My apologies."

I narrowed my eyes. How glib he sounded, like we were in a fencing match, and he had merely lost. But this wasn't a game.

"I know what you are," I said. "Necromancer."

He arched his eyebrows, though he didn't deny it. "Do you know *who* I am?"

"No," I admitted.

"My name is Wendel."

No longer nameless, he was more than just *the necromancer* now. I glanced into his eyes before forcing myself to look away.

"Thank you for telling me," I said, to disguise my unease. "I will make sure it goes on your grave."

He laughed, despite himself. "You won't have to wait long."

"You're bleeding out."

"Very observant." Pain sharpened his voice. His gaze wandered away to the forest. "I might die before you kill me. God, I'm disappointed in myself. What a commonplace death."

I have to save him.

My fingers tightened so hard around Chun Yi that the sharkskin imprinted my skin. To save him, I would have to touch him.

Necromancers were abominations. He could revive the dead and puppet them as his minions. His magic violated death itself.

"May I sit?" Wendel swayed on his feet. "I don't think I can…"

He fell to his knees swiftly, like a glacier cracking. A moment later, he collapsed on his side. His fingers splayed, he reached out and grabbed a fistful of snow as if to claw himself upright. A war dog's stiff corpse lay nearby. Its blood melted the snow where Wendel had fallen. His gentleman's clothing was altogether ruined now.

I sheathed my sword, my muscles shaking with fatigue. "Wendel."

He reached out again, groping blindly, and his hand closed on the war dog's paw. When he shuddered, the dog kicked its legs.

Fear jolted into my veins. I drew Chun Yi and stepped into a defensive stance. The dog climbed to its feet and growled at me despite its ruined, gaping throat. Its fangs glinted in the daylight. No breath clouded the winter air.

I braced myself as the dog charged. Paws pounding the snow, the dog veered for my left arm, jaws wide. I dodged right. The dog remembered its training and spun, nimble for such a huge mastiff—for such a *dead* mastiff.

I retreated, blocking the dog with my sword. The dog leapt high, aiming for my throat, and I brought Chun Yi up to meet him. With gritted teeth, I sliced through the reanimated corpse's neck and beheaded it cleanly.

The animal crashed to the snow. Dead again.

I wiped the blood from my blade and pretended my hands weren't trembling.

Wendel huddled sideways on the ground, his teeth chattering, clearly weaker for having used his necromancy. A widening bloom of blood stained the snow. There was something remarkably like fear in his eyes, but he smiled.

"Well," he said, "it was worth a try."

His eyes flickered shut before he collapsed. I edged closer to him and nudged him with the flat of my blade.

Nothing.

A shiver rippled down my spine and pooled low in my belly. Fear mingled with a dark desire to find out what he felt like.

I crouched beside him and searched for a pulse in his neck. His faint heartbeat raced under my fingertips. His skin was warm and soft enough, like any other person's. Not like a necromancer's. He was still handsome, even unconscious, and even covered in filth and blood. I shuddered and wiped my hand on the snow.

The burning cold almost erased the feeling of having touched an abomination.

2

I didn't want him to die.

Snowflakes drifted from the sky. They melted slowly on his cold skin.

Quickly, I slung my pack onto the ground and took out my healing supplies. He was bleeding too much from his arm. A blade must have nicked an artery, which would be fatal if I didn't help him. I knotted a tourniquet to slow the blood loss, then cut off the sleeve of his ruined shirt. He had been stabbed just above his elbow.

Wendel jolted awake.

He grabbed my wrist hard enough to hurt. His necromancy skittered like icy fire over my skin. I gasped at the shock of magic. His eyes betrayed his own surprise, as if he couldn't believe he was touching me.

When he spoke, his voice sounded more gravel than honey. "Why didn't you kill me?"

His words hit like a punch in the gut and took my breath away.

"Because I need you." I gritted out the words.

He stared at me with such quiet desperation that I couldn't tell him the truth. He clung to my wrist like he was drowning, and I was his only hope.

He wasn't wrong.

"Let me help you," I said.

When his eyes closed, his fingers loosened from my wrist. His hand fell back down to the snow before it curled into a fist.

"Don't take me back to them," he said.

"Who?"

He didn't open his eyes. "The Order of the Asphodel."

"Never heard of them." It was the truth.

Some of the tension eased from his body. "God, it's cold."

"You lost a lot of blood." I wrapped a bandage around his wound. "Can you walk without passing out again?"

"Perhaps."

I helped him stand. Deathly pale, he leaned on my shoulder while we walked.

I had borrowed a horse, a dappled gray mare who waited between the pine trees. Wendel reached out to the mare, letting her sniff him. The horse didn't shy away from him despite his bloodstained hand or his necromancy.

"Do you know how to ride?" I asked.

"Of course," he replied with a hint of arrogance.

He had to be rich. Or at least he came from a prestigious family.

I helped him climb into the saddle. Though his jaw tightened with pain, he didn't protest. I took the reins and led the mare through the forest.

We walked in silence, broken only by the crunch of footsteps in the snow.

"Where are you taking me?" he asked, so quietly I almost didn't hear him.

I glanced at him, worried he might pass out again. "You need a surgeon. There's an army camp not far from here."

"Which army?"

"The Empire of Austria-Hungary."

"You work for them?"

"Yes, for the Archmages of Vienna." On the lapel of my jacket, I straightened a golden flower pin—an edelweiss, the mountain blossom of the Alps. "They sent me to find a man who could raise the dead."

"That's why you need me." Bitterness tainted his voice, impossible to miss. "I wondered why you swooped down like a guardian angel."

My stomach clenched with guilt. "I'm a mercenary, not an angel."

"Tell me your name."

"Ardis."

"I won't forget it."

A thrill skittered down my spine when I turned my back on him—like I was turning my back on danger.

By the time we arrived at a tiny village, the snow fell as thickly as goose feathers. Soldiers for Austria-Hungary had pitched camp on the outskirts of the village. Smoke unfurled from scattered campfires between tents.

Wendel slumped in the saddle. With his head bowed, his long hair obscured his face.

"Wendel?" I asked.

He slid from the horse and crumpled on the ground. I rushed over to him, my heartbeat hammering, and checked his pulse.

Barely there. His skin felt like ice.

"Fuck," I whispered, before shouting, "I need a medic!"

I waited outside the field hospital tent.

The medics wouldn't let me inside. They had important work to do, they said, in a tone that invited no argument. I paced around the camp, polished my sword, and paced some more, feeling utterly useless. I'm better at killing people than healing them.

What would happen if Wendel died?

A knot tightened in my gut. I had heard terrible rumors. You didn't want to kill a necromancer. If you killed him, he would come back ten times stronger. If you killed him, he would lose the last traces of his humanity and become a monster that mercilessly hunted you down in revenge.

Was that true? I was afraid to ask the medics.

Finally, a medic emerged from the tent and beckoned me. "He's awake."

Relief rushed over me. I hadn't failed my mission.

And I was glad he was alive.

Inside the tent, faint light filtered through the canvas walls, supplemented by kerosene lamps. It stank of sickness and disinfectant. The wounded lay on makeshift cots, wrapped in bloody bandages, many of them lost in a morphine haze that dulled their pain. A patient near me shrank back, whispering a fearful prayer, and I knew he must be a rebel. As if I would murder him in a place of healing.

I found Wendel in bed.

He rested against a pillow like a prince lounging on a throne. Even more distracting, he was shirtless. He had a lean, hard body as pale as a marble statue. Scars marked his skin, a crisscrossing tally of all the fights he had survived before. How many times had he been hurt?

Wendel caught me staring and arched his eyebrows. Heat scorched my ears.

The medic glanced at a clipboard. "He's stable for now. The field surgeon repaired the lacerated artery in his arm."

Wendel waved at the bandage. "Am I done?"

"You need another blood transfusion," said the medic. "Without that tourniquet, you would have bled to death in minutes."

"I can't stay."

I crossed my arms. "You passed out. Twice."

The medic nodded. "He needs plenty of fluids and rest. Morphine for the pain."

Wendel said nothing, staring at me until the medic left. "I can't stay," he repeated. "If I stay, they will find me."

"Who? The Order of the Asphodel?"

His eyes burned with intensity. "Yes."

When he looked at me like that, shivers rushed over my skin, an echo of his necromancy on my body.

Holding my breath, I let it out in a rush. "We leave for Vienna soon."

"Soon?"

"Whenever you are well enough to travel."

He swung his legs over the bed. Thank God he was wearing trousers and wasn't naked. "We need to go back."

"Back to the battlefield?"

"I lost something very valuable there." Barefoot, he stood. "Excuse me."

I blocked his way. "No."

Taller than me by several inches, he stared down at me. His close proximity took all the air out of my lungs. I put my hand flat on his chest to stop him from leaving.

Touching him was a bad idea.

He kept his magic restrained; there wasn't even a tingle of necromancy. But I was still riveted by the feeling of his skin against mine. His heartbeat thumped under the palm of my hand and betrayed his true reaction to this intimacy.

Fuck, intimacy? That was dangerous.

"You can't stop me," he said.

His words sounded like both a threat and a statement of fact. He seemed, at best, mildly amused by my attempt to stop him from leaving.

How arrogant of him.

I kept my hand on his chest and pretended touching him didn't matter. "I didn't hunt you down just to let you go."

"You don't even know who I am."

"I'm beginning to find out."

The hard muscles in his chest flexed as he bent closer to my ear. "What do you want from me?" he murmured.

3

His dark voice sounded like a sinful temptation. I clenched my thighs against desire that pounded with every heartbeat. My body had never reacted like this before, though I was hardly an innocent virgin.

I needed to stay in control of the situation.

"I want you to cooperate," I said. "Come with me without fighting, and I will bring you to the Archmages of Vienna."

"Yes, ma'am." But he was smirking. "After we return to the battlefield."

"Not like this." I backed away from him, putting a safe distance between us. "Put some clothes on first."

"Of course. Whatever you say."

He sounded flippant, his eyes glinting, as if he enjoyed teasing me. I glared at him, but he wasn't looking at me now.

You don't even know who I am.

Who the hell was he? He had almost bled out on the battlefield, but he thought he could defeat me in combat. And he wanted to escape the Order of the Asphodel so badly he was willing to once again risk bleeding out.

Wendel dressed in a borrowed shirt and black long coat. He seemed steady enough on his feet, no longer in imminent danger of collapse. I watched him closely so he wouldn't escape, never mind how damn intriguing he was.

I returned to my gray mare, while he chose a raven black one with a wild mane.

We rode together through the snow.

"Tell me more about the Order of the Asphodel," I said.

His expression froze, as hard and brittle as ice. "How little do you know?"

"Next to nothing." I squared my shoulders. "Enlighten me."

"They come from Constantinople, though they claim to be older than the Ottoman Empire itself, and will likely outlast it at this rate."

"Constantinople? I've never been."

"I spent many years there." He met my gaze again, his eyes glinting.

"Why are you running from the Order?"

"Because I refuse to go back. Why do you fight for the Archmages of Vienna?"

"Money."

He laughed. "My compliments on the Hex. It really keeps these rebels in line."

The Hex had been cast by the Archmages of Vienna to negate gunpowder and stop a war. Fighting back, the rebellion against the empire had switched overnight to medieval weaponry and magic. We all had.

Wendel smirked as he kept talking. "Though the Transylvanians have a knack with scythes, pitchforks, and butcher's knives."

I winced. "A butcher's knife got you?"

"Yes," he said airily.

"God." My wince deepened.

"The Hex almost makes me miss guns. I was a good shot, you know."

"Why are you in Transylvania?" I asked. "You're a long way from home."

Wendel's smile didn't reach his eyes. "Constantinople isn't home. And the last time I checked, the Ottoman Empire and Austria-Hungary were allies. Which means, conveniently, we're allies."

"Good. I won't have to drag you to Vienna."

He arched his eyebrows. "You wouldn't dare."

"Just doing my job," I deadpanned.

A bitter wind stung my skin and flung my hair into my eyes. I braided it over my shoulder without even looking.

"How far have you strayed from home?" he asked.

I sighed. "You think I look exotic, and you want to know where I'm *really* from."

Everyone commented on my tawny lion-colored hair and unmistakably Chinese eyes. Some men even coveted me as if I were a rare jewel to collect.

"You have an American accent," he said, switching to flawless English.

"Oh."

"And you're beautiful."

His words fizzed like champagne in my stomach. It was impossible not to react to such a gorgeous, dangerous man. But I couldn't let him have more power over me.

"Don't waste your time on flattery with me."

"It isn't flattery if it's true."

He was still speaking English, and he had a posh accent, like the nobility of England. Was it a deception or the truth?

"You're staring at me again," he said. "And I'm not even shirtless this time."

My cheeks warmed. "You're very pale."

"Blood loss. That, and an inability to tan."

I laughed in disbelief. "How the hell are you still charming while half-dead?"

"You think I'm charming?" He smirked, his eyes glimmering. "And I'm not half-dead. Only a quarter dead."

"I think you're dangerous."

"Right again."

We reached the battlefield.

Wendel dismounted. He strode to a Transylvanian soldier in a bloodstained blue uniform. Snow had begun to bury the body. Wendel placed his hand on the soldier's neck. All the muscles in his shoulder and arm tensed.

The soldier blinked his unseeing eyes before sitting upright.

I clenched the hilt of my sword. My stomach soured.

Intensity etched Wendel's face. "Where is my dagger?"

The soldier stared ahead with clouded eyes. His blue lips moved before a gurgling noise came from his throat. He wasn't breathing. Or perhaps, the air moving through his lungs simply remained as cold as the winter sky.

"Remember," Wendel said. "You tried to kill me."

"The dagger—is by—the tree." The soldier pointed toward a pine. His gaze never left the necromancer's eyes.

"Thank you," Wendel said.

He let go of the soldier, and the man collapsed back into the snow. Dead again.

I swallowed hard. "That was the man who wounded you?"

"Yes," Wendel said.

He had a disgusted, disdainful look, one I had seen before on the faces of cats. He pawed at the snow beneath the pine, then held a blade high—a black dagger with ornate silver engravings of flowers on the hilt.

"This is Amarant. Do you know what that means?"

"No," I said.

"Undying."

Wendel slid his thumb along the flat of Amarant as if polishing away a fleck of blood. Ripples swirled through the black metal, the mark of Damascus steel, an art lost centuries ago. What dark curse imbued his dagger?

Ever since the Hex, hundreds of enchanted blades had materialized on the European black market. The Archmages of Vienna had anticipated this, though not the breadth of cruel creativity—a thousand and one ways to die.

My hand found Chun Yi again. At least my blade was honest metal.

Wendel sheathed his blade. He cut across the snowy field without a backward glance. I followed him through the whippy branches of willows. An ice-choked river flowed through the Transylvanian forest.

Kneeling, he washed his hands in the river with the solemnity of a ritual. Every movement was slow and meticulous.

He wanted to forget, didn't he? Bringing back the dead man.

My throat clenched. I resisted the urge to reach out to him, to care about him. "That water must be freezing."

"Concerned about me?" He held his hands up to inspect them. "Should I be touched?"

"I didn't save your life just so you could die of hypothermia."

His shoulders tensed. "You're right." When he stood, his pale eyes glinted in the light of the dying sun. "You saved my life."

The intensity in his stare took my breath away.

He dropped to one knee. "I swear undying loyalty to you until the debt is repaid."

4

is words sounded formal, as if he had memorized them from a book. I was speechless. Silence stretched between us. He kept kneeling before me, his face inscrutable, his dark hair stirring in the wind.

He almost looked like a man proposing marriage.

Finally, I laughed. "*Undying* loyalty? You're joking, aren't you?"

"Ardis." He had never said my name before. It curled low in my belly. "I would never joke about such a serious vow."

"But what does this even mean?"

"I pledge myself to protect you. I will do anything necessary."

Anything. I didn't doubt that.

"Well, fuck," I whispered.

Bring him back to Vienna. That was my mission. It ended

the moment I delivered him to the archmages. Then I would be done, and on to the next mission. But that never involved him falling to one knee and swearing undying loyalty to me.

When a crow cawed in a nearby pine, I flinched. Fatigue always frayed my nerves.

"Only until Vienna," I said. "I—I have work to do."

"Right." He all but rolled his eyes. "Back to business, killing for the highest bidder. I can help, you know. I'm good at killing."

"That's what I'm afraid of."

His smile was frosty. "Though I prefer to work with the dead."

"Get up." I exhaled a cloud of white. "We're going."

He stood, wincing, and clutched his wounded arm to his chest. "Where?"

"The train in Petroseni. It leaves in about an hour."

"We're riding there?"

"No." I glanced at the sky. "We're flying."

Diesel engines powered a zeppelin skyward.

Wendel closed his eyes and leaned against the wall of the zeppelin's utilitarian cargo hold. His borrowed long coat was slightly too big for him. The sleeves partly covered the white knuckles of his clenched hands.

Was he always this deathly pale?

"You need to drink something," I said. "The medic said plenty of fluids."

"I'm fine." Wendel opened his eyes a sliver. "I'm not going to die."

"Don't. That would be counterproductive."

"You Americans. Always so tactful."

He broke into a smile, his eyes sparkling, and I couldn't help smiling back. "Always."

God, what was wrong with me? This was a mission. He was my target. I forced myself to keep a poker face.

"How long of a flight is this going to be?" he asked.

"About thirty minutes. Do you hate flying?"

He shrugged. "I'm indifferent to flying." He glanced into my eyes. "Is thirty minutes long enough for me to hear your story?"

"Why?"

"You intrigue me."

I fidgeted against the cold steel of the floor. "You first."

Wendel let his head fall back against the wall. "I come from a good Prussian family, but I still managed to inherit bad blood."

Prussian. No wonder he spoke flawless German. The kingdom of Prussia, far to the north, ruled the German Empire.

"Is it inherited?" I asked. "The necromancy?"

He shrugged. "Apparently a great-great-great grandfather of mine had the talent."

"What's your family name?"

His jaw tightened. "They aren't my family now. They disinherited me years ago."

"For being what you are?"

"Obviously." His voice took on a bantering tone. "Your turn."

"My mother came from China."

"And your father?"

"I never met him." I shrugged. "He wasn't Chinese, of course."

Wendel's gaze lingered on my hair. My cheeks heated. If only I didn't look foreign wherever I went.

"I assume your sword also came from China."

"Yes. It's called a *jian*."

I drew Chun Yi halfway and let the light glint off the battered old blade, highlighting the two characters engraved below the cross guard. I couldn't read Chinese, but I knew they must be the name of the sword.

"These are the characters for Chun Yi. Pure Justice."

He raised one eyebrow with an impeccably sardonic look. "And how exactly did Pure Justice happen to fall into your hands?"

"It's a family heirloom." It wasn't entirely a lie.

"Heirloom?" His eyes glinted. "Shouldn't that sword be hanging over a mantelpiece?"

"It was." I paused. "Until I killed a man with it."

That caught his attention. "Did he deserve to die?"

My stomach twisted. "He wouldn't take no for an answer."

"I hope you killed him slowly." Shivering, he closed his eyes.

"Are you cold?"

His eyes stayed shut. "It's winter. We're all cold."

"You lost a lot of blood." I started to stand. "Let me—"

When he caught me by the wrist, his icy fingers shocked me. He was even colder than I had expected. Glacial, even.

"No," he said, in an intense murmur. "I don't need help."

Even after he released me, my skin kept tingling from the memory of his touch. I curled my fingers into a fist.

"If it bothers you," he murmured, "my hands are clean."

"I'm no stranger to blood on my hands."

Before he could reply, I climbed to my feet and left him leaning against the wall. I busied myself by scanning out the window, though I was only pretending to pay attention to how close we were to our destination.

I couldn't stop thinking of Wendel.

By the time the zeppelin landed in Petroseni, the sky had darkened to plum purple. My boots clomped on the landing ramp as I exited the zeppelin. In this Transylvanian town, half-timbered medieval houses clustered around the cobblestoned town square. The most modern building here was a train station of soot-blackened red brick, where plumes of smoke muddled the clouds.

"Ready?" I said.

Wendel nodded. He still looked pale, but at least he was steady on his feet.

The eight o'clock train idled on the track. Its sleek chrome sides gleamed in the last of the evening light, and the sharp aroma of diesel punctuated the air. An elderly man sold tickets inside of a booth

"How much for two sleeper tickets to Vienna?" I asked.

"Coach or first class, ma'am?"

"Coach."

Wendel waved a bundle of koronas in his hand. "First class."

The ticket-seller raised his bushy white eyebrows. "Are the two of you together?"

"Yes." Wendel peeled off a few bills. "A hundred and fifty koronas should cover it?"

"Certainly, sir."

I stared sideways at Wendel. I never traveled first class, since it drew too much attention. None of the other passengers ever looked at me like I belonged there, with my American accent and my Chinese eyes.

Wendel took the tickets, then walked to the first-class cars on the train. "Coming?"

I hurried to catch up as he handed the tickets to the conductor, who glanced between us with obvious curiosity.

"Your cabin is number seven," the conductor said, "down the hallway on the right."

Cabin? Singular?

Wendel offered his arm, playing the part of a gentleman, but I shook my head and climbed onto the train without him.

First class was indeed luxurious, with wood paneling on the walls and elaborate cut-glass shades on the lamps. I slid open the door to our cabin. Two bench seats in paisley velveteen faced each other. I fiddled with one until it folded out into a berth. At least we would be sleeping opposite each other.

If I could even manage to fall asleep tonight.

I folded the berth back into a seat and I sank onto it. My dirty boots looked out of place on the plush carpet.

Wendel walked into the cabin. His face was unreadable.

"Nice little stunt back there," I said.

"Stunt?"

"If you want to lie low, first class isn't the way to do it."

"I always travel first class."

I narrowed my eyes. "How lucky of you."

He slid the door shut. When he drew the curtains on the window, my heart began to pound. The cabin was too small; he was taking up too much space. He sat opposite me and leaned forward, his elbows on his knees.

With a whistle, the train jolted into motion and chugged from the station.

"Who *are* you, Wendel?"

A smile tugged at his lips. "They sent you to find me without telling you who I am?"

"They needed a necromancer. I assumed you were the closest one."

"The only one."

"Are necromancers so rare?"

"Yes." He laughed darkly. "What else did they fail to tell you? How easily they send you into danger."

"They sent me after rumors of a man who could raise the dead."

"Rumors? Nothing of my reputation?"

"I hadn't heard of it."

"They call me the Prince of the Undying."

"Prince?" I scoffed. "Isn't that a little pretentious?"

"Not if it's true."

I laughed. "You're joking."

"Before my family disinherited me and flung me to the assassins, I was once Prince Wendel of Prussia."

5

I stared at him without blinking. "Prince Wendel of Prussia?"

"Yes, a blemish upon the House of Hohenzollern."

"Castles and fabulous wealth?"

"Before I was disinherited."

He leaned back with his good arm draped over the seat. He had a casual arrogance that could only be described as royal.

"Fuck me," I muttered.

"Pardon?" He had a wicked glint in his eyes.

"Nothing." I grimaced. "What did you mean when you said your family flung you to the assassins?"

"The Order of the Asphodel is, above all else, a society of killers. My necromancy makes me invaluable to them. They first gave me the name the Prince of the Undying."

"No wonder they want you back."

"I don't belong to them."

I exhaled hard. "I don't want to fight them. An ancient society of assassins sounds like a really bad day."

"Ardis, do not doubt me. I promised you that I would protect you."

Tension thickened the air between us.

When I stood, he followed suit. The train swayed along a curve in the tracks, and I stumbled against him. I braced myself with both hands on his chest. He had the unexpected scent of rain on pines.

"Ardis," he said again, more gently.

He tilted his face as if he were a breath away from kissing me. His lips parted. His beautiful eyes smoldered with intensity.

Desire uncurled inside me. My heartbeat pounded between my legs.

A prince. I was touching a prince.

"I have no reason to trust you," I said.

"Then I will win your trust."

He sounded so earnest it scared me. He would never forget his vow of undying loyalty.

"Fuck." I sank back onto my seat. "I never should have taken this job."

"Why do you kill for profit?"

His question knocked me off balance. "I need the money. Not everyone can be fabulously wealthy. What's your excuse?"

He shrugged. "I don't get paid."

"Killing is a labor of love?" That sounded much too callous, and I regretted it.

Icy emotion froze in his eyes. "A matter of survival."

"Then we understand each other," I said.

The cold in his eyes melted. He seemed to be studying my face, and I felt my cheeks betray me with a blush.

"You are more than simply a mercenary."

"Are you more than a necromancer?"

He looked away. "I wish to be."

The warm glow of the dining car contrasted with the wind-driven sleet outside the train's windows. I leaned back in my chair, my spine aching, and relished this hard-won moment of rest. The polite murmur of conversation and the clink of silverware on porcelain were a far cry from the sounds of the battlefield.

"Ma'am?" said a waiter. "Could I start you with something to drink?"

"Just water," I said. "Thank you."

"Very well, ma'am. Please let me know if you need anything else."

I had to admit, I could get used to this first-class service.

At the table nearby, a woman wrapped in furs giggled at her companion, a portly man in a top hat. I doubted they had started their journey in Transylvania. More likely they were just passing through on their way to Budapest. They likely couldn't even see the rebel skirmishes from the railways.

Where was Wendel?

I hadn't seen him since our conversation in the cabin, when

he had excused himself and vanished elsewhere on the train. I could only hope he hadn't passed out, considering how he was still looking poorly.

"May I join you?"

I glanced up, armed and ready with a sarcastic comment—but it wasn't Wendel.

A slender man with sandy curls and a neatly trimmed beard stood there. He wore a well-cut charcoal suit with an edelweiss pin at his lapel. He looked a bit sunburned, and I wondered if he had been somewhere faraway.

"Oh," I said, "yes, I suppose so."

"Allow me to introduce myself." The man smiled at me and bowed. "I'm Konstantin Falkenrath. And I didn't mean to be so presumptuous, but I'm afraid this dining car is rather popular at this time of night."

"It's fine." I unfolded my napkin. "I haven't ordered yet."

"Are you dining alone?" Konstantin said.

I hesitated, then wondered why. It wasn't as if Wendel and I were going to dine together every night, or at all.

"Yes," I said. "Please, sit. And my name is Ardis."

"What a pretty name." His eyes were sky blue, a shade that reminded me of summer. "*Ardis* is derived from the same root as *ardent*, if I'm not mistaken."

"I wouldn't know."

I had chosen the name because it sounded right. But even after living for three years as Ardis, I would never forget my birth name. I was still Yu Lan inside, which translated to Jade Orchid, the Chinese word for the magnolia flower.

"Where are you from?" Konstantin said.

"America." That was vague enough.

"Oh? Which part?"

Chinatown, San Francisco was the place I called home. Whenever I stood in the street, I would breathe in the confused perfume of fried restaurant food and cigar smoke and ever-present sandalwood incense.

I blinked away the memories. "California."

He nodded. Thankfully, he didn't question me more.

The waiter returned with my water. "Anything for you, sir?"

"I'll have a gin and tonic." Konstantin didn't even look at the menu. "And I hear the asparagus and trout are excellent tonight."

"And you, ma'am?" said the waiter.

I stared at my menu, but it might as well have been written in ancient Greek. "The asparagus and trout as well."

"Good choice." Konstantin had a warm smile, the kind that made me return it.

I glanced at his edelweiss pin. "You work for the archmages?"

He steepled his fingers on the table. "I *am* an archmage."

I sipped my water to disguise my surprise. The man sitting across from me was one of my employers. Though I couldn't remember hearing of Falkenrath.

"Or I will be," he admitted, "once I arrive in Vienna. Then it will be official."

I raised my eyebrows. "You must be one of the youngest archmages there."

He looked down at his fingers. "Is it that obvious? I had hoped the beard would help."

"It does."

He stroked his goatee and made a face. "Do you think I should aim for long and gray?"

I laughed. "No."

"I have a few good decades left in me before that, I should hope."

I cocked my head. "I'm curious where you got that sunburn."

The waiter returned with Konstantin's gin and tonic. He sipped the drink before he smiled. "The Dodecanese."

"The what?"

"The where."

Konstantin flipped the menu over. On the back, there was a map of European railways. His fingertip rested on the Mediterranean.

"There," he said, "in the Aegean Sea. Twelve marvelous islands called the Dodecanese. The water there is a remarkable turquoise." He furrowed his brow. "Unfortunately, of course, the islands are still occupied by Italy."

"Why were you there?" I asked.

He broke into a boyish grin. "The Hex."

"I thought the Hex covered only Austria-Hungary?"

"Last year, when Italy invaded Tripoli, the Ottoman Empire turned to us for help. The archmages pledged their aid to extend the Hex." He ran his finger along the borders of the Kingdom of Serbia. "Everyone keeps fighting like dogs over the scraps of the Ottoman Empire. We will muzzle them until they obey."

Sipping my water, I almost choked.

Wendel stood in the doorway of the dining car. He narrowed his eyes at me before shaking his head and exiting the car.

What the hell was he doing lurking in the shadows?

The waiter delivered our plates with a flourish. On each, a tiny filet of trout rested in a sea of sauce, with no more than six grilled spears of asparagus on the side. Tender white asparagus, the kind they called *spargel* in German.

It was hardly a dinner. I resisted the urge to sigh.

"Believe it or not," I said, "I work for the archmages."

"Is that so?" Konstantin shook his napkin loose. "Please, tell me more."

"I'm a mercenary."

"The rebels in Transylvania really are troublesome, aren't they?"

I impaled a spear of asparagus on my fork. "Not so much after you behead them."

Konstantin laughed nervously. "Beheadings are hardly proper dinner conversation."

"You asked." I finished my trout in one bite.

"It was a rhetorical question."

I stared at my empty plate. "If I can speak freely, I'm not sure we're winning. More and more of the Transylvanians have learned how to fight with bows and spears. I'm even seeing decent swords out there."

Konstantin dabbed at his mouth. "An unfortunate consequence of the Hex."

"'Unfortunate consequence' isn't how I would put it."

He looked directly at me, his eyes keen with interest. "And how would you put it?"

Better not to insult one of the architects of the Hex. "There will be a war, and all the magic in the world can't stop it."

Konstantin sipped his gin and tonic. He peered out the window as we rocketed through the dark forests of Transylvania.

I dropped my napkin on the table. "I'm afraid I'm done for the night."

"No dessert?"

I shook my head, since I suspected it would be equally minuscule.

"Then good evening," he said. "I hope to see you again."

I mustered a polite smile. "Thank you for the company."

On the way back to our cabin, the train rattled over a bridge, and my meager dinner squirmed in my stomach. The train's staff had converted our seats to berths and even left a mint on each of our pillows.

Fancy. I tossed a mint into my mouth.

The door to the tiny bathroom stood ajar. I rapped on the wall.

"Yes?" Wendel said.

"It's me." I peeked inside.

He was bent over the sink, bracing himself with his hands, breathing shallowly. He stared at his own reflection in the mirror. Pain etched his face, and I discovered why. His wound was bare and bleeding again.

6

Wendel met my eyes in the mirror. "Ardis."

"What are you doing?"

"Doctoring myself." He held out his hand. "Could you pass me the alcohol?"

Ugly black sutures ran the length of his wound, and blood still seeped past the stitches and trickled down his arm.

"The alcohol?" he repeated. "To clean the wound?"

"You don't use alcohol to clean wounds. It's too strong."

"Oh?"

"Why did you take the bandage off?"

His outstretched fingers twitched. "The medic told me to apply a new one."

"On top of the old one." I shook my head. "You haven't stopped bleeding yet."

He lowered his head and made a noise like a growl. "I'll fix it."

"No." I grabbed the first aid kit from the counter. "I'm taking over."

"I said, I'll—"

"Shut up and let me do this before you pass out."

"I'm not going to—"

I dabbed at the wound with a damp towel. He sucked in his breath with a hiss.

"I doubt you have any more blood to spare," I said. "I'm impressed you lasted this long without keeling over."

His face hardened. "You underestimate me."

I refused to be intimidated by him. "Hold still."

"I am." He glared at me. "It's this train swaying back and forth."

I finished cleaning the blood, then washed my hands. Pink water swirled down the drain. I wrapped another bandage around his arm. He clenched his hands, grimacing, but he let me continue.

"Are you always this sadistic?" he asked.

"Are you always this delicate?"

He scowled. "I'm so glad you aren't a nurse."

"Me, too."

His scowl deepened. "How was dinner with the archmage?"

"Do you know him?"

He snorted. "I think not."

"Then how could you tell—?"

"Anyone who stinks of so much foul magic must be at least an archmage."

"A necromancer, complaining of foul magic?"

Disdain cooled his eyes. "The archmages toy around with spells and tricks memorized from books. Necromancy is a natural magic."

"There's nothing natural about raising the dead."

"Natural meaning inborn. Inherited." He let out a long, slow breath. "Though I know you think necromancers are monsters."

My stomach twisted. It was the truth, but not the whole truth.

"Believe me," he continued, "the Archmages of Vienna hate necromancy more."

"What will they do with you?"

"I don't know."

It was dangerous to care about him. To feel *anything* for him.

I fastened the bandage and stepped back to inspect my work. He looked at his ghostly reflection in the mirror.

"Damn cold in here," he mused.

When the train jolted on the tracks, he stumbled forward and caught himself on the sink. He didn't look like he was going to stay upright much longer. I held his elbow and helped him lie down on his berth.

"Not going to pass out?" My voice didn't have much bite in it.

He mustered enough strength for a sarcastic smile. "God, maybe I will. This berth is comfortable. And look, two pillows."

"Hell no," I muttered. "I recognize a trap when I see one."

He laughed. "Good night, Ardis."

I escaped into the bathroom, locked the door, and splashed my face with cold water. Gasping, I stared at myself in the mirror. I could do this. I could last until Vienna without surrendering to this forbidden temptation.

The train rattled further into the forest and deeper into the gathering night. I rested in my berth while Wendel slept. He wasn't wearing a shirt, and his body looked like fine marble in the moonlight.

He had tossed off his blankets despite the chill. Was he feverish?

In the back of my mind, a thought lingered like a primitive fear. Don't close your eyes with a necromancer nearby.

Exhaustion muddled my thoughts. My eyelids drifted lower.

"Ardis."

A screeching hurt my ears.

"Ardis!"

I jolted upright. Fully awake.

Wendel stood by the window, the curtains clenched in his fist. The screeching had to be the train's brakes. I jumped down to the floor.

The train lurched to a halt. I stumbled. He caught my arm to steady me, but momentum flung us both into his berth. He fell onto his back with me straddling him. His eyes darkened, his pupils blown.

Oh, God.

Heat rushed through my body. He was right there between my thighs. His cock began to harden beneath me in an instant.

Oh, *God*. He was bigger than I expected, and I fought the urge to rock my hips.

"Ardis," he rasped.

I leapt off him as if scalded. "Sorry!"

He cleared his throat, though he still sounded hoarse. "I'll live."

I might die of mortification first.

"What happened?" I remembered how to breathe. "Why did we stop?"

He looked out the window, where moonlight poured over the forest. "We must have found one of the holes in the Hex."

"Holes? I thought those didn't exist."

He smiled thinly. "Ah, but I heard gunshots."

There was a definite note of satisfaction in his voice, like he was pleased that the magic of the archmages had failed in this area.

"Get dressed," I said. "We're going outside."

"Yes, ma'am," he said sardonically.

Wendel buttoned his shirt and shrugged on his long coat. I laced my boots, grabbed my sword, and hurried out the door. I glanced back just as he slipped his strange black dagger into the pocket of his coat.

In the hallway, a conductor stopped us. "Ma'am, sir, there's no cause for alarm."

"Gunshots?" Wendel sounded gleeful.

I held up a hand. "I'm a mercenary with the archmages, and it sounds like there's been a problem with the Hex here."

The conductor hesitated, but stepped aside.

"Impressive," Wendel said. "You pull off the voice of authority well."

I marched down the hallway and entered the swaying passageway between cars. I slid open the door and walked onto the narrow steel platform just as the train chugged to a halt, hissing and puffing diesel smoke.

Beside me, Wendel leaned over the railing. "So that's why we stopped."

I peered into the darkness. The headlights of the train illuminated a truck parked directly across the tracks. A scattering of people stood around the truck, the unmistakable silhouettes of guns in their hands. The beams of their flashlights and lanterns crisscrossed the chilly fog.

"Rebels," I said. "Do they think they can hijack this train?"

"Apparently. There *are* a lot of wealthy passengers on board."

"And the archmage."

"Oh?" He gave me a look. "Don't tell me you plan to protect him from those—"

"*We* will. You work for me now, remember? And you better be good for a fight, because it looks like they want one."

He sighed a long-suffering sigh. "Whatever you say."

One of the conductors hopped off the train and landed in the snow. He approached the rebels with his hands held high. His words were unintelligible to me. The rebels aimed their lights at the conductor's face. Then their guns.

"What is he doing?" I muttered.

"Negotiating?" Wendel suggested.

"I count seven rebels. And it looks like all of them have guns."

"Seven?" He shrugged. "Just signal when you plan to attack them."

"What do you propose?" I stared sideways at him. "Show ourselves and get shot?"

"Who said anything about showing ourselves?"

After a shout, a gunshot cracked in the night. The conductor crumpled in the snow, blood spreading beneath him.

"That sounds like a signal to me," Wendel said.

He leapt over the railing and hit the ground running.

"For fuck's sake," I whispered.

Wendel loped across the snow, straight into the darkness of the trees. I jumped after him. My boots fractured the hard crust of ice on the snow, and I dropped into a crouch, still hidden from the rebels.

The rebels were walking nearer, though, along the length of the train.

Wendel reached into his coat and drew the black dagger. With a hissing whisper, tendrils of smoke crawled from Amarant and curled around his arm, his body, his face. His outline faded to nothing more than a shadow.

My breath snagged in my throat. I had never seen such dark magic.

Nearly invisible, the necromancer stole along the edge of the trees. I lost sight of him, and followed his footprints in the snow. He circled around behind the rebels and crept nearer through the forest.

What was he doing? Did he think he could outmatch seven men with guns?

7

I tightened my grip on Chun Yi, ready to fight or flee if the rebels tried to corner me. Flashlights swung in my direction. I flattened myself against the cold steel of the train, holding my breath so it wouldn't steam the air.

Wendel lurked behind a rebel man with two pistols. The rebel turned his head. In one sweeping lunge, Wendel smothered the rebel's mouth and slit his throat. Blood spurted from the rebel's neck and splattered the snow. He collapsed. Wendel knelt, never lifting his hand from the rebel's mouth.

Shadows from the black dagger swarmed thick and dark over Wendel's skin.

He raised the man from the dead.

The corpse staggered to his feet. Blood slicked his chest. His pistols thudded in the snow. Wendel snatched both guns, then vanished into the shadows. The dead man stood waiting for his command.

The Prince of the Undying.

The name suited Wendel. He fought with such elegant brutality it took my breath away.

The rebel captain shouted in Romanian, and it took me a moment to understand. "Search the train! Take no prisoners."

Maybe they didn't know about Konstantin, and only wanted to send a message to Austria-Hungary at the cost of innocent lives.

"Ardis." Wendel's footsteps crunched the snow behind me. "Are you a good shot?"

"I'm American, remember?"

Cloaked in unnatural shadows, his smile had a sinister beauty. He tossed me a pistol. I caught it and sheathed my sword.

"Only six rebels left," Wendel said, "now that one of them is mine."

"We're still outnumbered."

"They won't see us if you stay close to me."

A rebel raised a lantern in the face of the dead man. Light revealed red on white, blood dripping into snow.

The rebel stumbled back. "Captain! Luca is hurt!"

Wendel let out his breath.

The dead man—Luca—swung his arm at the rebel and knocked him off his feet. The rebel flew back, skidding across the snow, and the lantern flickered out. The five other rebels ran to his side.

"Keep back," their captain commanded. "Luca isn't hurt. He's dead. Walking dead."

Luca swayed on his feet, then charged the rebel captain.

Three gunshots to the chest didn't stop the undead man. He plowed onward as the rebels shouted and scrambled out of his way. At last, the captain had the idea to unsheathe a brutish saber. Without ceremony, he severed Luca's spine.

The dead man thudded on the ground.

"Necromancy," said the captain.

I hefted the pistol in my hand and judged the distance to the rebels. They clustered together now, their guns cocked and loaded.

Killing Luca might have been a bad idea.

"Take out as many as you can," I said. "When they return fire, we take cover."

Wendel swapped his dagger and his pistol in his hands. The shadows hiding him swirled like storm clouds. "Ladies first."

I leaned out from behind the train and sighted down the barrel of my pistol. I aimed for the captain's head.

It had been a year since I last fired a gun.

I squeezed the trigger.

My shot went wide, hitting the captain in his shoulder, but it was enough to stagger him. Wendel shot twice. A miss, then a crippling hit. The remaining five rebels returned fire. Bullets ricocheted off the sides of the train and buried into tree bark. I dove into the snow and crawled under the train.

Wendel slid after me. He dropped his gun.

"What are you doing?" I hissed.

"Take my hand. Trust me."

I already trusted him. Why? I didn't know, beyond an instinct deep in my bones, but that was enough for me to obey.

Shadows crawled from his skin to mine and slithered over

my body. It felt like being dunked in cold water. The darkness covered my face, and I gasped, claustrophobic for a second. My vision rippled before returning grayer than before. When I looked at my own hands, they were all but invisible.

The rebels ran toward us, their boots kicking up bloody snow.

"Find them!" their captain shouted.

"Don't let go," I whispered.

Wendel's hand tightened. "I won't."

His voice sounded so protective, I shivered. No one had ever taken care of me like this before. I always fought alone.

Flashlights shone under the train, just to the right of our hiding place, then swept closer. Wendel scrambled out on the other side and pulled me with him. We ran along the train. I peeked between the cars.

A rebel looked in my direction. His gaze slid right over me.

I raised my gun and shot the rebel square in the chest. Before he even had time to fall, I was running away with Wendel.

Four rebels left. Including the captain, if he wasn't too wounded to fight.

"Slow down," Wendel whispered.

"Why?"

"Too loud."

"Too late for that."

I darted between the cars, sighted a rebel, and fired. My pistol jammed. I tossed it aside and unsheathed Chun Yi. The rebel fired his rifle, missing wildly, and I dropped Wendel's hand. Shadows vanished from me before I launched into an attack.

The whites of the rebel's eyes gleamed.

I drove Chun Yi into his heart and kicked the rifle from his hands. Wendel swooped in and, with a kind of macabre grace, touched the man as he died. The rebel never hit the ground; he never breathed again.

Life flickered from the man's eyes, replaced by the flat gleam of death.

"Attack them," Wendel told his minion.

The undead man advanced at a shambling run and turned on his former comrades. The captain hacked at him with his saber, but it took several swings before he felled the undead.

Three rebels left. They started to panic.

"Find the necromancer!"

"I don't see him anywhere, Captain."

"God, do you hear the crows?"

The whooshing of wings and caws foretold the arrival of the sleek black birds. A murder of crows perched in the trees. They surrounded the necromancer. Shadows tattered and fell away from him.

The rebels crossed themselves and gibbered prayers. Their captain stared at Wendel, transfixed, like a mouse before a viper.

"Run," I said, "or we will kill you all."

Wendel spread his arms. "And I will bring you back."

The rebels fled to their truck. They leapt inside the cab, gunned the engine, and roared off the railroad. Slush sprayed beneath the tires. The truck fishtailed and careened until it found the gravel road, then sped into the night.

I grinned at Wendel, giddy from our victory. "We won."

He smiled back, still breathing hard. Crows wheeled overhead. The sulfuric tang of gunpowder lingered in the air.

"So many crows," I said. "I wonder why."

He cocked his head. "You haven't heard the stories? Crows are an omen of evil. When you see them, death isn't far behind."

"They can sense your necromancy?"

"Yes." He smirked. "If it were up to me, I would have chosen a quieter omen."

When Wendel walked back to the train, I followed without thinking, like I had followed his lead in battle.

"I'm impressed," he said.

"By what?"

"You fought well."

Adrenaline still sang in my blood. My muscles were shaking from unspent energy. When he touched my shoulder, I stopped and stared at him. Waiting. My mind stopped functioning with him so close.

Thank you. Say thank you.

"Ardis," he murmured.

By the light of the moon, his eyes looked smoky green on the edge of gray. Why was he so heartbreakingly beautiful? His gaze raked my body before lingering on my mouth. His lips parted though he didn't speak.

Tension froze between us like ice.

It shattered when I kissed him.

He returned the kiss with hard ferocity, as if he still wanted to defeat me in combat. His fingers twisted in my hair and held me exactly where he wanted me. His other hand pressed into the curve of my lower back, a possessive imprint over my spine.

He wanted to conquer my body.

I gripped his shirt with my fists and held on. When I arched my hips, desperate to find his hard cock, he growled and trapped me against the train. The heat of his body scalded mine and overrode the feeling of cold steel.

The crows took flight, cawing, and whirled overhead.

We jolted apart. My heartbeat was pounding. Every muscle in his body tightened like those of a predator about to spring.

A man stood on the train platform and stared down at us.

Konstantin.

8

The cold night air did little to cool my burning face. How much had Konstantin seen? Why had I been so reckless?

"Release her," Konstantin commanded.

Wendel retreated with a sneer of disdain. "Where were you, archmage? Sleeping? Did you have sweet dreams?"

"Silence, necromancer."

"I don't do tricks on command."

"Stop." I stepped between them. "Wendel, we're not here to pick a fight. We barely got out of the last one alive."

Wendel snorted. "The *guns* did add an element of challenge to the battle."

"A minor imperfection in the Hex." Konstantin waved away his comment. "A structural repair of the underlying magic shouldn't take me more than an hour to implement. In fact, I should start work on that immediately."

Wendel swept his arm into a parody of a bow. "Good luck, archmage."

He vaulted onto the platform and vanished inside the train. I climbed the stairs, but Konstantin blocked my way. He touched my arm with a concerned look.

"Are you all right, Ardis?"

"I'm fine."

"Did he force himself on you?"

God, he had seen the kiss.

I wanted to cringe, but I squared my shoulders instead. "It was my fault. I won't be so unprofessional again."

He studied my face. "Why didn't you tell me you were the one tasked with bringing the necromancer to Vienna?"

Surprise jolted me in the gut. "You knew?"

"I requested him."

"But why?"

"His necromancy may prove invaluable to the Archmages of Vienna."

"Am I allowed to know more?"

"That's confidential, I'm afraid."

They trusted me enough to find the necromancer, but nothing beyond that.

"Understood." I clasped my hands behind my back. "Though I'm curious why you need the Prince of the Undying."

Konstantin's sharp intake of breath wasn't lost on me. "*He's* the Prince of the Undying?"

"That's what he told me. Prince Wendel of Prussia, from the House of Hohenzollern, though he was disinherited by his family."

"That makes him more dangerous. He's a man with nothing to lose."

"Can you tell me about the Order of the Asphodel, or is that also confidential?"

Frowning, Konstantin rubbed his beard. "Rumors describe the Order of the Asphodel as an ancient society of assassins, with a particular interest in black magic. Officially, the Archmages of Vienna deny the existence of the Order of the Asphodel, though unofficially, it's something of an open secret."

"They want Wendel back."

Konstantin's frown deepened. "Back?"

"He's running from them. I don't know why."

"Find out and tell me."

"Yes, sir."

Konstantin turned to go. "Ardis? Don't trust the necromancer."

"I won't." The words tasted bitter in my mouth.

Lingering, I watched the dawn. Railway employees had started hacking at the frozen earth to dig graves for the dead. One of the men covered their fallen conductor's eyes, but left the rebels to stare at the sky.

Wendel wasn't in our cabin. After checking the dining car, I ventured into the lounge car. Judging by the forest green carpet, leather chairs, and lingering scent of cigars, the lounge was meant to be a bastion of masculinity.

Wendel sprawled in a chair, a glass of green-gold liquid in his hand. "Please, sit."

My heartbeat started to pound when he glanced at my mouth. Remembering our kiss? Or imagining something less innocent?

I didn't want to get too close to him.

"What are you drinking?" I asked.

He lifted the bottle to his face to inspect its contents. The color of the liquor within resembled his eyes remarkably. "Absinthe."

"Why?"

"You heard the medic. Plenty of fluids."

"Alcohol isn't a good idea."

"Why not?" He sipped his drink. "It helps to dull the pain."

Why was I holding my breath? It escaped me in a sigh. I took the bottle of absinthe from the side table, then helped myself to a glass. The absinthe scorched my throat and I winced at the burn of alcohol.

"Not bad," I rasped, swallowing back a cough.

"Brave of you." He dipped his head. "I never drink absinthe straight."

I glanced at his glass. His drink was paler than mine. I spotted a bowl of sugar cubes on the table, alongside a carafe of ice water and a slotted silver spoon. Right. Drinking absinthe properly was almost a ritual.

"I never drink absinthe," I admitted.

His eyes glinted when he smiled. "An absinthe virgin?"

My cheeks heated at his choice of words. Time to change

the subject before this went too far. "Why are you running away from the Order of the Asphodel?"

Darkness shadowed his eyes. "The archmages really should hire better spies."

"I'm not a spy." I held the bottle of absinthe out to him. "Clearly."

When he took the bottle, his fingertips touched mine. A shiver of electricity skittered down my backbone. Latent necromancy in his skin, or the undeniable desire that simmered between us like magic?

"Will you go home to Prussia?" I asked.

He knocked back the last of his drink. "Why the hell would I do that?"

"Because of your family."

His eyes hardened at the word *family*, telling me already that I was wrong. "I don't exist, Ardis. Not to them. You won't find me on any of their family trees. I'm not a part of their lineage anymore. If I die, they will have an easier time erasing me from their reputations. An easier time forgetting."

I swallowed past the ache in my throat. "When a necromancer dies, does he die like a normal man?"

"God, I hope so."

His beautiful eyes looked molten with emotion. His honey-gravel voice, the intensity of his stare, and the way he looked at me were all dangerous. Tension stretched taut between us like a string about to snap.

"Wendel, I need to apologize."

"For?"

"Kissing you was a mistake."

He swirled the absinthe in his glass. "Because I'm an abomination?"

"Because you're forbidden."

"But forbidden fruit tastes so much sweeter."

He set down his glass with a decisive clink. When he leaned forward, his elbows braced on his knees, the scent of him surrounded me. Absinthe, like bitter licorice, mingled with his masculine warmth. God, he smelled good.

I resisted the urge to kiss him again. Would his lips taste like absinthe?

"Why do you want me?" he asked, in a deadly murmur.

"The archmages need a necromancer." I hated how breathless I sounded.

"No. *You*."

Liquid desire rippled through my belly. I curled my hands into fists. "I don't."

"Don't lie to me." He leaned even closer, his eyes glittering. "You believe me to be an abomination, and yet you still can't stop touching me."

Fuck, he wasn't wrong.

"You aren't untouchable." I tossed the words at him without any real malice.

"A necromancer often touches the dead more than the living. But don't worry, I keep my hands clean. I haven't defiled you yet."

Yet. That one little word coiled in my stomach like a snake.

I wanted him to defile me. The dark urge darted through my mind. My fingernails bit harder into my palms.

"What makes you think I'm any less dirty?" I asked. "My hands have been stained by the blood of countless men."

"Are you threatening me?" He raised his glass as if toasting me.

"Trust me, you would know if I was."

He cocked his head, his mouth bent between a smirk and a sneer. "Do you want to kill me or kiss me again?"

"Neither."

"You aren't a very good liar." He drained the rest of his absinthe, then licked his lips. "Tell me the truth."

"You first."

"Truthfully, you surprised me when you kissed me. Desperate enough for even a necromancer."

Heat flared inside me, chased by cold shame. "Go fuck yourself."

"Is that an invitation?"

Before he could reply with yet more sarcasm, I strode out of the lounge car. I retreated to our cabin, slid the door shut, and locked it for good measure. Legs trembling, I paced between the seats like a wild animal in a cage. Instinct urged me to run back to Wendel and fight him—or fuck him.

God, I needed to get out of here before he came back to our cabin.

I didn't trust him.

Or myself.

9

Where was Konstantin?

I hunted for him until I finally found him outside the train. Snow dazzled me in the morning sun. A dozen or so passengers clustered around the archmage. Gentlemen, mostly, with their cigar smoke curling into the cold, but a few ladies too, who were fanning themselves as if waiting for a show to start. A flighty lady in a fox-fur coat nearly stepped on a blood splatter in the snow and shrieked dramatically.

"Watch your step!" Konstantin called out. "My preparations are nearly complete."

"Don't meander too close," a gray-bearded gentleman told me. "I'm afraid this is rather too complicated for a feminine mind."

Fuck you, I thought to myself.

Konstantin waved me closer. He wore leather-and-steel

bracers that left his fingers bare—it's armor common to arch-mages, though I knew little about its function. He had set up an apparatus about the size of a bread box, constructed of steel and polished maple wood. Brass knobs circled a glass window that flickered violet-white with caged magic.

"Technomancy?" I asked. "To repair the Hex?"

"Precisely." Konstantin lowered a pair of goggles over his eyes. "Imagine sewing a patch to the enchantment in the sky."

"How can I help?"

"Make sure nobody wanders too near. I don't want to singe a wayward duchess."

"Understood."

"Good!" His bracers clinked when he clapped his hands. "Let's get started."

I walked back to the crowd. The gray-bearded gentleman who had been rude to me scowled at my return.

"Keep your distance." I kept a relaxed hand on my sword. "Orders of the archmage."

"Why?" asked the lady in the fox fur. "Is it terribly dangerous?"

I shrugged. "Very."

Behind me, there was a pop like a small firecracker.

"That's not quite right," Konstantin said. "Let me adjust things a bit..."

Bluish smoke wafted above his head. He fiddled with the apparatus, then cupped his hands heavenward. Between his palms, an arc of violet-white lightning lashed out like a viper and crackled into the clouds.

A bone-deep hum resonated through the forest. It vibrated in my ribcage and quivered the needles on the pines.

"Stay back!" I warned the watchers, but I couldn't hear my own words.

Their wide eyes reflected the violet-white magic.

Konstantin split the lightning between his hands. He raised his arms and directed the magic at the sky, letting it linger more in certain places, less in others, as if smoothing over invisible cracks in the Hex.

When he clenched his hands, the magic sizzled out with a flash.

In the deafening silence, polite applause pattered.

"Thank you," Konstantin said. "Ardis?"

"Yes?" When I returned to him, he handed me a pistol.

"Would you do the honors of testing the Hex?" He faced his audience with a theatrical bow. "And now my lovely assistant will prove that the magic I have just constructed nullifies the power of gunpowder."

Lovely assistant? That was a bit much.

I aimed the pistol skyward, since I only trusted magic so much, and pulled the trigger. The gun misfired with a *click* while the spidery tickling of the Hex crawled over my fingers. A shudder shook my body.

More applause from the audience.

Konstantin smiled. "Excellent!"

I inspected the pistol. In ordinary circumstances, the misfire could in fact be a hang-fire—a delayed discharge—but these were obviously extraordinary circumstances. I set the safety and ejected the round from the chamber. The brass of the bullet was tinged blue, a telltale sign that it had been altered by the Hex.

The crowd wandered back to the train, already bored of magic.

"Thank you," Konstantin said when I returned the pistol. "Have you learned more about the necromancer?"

I clenched my jaw. "Only that he's an infuriating bastard."

"Care to elaborate?"

"He evades any useful answers to my questions."

"The Order of the Asphodel may pose a significant threat to our plans. We need to reduce the number of unknowns."

"Meaning?"

"We can't lose the necromancer. Talk to him. Get him to spill his secrets."

That didn't rule out seduction, which was probably the only way to strip away the armor of Wendel's arrogance.

A knot tightened in the pit of my stomach. "Yes, sir."

With the Hex patched and the dead buried, the train huffed into motion. It rattled from the mountains down into fields of frosted stubble. Clouds streaked the crisp blue sky. Flocks of crows flew alongside the windows.

In the dining car, I devoured toast, poached eggs, bratwurst, and strudel. At least they had good food here. My hunger satisfied, I drank my coffee and studied a newspaper that was only a few days old. I still struggled to read German, though I stared intently at the ornate Gothic letters until I recognized a few words.

"*Amerika*," I whispered.

The newspaper had a photograph of the president, Woodrow Wilson, who had been elected after I had left home. I hadn't seen San Francisco for three years. I didn't know when I might see it again.

It had been a death that brought me to Europe, and a hope that kept me here.

My fingers found the thin chain at my neck. I opened a silver locket and traced the pair of tintype photographs inside.

On the left, my mother looked out with shadowed eyes and a mysterious smile.

On the right, a pale-haired man stared gravely at the camera.

My father, Leo.

But Leo couldn't be his real name. He had revealed little to my mother during the fleeting time they had been together.

Including the double-headed eagle tattooed on the back of his neck.

When I was younger, I dreamed this eagle would lead me straight to my father, but it could belong to any number of empires or kingdoms. Everyone from the Byzantines to the Russians seemed fond of the symbol.

I sighed, a brief indulgence of sadness, and hid the locket once more.

"May I join you?"

Wendel rested his hand on the chair opposite me. He had an expression of mild interest. Morning sunlight slanted through the windows and glinted in his eyes. I lost a moment marveling at their greenness.

Damn him and his beautiful eyes.

I shook the newspaper straight with a snap. "Of course."

Sitting, he unfolded his napkin. "I would say good morning, but I think we both got too little sleep for that to be true."

Silently, I stared at the newspaper without reading it. Anger still simmered inside me from our earlier skirmish.

Go fuck yourself.

Is that an invitation?

"Let me apologize for being unnecessarily rude." A smile quirked his mouth. "Or necessarily rude."

"Did you come here to joke?"

"No." Wendel sobered. "Damn, let me try again." He stared out the window.

"I'm waiting," I said coolly.

"I'm not used to anyone wanting to touch me, but it was wrong of me to imply desperation on your behalf. I'm sorry."

He sounded so sincere that it was impossible to stay angry at him. But of course he had dodged around the truth: I had gone far beyond touching him. Remembering our kiss evoked shivers down my spine.

"Truce?" He offered his hand to me. He had a half-smile on his face, but his pale eyes said so much more.

I gave him a brisk handshake, the safest option. "I wasn't aware we were at war."

His half-smile became a whole one. "Touché."

Touché. To touch. Did he mean that to be a pun? A handshake felt like a loaded gun, knowing what magic crawled beneath his skin.

I released him and pretended to be obsessed with the menu.

Wendel waved over the waiter. "The omelet. And coffee."

"Coffee for me, too, thanks," I added.

The waiter poured us each a cup, then left us alone. I blew on the black liquid to cool it before sipping.

"God," I said, "I need the caffeine."

Wendel studied my face. "You *do* look as tired as I feel."

"We were up nearly the whole night."

"For all the wrong reasons." He deadpanned it perfectly, a wicked glint in his eyes. "I did entertain the thought of going back to bed."

10

Was he serious? Or just teasing me?

Curiosity flickered in his eyes. He slid his thumb along the rim of his coffee cup, the muscles in his jaw tightening. Heat rose inside me like a slow boil. Wasn't I supposed to be the one seducing him? His close proximity turned everything upside down. Flustered, I focused on my newspaper instead of him.

"You read German?" he asked.

My heartbeat calmed down. "Badly," I admitted.

He walked his fingers across the table and tugged the newspaper to him. "It's all boring anyway. Just the bickering of cousins who are kings."

"And you don't care, being a prince?"

"A prince who never was, and never will be." He said it flippantly and thumbed through the newspaper. Then he cocked

64

his head. "Perhaps I spoke too soon. Well, Ardis, it looks like politics isn't so boring after all."

"What happened?"

He jabbed the headline. "Didn't you read this?"

"Not before you stole the newspaper from me," I scoffed.

He cleared his throat. "'Heir to Austrian Throne Attacked,'" he read. "'Archduke Franz Ferdinand Survives Stabbing.'"

I straightened in my chair. "Who did it?"

"My money is on the Serbs." He shrugged. "It looks like the Archduke was hunting in Bosnia with local dignitaries, killing deer in the name of diplomacy. Franz can thank the Hex he's alive. A Serbian lunatic knifed him in broad daylight, but only wounded his Imperial and Royal Highness's arm."

That secret society in Serbia must have sent the assassin. "Was it the Black Hand?"

"Yes." He glanced into my eyes. "You knew?"

I sipped my coffee. "The Black Hand has been helping the Romanian rebellion, even if the King of Serbia won't dirty his hands."

"He isn't stupid. Serbia hasn't got the army to fight Austria-Hungary."

"Neither do the Romanians, but that hasn't stopped them. Not even the Hex."

"Sir?" The waiter returned to our table. "May I have a word with you?"

Wendel arched one eyebrow. "Yes?"

The waiter cleared his throat. "I'm afraid your presence in the dining car is making the other passengers uncomfortable.

We would like to recommend that you dine alone in your cabin. Complimentary room service."

At several nearby tables, diners stole glances at the necromancer and whispered among themselves. I suspected that a particularly red-faced family of five had been the ones to make the complaint to the waiter.

Wendel's eyes hardened, but he tossed his napkin onto the table.

"Excuse me?" I asked. "We aren't leaving."

The waiter's thin mustache twitched. "This dining car is welcoming to guests of all ages. Surely you understand why people with more delicate constitutions—children, the elderly —might be offended by his profession."

"I don't understand the welcoming part. Offended, yes."

"Ma'am—"

"We're paying guests. We have every right to eat here."

The waiter sniffed. "I'm afraid you may be mistaken, ma'am. There are fewer of your American liberties here."

I leaned back in my chair. "You saw his offensive profession last night. If it weren't for the two of us, you would all have your throats slit by rebels. You should be thanking us. How about some hospitality?"

Wendel pushed his chair from the table. "Ardis, enough."

"Fine." I followed him from the dining car back to our cabin. "What an asshole."

"I can only hope you don't mean me."

"No, the waiter. He didn't even serve you!"

Wendel locked the door behind us. The click sounded loud despite the noise of the train rattling over the tracks. My gaze kept getting dragged back to his lips. If I kissed him, would he still taste like absinthe?

"Why are you here?" he asked.

I sat down on a seat. "Because you booked a single cabin, remember?"

He arched his eyebrows. "The waiter didn't ask you to leave the dining car. You can go drink your coffee in peace."

"Aren't you hungry?"

"Not enough to return to the dining car." He twisted his mouth. "It wasn't as if I resurrected skeletons at the table."

My jaw dropped. "Skeletons? You can resurrect skeletons?"

"No." Wendel lounged on the seat opposite me. "They tend to fall apart into bones."

I needed to keep him talking. Maybe he would answer more of my questions and tell me why he was on the run.

"Have you always known you were a necromancer?" I asked.

"No. Not always."

"When did you find out?"

He looked out the window, his gaze far away. "There was a cat. A kitten, really. A gray tabby with green eyes. I had him when I was little, and I named him Maus. My mother made me keep him in the stables. She wasn't fond of cats. I would visit him every day after I finished lessons with my tutors. One day, Maus vanished. The stable boy told me that the cat had been kicked by a horse. Killed."

"God," I whispered.

I knew where this story was going. I crossed my arms across my chest and resisted the urge to touch him.

"I went looking for Maus," Wendel continued. "I found him lying by the rubbish heap. His body was so pathetic. Tiny and limp. I went to pick him up. I remember wanting to touch him one last time. When I petted Maus, he woke up."

My throat ached until it was hard to speak. "You didn't know, did you?"

"I didn't." His voice roughened. "I brought Maus to my mother and father. I didn't understand why they were so angry with me, or why they told the groundskeeper to bring Maus into the woods and burn him to ashes."

Tears stung my eyes. "How old were you?"

"Eleven. That was a month before they said goodbye."

"They sent you to the Order of the Asphodel?"

"Yes." He laughed bitterly, though his eyes glimmered with emotion. "Because, by then, I was hopeless. Ruined. All because I wanted to touch my cat one more time. Even if he was dead, he was still Maus."

Looking at him, it was easy to imagine him as a boy, all those years ago, full of heartbreak and regret and pain.

I reached out to him, no more than my hand on his knee.

His face was at once open and closed. A guarded, brittle hope softened his mouth and eyes. I had found him bleeding out on the battlefield, but I had never seen such vulnerability until this moment.

"Wendel," I said. "I'm sorry."

"I won't lie. When I first discovered my talent for raising the dead, I was...unhappy."

"You were just a boy."

"Not yet old enough to appreciate my magic. Necromancy

is fascinating." His velvety voice brought shivers down my spine. "With it, I can recover long-lost memories. I can speak to the dead who left this world days, weeks, even centuries ago. There's a certain repulsive elegance to being a necromancer."

He tilted his head as if noticing, finally, that my hand rested on his knee. He curled his fingers around mine. I expected him to pry my hand away, but he held me there instead, his grip strong yet gentle.

"And yet you keep touching me," he murmured.

He looked deeply into my eyes, searching for my innermost desires. My heartbeat pounded against the cage of my ribs like a trapped bird seeking freedom. I ached for more than just a touch of his hand.

When he lunged across the distance between us, I gasped.

Bending over me, his arms caged me against the seat. He captured me in a fierce kiss. His mouth devoured mine with the desperation of a starving man. Desire flooded me in an instant and scorched away any sorrow. I clung to him with my hands in his hair.

Silk. His hair was like silk. It contrasted with the hard muscles of his body.

Fuck, his muscles weren't as hard as his cock. I arched my hips and ground against him, rewarded by a grunt low in his throat. I wanted to free his cock and see it jutting against his princely black clothes.

"Ardis." The gravel in his voice turned it into a growl. "You're playing a dangerous game."

"That's exactly why I want you."

He grabbed me by the wrist before I could touch the bulge of his cock. "Because you want to manipulate me?"

"No."

"You're lying to me. Again." He curled his lip. "The archmage sent you?"

"No!" I sucked in an unsteady breath. "I'm a mercenary for the Archmages of Vienna, but I'm not a whore."

My own mother ran a brothel in Chinatown, San Francisco, for Christ's sake, which was enough to convince me to never enter that line of work. I preferred killing strangers to fucking them, as mercenary as that sounded.

"Aren't they paying you?"

I glared at him. "To bring you back alive, not to fuck you."

"Who says I would fuck you?"

"Your cock says otherwise."

He laughed darkly. "I'm tempted to slide my fingers into your sweet pussy and find out just how wet you are right now."

Drenched. That was how wet.

I locked stares with him. "Only if I can find out just how hard you are right now."

II

is quick intake of breath gratified me. His pupils widened until darkness swallowed almost all of the green in his eyes. He stroked his hand along the nape of my neck. Necromancy shivered like icy fire from his fingers.

I shuddered at his magic. His power over death both thrilled and terrified me.

"Are you afraid of me?" he asked.

"Yes."

"Ardis." His voice fell to a rough murmur. "I vowed to protect you. I would never hurt you, not even if you betrayed me."

He found a way through my defenses with a few well-placed words.

I couldn't look away from his eyes. "Why would I betray you?"

"Because you're a mercenary, and I'm nothing more than a necromancer you need."

"That's not true." I swallowed hard. "My job would be a hell of a lot easier otherwise. God, I wish I could stop wanting you."

His lips parted. "We shouldn't do this."

"Of course not."

But I dragged him down regardless.

When he kissed me, it was slow and indulgent. One of my hands twisted in his hair, the other sliding beneath the hem of his shirt. The hard muscles in his abdomen tensed beneath my touch. He was still restraining himself, I could tell.

I wanted him to shudder with pleasure, the arrogant elegance of him unraveling into something raw and primal.

A knock rapped on the door to our cabin. We broke apart with a gasp. Wendel was pale enough that it wasn't hard to miss the flush in his cheeks. He tucked in his shirt and raked his fingers through his hair. I tugged my clothes straight before answering the door.

Konstantin.

He glanced between us with sharp blue eyes. My skin heated with embarrassment. How much did he suspect?

"May I have a word with you?" When I stepped forward, Konstantin shook his head. "Not you, the necromancer."

"Me?" Wendel twisted his mouth. "What have I done to deserve this honor, archmage?"

Konstantin met my gaze. "Ardis, would you give us a moment?"

"Of course."

I stepped out into the corridor. Konstantin shut the door behind me. Like a bodyguard, I leaned against the wall with my arms folded. I wasn't trying to eavesdrop, but I wasn't trying *not* to eavesdrop, either.

Their muffled voices carried through the door in fragments.

"...can't do this without you."

"Why?"

That was Konstantin, followed by Wendel.

A conductor strode down the corridor. "Ladies and gentlemen, we will be arriving in Budapest shortly. Please gather your belongings and make your way to the exits." We nodded at each other as he walked further down the train.

"Archmage, you surprise me."

"Is it so surprising? Your necromancy...to Project Lazarus."

Project Lazarus? What the hell was that?

The brakes of the train whined as it slowed, approaching Budapest. Outside the windows, patchwork fields yielded to city streets punctuated by clock towers and church spires. A grand train station loomed ahead.

The puffing of the train and the chatter of disembarking passengers filled my ears.

"Welcome to Budapest," said the conductor. "Please watch your step as you exit."

A few minutes later, a whistle blew. The train chugged from the station again.

Out of the corner of my eye, a grizzled man approached. He wore a gray cloak over an outdated suit. At his belt, he had a scabbard for a curving sword—a scimitar from the Ottoman Empire, if I had to guess.

"Excuse me." The stranger spoke with an accent I couldn't place. I pressed against the wall to let him pass, but he stopped and looked me over. "Could you help me? I'm looking for a man named Wendel."

Fuck. This couldn't be good. "Sorry, no."

The stranger's mouth twitched as if he knew I was lying. Without another word, he disappeared into the next car of the train.

The Order of the Asphodel. Who else would be looking for Wendel?

I knocked on the door.

Konstantin answered, though he frowned at me. "Yes, Ardis?"

"A man is looking for Wendel."

Wendel jolted to his feet. "Who?"

"He had a sword. A scimitar, I think."

With a hard exhale, Wendel let his hand slide down his face. His eyes focused somewhere far away, as if he were already thinking of the battle ahead.

"Did he go left or right?" he asked me.

"Right. Who is he?"

Wendel said nothing.

Konstantin caught the necromancer by the shoulder. "Think of the consequences."

"You don't own me, archmage."

Wendel shrugged off his hand and strode after the stranger.

"Ardis," Konstantin said. "Keep an eye on him. Report back to me. Don't let *anything* happen to the necromancer."

"Understood."

I followed Wendel down the corridor. He must have heard my footsteps, but he didn't look back when he spoke.

"Let me do this."

A cold thrill shivered down my spine. Wendel slid open the door separating this sleeper car with the next. The stranger stood with his back to us. He turned around with his hand on the hilt of his scimitar.

"There you are," he said.

Wendel froze. "An assassin, I presume."

The stranger didn't deny it. "You can call me Sven. You know who sent me."

"What do they want?"

"You." Sven's thumb traced the pommel of his scimitar. "You failed to report back after the battle at Petroseni. They thought you had been killed." He grunted. "They wondered if you had returned from the dead."

Wendel's laugh was scathing. He spread out his arms in a taunting gesture. "Sorry to disappoint. I'm still breathing."

"Not for much longer, princeling, unless you come with me."

"That's a pathetic threat. We both know the Order prefers me alive."

Sven sized me up. "Who's she?"

I clenched my jaw. I knew my weaknesses, and bluffing was one of them.

Wendel's gaze connected with mine for a second. "You know how I like my women. Beautiful and dangerous."

Beautiful? He thought I was beautiful? My stomach fluttered. He wanted to protect me, didn't he? It was safer to pretend I wasn't a mercenary for the archmages.

"Say your goodbyes." Sven unhooked handcuffs from his belt. He edged toward Wendel as if cornering a predator that might lash out at any moment.

"Hurry up." Wendel sighed. "It's a long way from Vienna to Constantinople."

Sven locked the handcuffs around his wrists. "Where's your fancy dagger? Lose it?"

"In my pocket. Don't tell me, it's worth more than I am."

"Damn right." He patted Wendel down. "Here we—"

Wendel swung his arms over Sven's head and lunged behind him in a stranglehold. The chain between the handcuffs choked the assassin's neck. Sven ran backwards and slammed Wendel against the wall. Savagely, Wendel wrenched the handcuffs even tighter. Sven slammed him against the wall again, but couldn't shake him.

Sven's face turned red. He fumbled for his scimitar.

"Disarm him!" Wendel said.

I swung my sword at Sven. Our blades clashed in a ringing of steel. Sven drove me back with his brute strength, but I slid my sword down his scimitar and locked them at the cross guards. When I twisted hard, I knocked his scimitar clean out of his hands. His blade flew sideways and clattered on the floor.

Wendel kept choking him. "Thank you."

Sven's face darkened to purple. He dropped to his knees and tried to throw Wendel overhead, but he was too weak. The assassin's eyes flickered shut. He slumped, supported only by the chain around his neck.

"He's out cold," I said.

But Wendel gritted his teeth and didn't let go. Shadows darkened his eyes.

"Wendel, you can stop."

Still, he didn't let go.

"Wendel!"

At last, he released the assassin. He pressed his fingers to Sven's neck as he fell. Was he checking his pulse?

But then Sven sat upright.

12

"Free me," Wendel commanded.

Sven grabbed a key from his pocket. His eyes looked empty as he unlocked the handcuffs. Done, he stood motionless.

Wendel rubbed the welts on his wrists. "Jump off the train. Walk—crawl, I don't care—until you can't anymore."

Sven climbed to his feet and shambled toward the door. Wendel shadowed the dead man down the corridor. Sven groped for the door, yanked it open, and lurched outside. He plodded to the platform before he leaned over the railing. He teetered from the moving train and fell into a ditch.

Sven crawled from the ditch and dragged himself away from the tracks. Wendel watched until the dead man vanished. His eyes had lacked emotion earlier, when he was killing the man, but they smoldered now.

"Fuck," I whispered, clinging to the cold iron railing. "Was that necessary?"

"He had to be stopped." Wendel glanced at his hand, red and slick with blood. "That could have been a cleaner kill."

"But he wasn't bleeding."

"Ah." Red stained the sleeve of his shirt. The fight must have torn the stitches over his wound. "I'm starting to feel it."

His head bowed, Wendel clutched his arm and trudged back into the car.

I kept pace alongside him. "You didn't have to kill him."

"He was working for the Order."

"*Working*. You were just another job to him."

He shot me a glare. "And you have a moral objection to killing on the job?"

I shut my mouth rather than admit he was right.

We encountered Konstantin in the corridor. "God." He blanched at Wendel's bloody knuckles. "What happened?"

"He killed the assassin," I said grimly.

Wendel gestured to his wound. "Can you heal me, archmage?"

"I'm not a doctor!" Konstantin protested.

"You *do* know at least some medical magic? I'm rather short on alternatives."

"All right." Konstantin grimaced. "Follow me."

Konstantin brought us to his cabin, which was also in the first-class sleeper cars. He fetched a small suitcase from the luggage rack. Kneeling, he unbuckled the clasps and revealed it wasn't a suitcase at all, but an apparatus built into its own carrying case. I hadn't seen it before when he patched the Hex.

"I almost didn't bring this," Konstantin said. "Luckily for you, I did."

Wendel eyed the apparatus. "What does it do?"

"Temporal magic."

"Archmages and their technomancy gadgets," Wendel muttered. "I suppose it came to this, making a deal with the devil."

"And you think that *I* am the devil?"

Wendel shrugged off his coat and unbuttoned his shirt. Wet with blood, the cloth clung to his wound. He hissed through his teeth as he peeled it away. I couldn't help wincing. That had to hurt, especially after his adrenaline waned.

"Do you think two weeks will be enough?" Konstantin asked him.

Wendel hesitated. "Make it a month."

"That will double the pain."

"I know."

I frowned. "How will temporal magic help?"

Konstantin tugged on his leather-and-steel bracers. "This magic accelerates the healing time of the wound, but it also accelerates the sensations of that time. Wendel will feel a month of pain in one instant."

"Wonderful bedside manner," Wendel muttered.

"You're welcome," Konstantin fired back.

Wendel unbuckled his belt and lay down on the seat. Blood kept trickling from his arm. He put his belt between his teeth and bit down on the leather, like he had done this before and knew exactly how badly it hurt.

"Ardis?" Konstantin said. "You may want to hold his wrists."

I glanced at Wendel, waiting for his consent, and he nodded. My fingers curled around his wrists. His pulse raced beneath my touch, though he was doing an excellent job of keeping his emotions from his face.

Konstantin shaped an invisible sphere in his hands. Between his fingers, a green glow flickered into a burning ball of light. He inspected the magic, his eyes gleaming with fierce concentration, then poured it onto the wound with a terrible sizzling.

Wendel bit the belt to stifle a scream.

He was stronger than me, though he must have been holding back. I put my weight into pinning him. He threw back his head, the tendons in his neck taut, and moaned through his clenched jaws. Sweat glittered on his skin, which was feverish beneath my fingers.

"And...done." Konstantin lifted his hands.

Wendel collapsed on the seat before sliding onto the floor. He spat the belt from his mouth. Shudders wracked his body. He curled sideways, breathing in ragged gasps, and hugged himself like he wanted to keep himself from falling apart.

An urge to protect him rushed through me. He was a deadly killer, but sometimes he just looked so...*broken*.

Kneeling, I touched his shoulder. He met my gaze, his eyes focusing, as if seeing me for the first time. Like that day I saved him on the battlefield and he clung to me.

"Are you all right?" I murmured.

"I will be." Pain still roughened his voice. "Thank you for asking."

A hint of sarcasm. Good.

Nothing of his wound remained except for a long scar across his arm, and the crimson that still stained his pale skin.

Konstantin pulled off his bracers and frowned at the blood on his fingers. He opened the door to the bathroom and washed his hands in the sink. Reflected in the mirror, curiosity sharpened his eyes.

The tension between me and Wendel had to be obvious.

Wendel grabbed the edge of the seat and hauled himself to his feet. His hair shadowed his face and obscured his expression.

"Blood everywhere," he muttered.

Konstantin stepped aside to let him into the bathroom. Wendel stared into the sink, his eyes distant, while he washed the blood from himself. He gave special care to his hands, picking beneath his fingernails, scrubbing at his knuckles. Long after he looked clean, he let water wash over his skin.

Was he thinking of how he had killed Sven? Or brought him back?

As Wendel turned off the water, I glimpsed a grim kind of hope in his eyes. Together, we returned to our cabin.

I locked the door behind us. "Tell me the truth."

"Be more specific," he said.

"Why are you running from them?"

His jaw clenched; his hands curled into fists. He still wasn't wearing his shirt or coat, and he tossed them onto the seat.

Somehow, he looked even more tense than he had during battle.

"You wouldn't understand," he said.

"Is this the first time you fought them?"

"No." He swiped his hand over his eyes like he wanted to erase everything he had seen. "Far from it. But they always expect me to come crawling back. No matter what they do to me. No matter what I have done."

I couldn't stop staring at the scars on his body. "How have they hurt you?"

"I don't wish to talk about this." He shrugged on his shirt and began buttoning it. "There's no point in telling you about the sins and punishments of my past."

They had punished him. Badly enough to scar his body, badly enough for him to kill the man who hunted him down.

I swallowed hard past the ache in my throat. "You said I wouldn't understand, but that's not true. I know what it means to run away from pain and unjust punishment."

"Do you?" His haughty tone needled me.

"I'm an outlaw in America. Wanted for the murder of a man so rich he thought I wouldn't refuse him. So rich that the police called it murder, not defense. My life wasn't worth as much as his."

Wendel froze halfway through buttoning his shirt. He looked at me with a fierce, protective look in his eyes. "I would have killed him a thousand times for you."

Shivers rushed down my spine. I believed him, and worse, I liked him even more. Who wouldn't want a dangerous, beautiful man promising to kill their enemies?

But I couldn't confess this to him.

Couldn't admit how much I wanted him to protect me.

"Will the Order of the Asphodel keep coming for you?" I asked.

"I fear only death will stop them."

13

I sat alone in the observation car, my hand lingering on my sword. Scenery flickered past the window with the dark purples of evening. The rattling of tracks under the train reminded me of a clock ticking down.

Vienna wasn't far away. I needed to bring Wendel to the archmages and say goodbye to him forever. I needed to forget him.

But I could *never* forget him. Whenever I closed my eyes, I saw his face.

Sleep dragged me under.

"Ma'am?" Someone touched my shoulder. "Excuse me, ma'am?"

I jolted awake. A conductor leaned over me. My hand had jerked to the hilt of Chun Yi, and I forced myself to relax.

"Where are we?" I asked.

"Vienna. This is our last stop."

Adrenaline flooded my blood. "Fuck," I whispered. I overslept.

I sprang to my feet, ignoring the conductor's protests, and sprinted to our sleeper car. Our cabin was empty.

Wendel was gone.

I ran for the exit and jumped from the train.

Plunged into a crowd, I fought to orient myself. The ceiling of the Vienna train station was vaulted overhead. Iron and glittering glass held the night sky at bay. All around me were people, swarms of people.

None of them were Wendel.

I zigzagged through the crowd. Our train had halted at the rightmost platform in the station, which meant I had a lot of ground to cover.

Had Wendel escaped at the earliest possible opportunity?

He had sworn a vow of undying loyalty to me, which meant he wouldn't run away from me—unless he was lying through his teeth.

Or had the Order of the Asphodel captured him already?

I scanned the lights overhead. There wasn't enough darkness here for the shadows of his dagger to be effective. If I were trying to escape, I would have disguised myself and left the train station as fast as possible.

Keeping my head down, I followed the flow of the crowd out into the night.

Rain hushed from the sky over Vienna. Puddles glittered with the lights of the city, and spray hissed from the wheels of passing automobiles. I flipped up the hood of my jacket and strode to the center of the plaza.

I had lost Wendel. And I—

"Ardis."

A voice in the crowd hissed from not too faraway. Where?

"Ardis!"

A hand closed on my wrist. I spun around—Wendel.

Relief crashed over me in a wave.

He dragged me from the plaza and into the darkness. He pushed me against the bricks of a wall, his grip tight on my wrist.

My breath left me in a rush and fogged the air. "Where were you?"

Rain sliding down his face, he looked into my eyes. In the shadows, we were all but invisible to the passersby on the street.

"I had to protect you," he said.

He kissed me, hard and fast, the length of his body pressing against mine. My hands locked behind his neck. Shivering electricity washed over my skin—his necromancy, or my nerves coming alive under his touch.

When we broke apart, I asked, "Protect me from what?"

"Not what." He shook his head. "Who."

Dread choked my throat and made it hard to breathe. "Assassins?"

His jaw clenched and he nodded.

"How many?" I asked.

"It doesn't matter. They're dead."

"God." I blinked rainwater from my eyes. "How long have we been in Vienna? Minutes?"

His fingers tensed around my wrist. "They were waiting for us."

"No. Not us. *You.*"

His throat worked as he swallowed hard. "You're right." His voice sounded husky. "You're in danger because of me."

When he released me, the warmth of his hand faded in the cold. He bowed his head, his rain-soaked hair obscuring his face. His shoulders slumped in the posture of a man who had admitted defeat.

It hurt to watch him like this. "We can't stay here."

"Take me to the Archmages of Vienna."

The night was still young when we arrived at the Hall of the Archmages.

Our boots clicked on the marble floor, the sound echoing under the vaulted dome. Wendel glanced heavenward at the dome's celestial mosaic of blue-and-gold tiles, then down to the halberds of the guards.

Ornamental, of course, and useless as weapons in battle.

"The archmages certainly love pomp and circumstance," Wendel muttered.

Once, I had found this all magnificent, but now I was too tired to give a fuck. My eyes were gritty, my muscles exhausted, even though it couldn't be past seven o'clock. It felt like I had spent an eternity with Wendel.

It was time to say goodbye.

We might never see each other again. My throat ached, our impending separation transmuted into physical pain. I brought him deeper into the warren of corridors. My pounding heartbeat sounded louder than our footsteps.

Finally, we reached the office of my employer: Archmage Margareta.

When I knocked, she called out, "Enter."

I opened the door.

Archmage Margareta stood by the fireplace and stoked the indigo-burning flames. An elderly woman, she wore her pewter hair in an intricate braid. The red color of her robes signaled her expertise in incendiary magic.

I cleared my throat. "Ma'am."

"Ardis." When she turned around, her frosty blue eyes latched onto Wendel. "You must be the Prince of the Undying."

He swept into a curt bow. "I am."

"What is your name?"

"Wendel von Preussen."

Her joints stiffened by age, Margareta lowered herself into a leather chair behind her desk. "A Prince of Prussia."

"Correct, though I was disinherited."

"Please, sit." Margareta waved her hand imperiously. "Both of you."

Wendel pulled out a chair for me, playing the part of a gentleman. My stomach twisted into a knot when I sat down.

Why did he look so aloof? Like he didn't care?

Wendel lounged in his chair as if it were a throne, with all the indolence of a prince. "Why am I here, archmage?"

"Pardon me, I failed to introduce myself. My name is Archmage Margareta."

He arched his eyebrows at her frosty tone. "Noted."

"We require your services as a necromancer." Archmage Margareta steepled her hands on the desk. "The details are confidential."

I cleared my throat. "We met Archmage Konstantin on the train."

"Did you?"

"I overheard something about Project Lazarus."

Margareta sighed. "I would suggest not eavesdropping next time. If you overheard any interesting details, forget them."

Embarrassment scorched my ears. "Yes, ma'am."

Margareta slid open a desk drawer and tossed a coin purse to me. "Your payment for a successful mission."

I caught it in my hands. The heft of the coins meant they had to be gold. "Thank you."

Wendel arched his eyebrows. "Speaking purely as the Prince of the Undying, I hope I'm worth at least a small fortune."

"Not as much as you might expect," I muttered.

"Pity."

Margareta pursed her lips at our banter. "Wendel, we will cover your room and board at the Imperial Palace Hotel. It's located across the street, and I believe even a disinherited prince should find it satisfactory."

Wendel tilted his head. "She stays with me."

"I hardly think you need a bodyguard, considering your reputation, and it would be rather improper—"

"No," he cut in. "I vowed to protect her."

"Why?"

"She saved my life."

Margareta shot a glance at me. "Is that true?"

I forgot how to breathe for a moment. "Yes. I did. But—"

"I insist." Wendel looked into my eyes without blinking. "I swore a vow of undying loyalty, Ardis, and I intend to keep it."

Shivers rushed over my skin at the intensity of his words. "You don't have to do this."

"I do."

"I survived without you before."

"You won't win this argument." He had the supreme confidence of royalty.

What a bastard. But I couldn't deny the flicker of excitement inside me, burning brighter with every heartbeat.

"Ardis?" Margareta cleared her throat. "Are you willing to accept?"

I swallowed hard. "Yes."

I had never entered the Imperial Palace Hotel before.

And definitely never with a disinherited prince. Wendel walked into the hotel with vague disinterest, like he had seen grander luxury. He scarcely glanced at the marble underfoot or glittering crystal chandeliers overhead.

I wondered if he had spent his childhood in lavish castles in Prussia.

Wendel opened the door to our room. "After you."

My boots sank into the plush carpet inside. I ran my fingers over the gilded wood and crimson silk of the couch nearest to me. Even the air had the scent of wealth: freshly washed linens and a citrus blossom cologne.

Wendel shut the door behind us. The lock clicked.

I stopped dead in my tracks. "There's only one bed."

"Of course."

After shrugging off his jacket, he tossed it onto the couch. His fingers made quick work of the buttons on his shirt.

My heartbeat pounded so hard my hands were shaking. "What are you doing?"

"I need a bath."

He wasn't even looking at me while he undressed, but I couldn't tear my gaze away. He unbuckled his belt. The masculine strength of his arms mesmerized me. Every vein and tendon was a work of art. He turned his back on me before I glimpsed his cock, and I was instead rewarded by his muscular ass.

God, he was gorgeous.

He strolled to the bathroom without a backward glance. "Care to join me?"

14

He walked into the bathroom without me, leaving the door ajar.

I didn't follow him, even though desire pounded inside my aching body. If I did, I would be crossing the point of no return. Nothing would ever be the same again. The sound of rushing water focused my attention.

Unable to resist, I spied on him through the crack in the door.

The luxury of the bathroom should have been dazzling, with its slabs of milk-white marble and gleaming copper fixtures, but his naked body was breathtaking. He wasn't in the clawfoot bathtub, but instead in the marble alcove of the shower. Rivulets trickled down the lean muscles in his abdomen and the sharp vee of his hips.

His cock bobbed as it hardened.

I stared, transfixed, gripping the doorframe.

He began washing himself. I had never been so jealous of a bar of soap before. His strong hands thoroughly worked the length of his shaft. He let his head fall back against the marble, his eyes halfway closed.

"Ardis."

Watching him pleasure himself felt forbidden. "I can go."

He locked stares with me. "Don't."

My fingernails bit into the wood of the doorframe. He kept touching himself, his eyes drunk with lust, his lips slightly parted. His knuckles tightened as he jacked himself off, rougher and quicker than I expected.

A groan escaped his clenched teeth. The muscles in his abdomen tensed, and he cupped his balls with his other hand.

He didn't stop until he came in great spurts across the marble.

Never breaking eye contact with me.

Pearly white dripped down the shower and his hand. He fell back against the wall and struggled to catch his breath. Water washed away the evidence of his pleasure. I had a secret urge to lick him clean instead.

"I can't stop thinking of you," he confessed. "Night after night, I stroked myself in my fist, desperate for any relief."

"Even on the train?"

"Yes."

"Where?"

"The bathroom. In the sink and across the mirror." He laughed, a raspy sound. "It took me a long time to clean it all."

Imagining him coming again and again filled my mind with filthy images. My legs turned liquid with desire. I had never been so aroused in my life. *Fuck it.* I shoved open the door and crossed the threshold.

He walked out of the shower, dripping wet, and dragged me into his arms. His mouth collided with mine in a kiss.

He broke the kiss long enough to say, "Tell me what you want."

"You."

"You want me to fuck you?"

My fingers tightened in his wet hair. The words *fuck you* sounded like pure and utter sin in his husky voice. My pussy was hollowed out and aching.

"I need you inside me."

"Wait." He pulled away. "We need to be safe."

"Protection?"

"I have preventives."

"So do I."

We had both anticipated this moment. An overwhelming sense of destiny sang through my blood. We belonged together.

He left the bathroom and returned with a tin of preventives. His cock was already halfway hard again. It had been only minutes.

"Why aren't you naked?" he asked.

I smirked at his imperious tone. "I thought you might like to help."

Between kisses, he unbuttoned my jacket. He fought the last button until I did it for him. He tossed my jacket away as if it had insulted him personally.

"Take off your clothes," he commanded.

"Yes, Your Highness."

"Your *Royal* Highness." His eyes glinted with wicked laughter.

I removed the rest of my clothing until I stood naked before him. His gaze lingered on every curve of my body.

"Beautiful," he murmured.

His words giddied me like absinthe. He dragged me into the shower and pinned me against the marble. My back hit the cool, polished stone. He kissed me like he couldn't kiss me enough. He paused only long enough to roll a preventive on his cock. Excitement rushed over my skin in a cascade of shivers.

"Fuck me," I demanded.

When he lifted me against the wall, I hooked my legs behind his hips. I was completely at his mercy. He angled his cock in his fist and locked stares with me. The intensity of his beautiful eyes took my breath away.

His cock invaded me until I didn't think he would fit. When he penetrated me fully, I cried out at the deep sensation.

My back arched from the marble. My pussy ached so sweetly I wanted to cry.

He braced me against the wall and began to fuck me with ruthless precision. Every thrust felt calculated to torment me. He hit exactly the right places to wind me tighter and tighter until I clawed at his shoulders. His control on his necromancy started slipping. His magic shivered over my skin like burning cold.

"More," I begged.

He slipped his hand between us and circled my clit with his finger. He locked away his magic again, but I shook my head.

"Don't hold back," I said.

He glanced into my eyes with obvious wonder. "You want my necromancy?"

"I want all of you."

He let out more of his magic, and I shuddered at the rush of icy fire. My nerves came alive under his touch. He searched my eyes as if he still couldn't believe I wanted all of him, including his necromancy.

"I love how you feel," I said.

Encouraged by my words, he fucked me with his fingers and his cock. He played my body like a violin. Every one of my muscles tensed. I was right there, right on the brink. I muffled my scream against his neck.

My climax crashed through me like a flood.

He kept fucking me, without mercy, until an even stronger climax hit me hard. I rode out wave after wave of ecstasy. The muscles in his ass tensed as his hips jerked forward. Groaning, he closed his eyes.

His cock throbbed hard, pumping out his seed, as he came deep inside me.

Gasping, we both stayed that way for a moment, our bodies still locked together. Slowly, he slid out of me. My pussy protested the loss of his cock. When he put me down, my knees almost buckled beneath me.

I laughed. "My legs are shaking."

He grunted, still wordless, and lifted me into his arms instead. I hooked my arms behind his neck and held on. He turned off the water and carried me out of the shower. He set me down by the bed.

After he took care of the preventive, he brought me a towel.

He started to dry me off. My tender skin was aware of every callous on his long, elegant fingers. Little shivers jolted through me every time he touched me.

He tossed aside the towel. "Bed."

My eyes widened. "You want more?"

"I was celibate for an eternity," he admitted.

"Why? Vow of chastity?"

He snorted at my teasing. "No one interested me. Not until you."

"I find that hard to believe."

"Why?"

"You're so fucking handsome. There weren't any women who flung themselves at you?"

"Plenty of women." He tilted his head. "And a few men."

Surprise darted through me. "You mean...?"

He looked at me for a long moment. "Both."

His confession startled me. Most places, it was illegal for a man to love another man. He had no reason to be so vulnerable, and yet he chose to share this truth about himself with me. He cared if I knew who he was.

"Thank you for telling me," I said.

"You have no qualms?"

"None."

I tugged him onto the bed with me. We sank into the heavenly soft linens. My pillow cradled me like a cloud.

He held himself over me and kissed me deeply. His cock nudged my hip.

"Damn," I said. "Already hard again?"

"Maybe I should try being celibate more often."

Laughing, I swatted his shoulder. He rolled another preventive over his cock and parted my thighs with his knee.

He glanced into my eyes. "Would you like me to fuck you more?"

"Hell, yes."

"Good." His face looked nearly pained with desire. "I need to be inside you."

This time, he fucked me slowly, at an indulgent pace to match the luxury around us. When he wrung yet another climax from me, bliss obliterated all thought. He kissed me hard and relinquished his control.

The full force of his necromancy hit me as he came. His cock throbbed inside me as his magic rushed as deep as my bones. The raw intimacy of it brought tears to my eyes. I closed them tight and clung to him.

"Ardis," he murmured. "Are you crying?"

"No," I lied.

"Have I hurt you?"

"No, I'm just... I think my mind melted. I came one too many times."

He chuckled. "No such thing."

Joking was easier than confessing my true emotions to him. I was on the edge of falling for him, and that terrified me.

15

After the best sleep of my life, I woke up in his arms.

I had been thoroughly fucked last night. Maybe that was the secret.

Buttery sunlight streamed through the sheer white curtains. When I stirred, his arms tightened around me. He held me in such a protective way that my stomach fluttered. He kissed my neck just below my ear.

My fingertips traced a long scar across his chest. More scars marked his back, his arms, his thighs—some invisible to all but my fingertips. His muscles tensed under my touch. What memories did he have?

"Should I stop?" I asked.

"No." He hesitated. "Do they bother you? My scars?"

"Your body is gorgeous."

He kissed me again, then sighed. "I need to go."

"Can't you stay a little longer?"

"I promised the archmages I would start work on Project Lazarus today. Konstantin insisted on this ungodly hour."

While Wendel dressed, I counted my payment for bringing him to Vienna. The gold coins glinted against the bed linens. He fastened his cufflinks with a smirk.

"Still not enough," he said.

I rolled my eyes. "You act like having a bounty on your head is a good thing."

"I should be worth at least twice as much."

"Three times, considering your skill in bed."

He laughed, his eyes bright. "I wasn't going to say it. I thought it sounded too arrogant. What will you spend it on?"

"My sword. The sharkskin on the hilt has been getting a little cracked."

"How mercenary of you." He shrugged on his jacket and straightened his collar. "I wish we could spend all day together."

"Or at least breakfast."

"Tomorrow," he said, which felt like a promise. "And tonight, dinner?"

Early morning in Vienna. The city had never looked so beautiful before.

Mist drifted above church steeples and red-tiled roofs. The

smoke of diesel-powered autos clouded the bracing chill of the winter air. My feet floated over the cobblestones. I hummed softly to myself under my breath.

After years of nothing but survival, I was happy.

The Viennese walked briskly along the streets near the Saturday market, many of them glancing curiously at me as I passed. I knew my jacket didn't do much to hide my dusty clothes or the scabbard on my belt.

And, of course, there was nothing I could do about looking foreign.

Hunger gnawed at my stomach. Breakfast with Wendel would have been lovely. Delicious smells wafted from a bakery. Locals had already lined up for the day's bread. When it was my turn at the counter, I smiled.

"*Guten morgen,*" I said.

The freckle-faced baker nodded. "What would you like?" he replied in English.

"The strudel."

"Apple?"

"Please."

He insisted on speaking English, like my German wasn't good enough. Was my accent still so poor? I had a knack for languages—everyone told me so—but I had only been speaking German for three years.

What did I sound like to Wendel? An American yokel, butchering his language?

"Ma'am?" The baker was holding out the strudel.

I blinked a few times. Was I obsessed with Wendel?

Yes, but I don't know how to stop.

"Thank you."

"Why are you in Vienna?"

I let my jacket fall away from my sword. "I'm a mercenary for the Archmages of Vienna."

The baker broke into a lopsided grin. "I want to fight, not bake strudel."

"The Hex will protect you."

"When they tell us there is a real war, I will join you." The baker gave me a thumbs up. "Teach those rebels a lesson!"

For his sake, I hoped there would never be a war.

I devoured the strudel while I walked through the streets. It wasn't the polite thing to do in Vienna, but I was too hungry to care. I entered the Saturday market clustered in the shadow of a cathedral. Merchants hawked potatoes, eggs, beeswax candles, walking sticks, and evergreen garlands for Christmas.

I wasn't interested in such wholesome wares. I was looking for a swordsmith.

Past the market proper, down a crooked medieval alleyway, I spotted a shop with a wrought-iron guild sign that depicted a gilded serpent entwined around a sword. I tugged open the heavy door and let myself into the shop.

The vague light of kerosene lamps glimmered on glass cases full of blades. I leaned in for a closer look. Daggers and swords rested on black velvet. Some glistened with the telltale iridescence of an enchantment forged into steel. A man with quick eyes and a devilish mustache leaned behind the counter, picking his teeth.

"Excuse me," I said. "I need some work done on my sword."

At the word *sword*, the man straightened from his slouch. He eyed me up and down, then smiled with his toothpick in his mouth. "You?"

Was he about to say something stupid? I suspected as much. Maybe a glimpse of my sword would convince him I was here on important business. I slid Chun Yi halfway from its scabbard and let the blade glint in the light.

"Me," I said.

The man stared at the sword. "Oriental?"

"Chinese."

"Like you?"

"I'm half." I kept my tone brisk and businesslike. "Can you fix it, or do you only handle Austrian swords here?"

The man twirled the toothpick with his tongue before offering his hand. "The name's Vigoren. Finest swordsmith in all of Vienna."

I would believe that when I saw it.

I gripped Vigoren's hand for a brisk shake. "Ardis."

"Never seen a blade like yours before." He held his palms skyward. "May I?"

I unbuckled Chun Yi from my belt and laid the scabbard in Vigoren's hands. My finger traveled along the cracks in the sharkskin.

"See the damage, there?"

"I do." His brow furrowed. "How old is this sword?"

"Old? At least a hundred years. I take good care of it."

Vigoren slid Chun Yi from its scabbard and tapped the

blade with his fingernail so it sang. He stared along the length of the sword, squinting, then inspected the pair of Chinese characters engraved on the blade.

"Is that Chinese writing?" he asked.

"Yes, the name of the sword." I couldn't read Chinese, but my mother had told me.

"What does it mean?"

"Chun means *pure,* and Yi means *justice* or *righteousness.*"

"I had hoped it described the enchantment."

I blinked. "Enchantment?"

"This sword must be well over a hundred years old, considering how weak its magic has become. But I should be able to—"

"It's not enchanted."

Vigoren laid Chun Yi on the counter. "Excuse me?"

"It isn't a magic sword."

The swordsmith scoffed. "You can't be serious."

I crossed my arms. "Chun Yi has been my sword for three years now. Not once have I ever seen an inkling of magic."

"There's clearly an enchantment forged in the blade. It's old, but it's there."

Excitement hopped inside me like a cricket. "Can you show me?"

Vigoren unhooked a small lantern from the wall behind him. The glass in the lantern looked cloudy and greenish.

"A will o' the wisp lantern might show us more of the enchantment."

He lit the white candle within the lantern. It burned with a pungent sweetness like sagebrush. He held the lantern over Chun Yi. When the scarred old blade flashed in the light, I gasped. Shimmering green glowworms of magic crawled over the sword, creeping over the metal, burrowing into its heart.

"Jesus Christ," I whispered. "I had no idea."

16

Vigoren grinned. His face looked ghostly by the light of the will o' the wisp lantern. "That's some kind of binding spell. Not like any I have ever seen before, but we can expect exotic magic in an exotic sword."

Had my mother known about the magic forged into Chun Yi? She never mentioned an enchantment. On the long journey from China to America, she brought the sword and the clothes on her back. I had always assumed the sword was a family heirloom, with no value beyond its age and its deadly steel.

I slid my hand along the counter until my fingers rested on the sword. The glowworms crept from the blade to my skin. They didn't feel like anything, though they were definitely crossing onto my hand before fading.

"Binding?" I asked. "What is the spell binding?"

When Vigoren blew out the lantern, the glowworms vanished. "If you look closer at the blade, there's a particular waterfall pattern that only occurs when magic is folded into the metal. Certain mages can read the steel to determine an enchantment's purpose, but with this sword, I suspect only a Chinese mage would know."

I lifted the sword. "Can you unbind the magic?"

"It would be my pleasure." Vigoren smiled. "It won't be more than a moment."

Damn, that was fast. I should have splurged on a sword-smith years ago.

Vigoren disappeared into the back of his workshop.

In the glass case near my right, I inspected the lineup of antique rapiers. I didn't like the thrust-and-parry style of fencing, but I had seen one or two mercenaries who had made a living out of killing that way.

Not that mercenaries had long careers. They always seemed to die young.

I shadowed a swordswoman for a year in an informal apprenticeship, until my tough-as-nails mentor took an arrow in the belly and died not two weeks later. Thinking about it still made me feel numb.

When Vigoren returned, he offered me Chun Yi, pommel-first. "Try it."

I swept my sword from its scabbard.

Nothing happened. Chun Yi still looked dull and battered. Frowning, I gripped the sharkskin hilt tighter and swung the sword so it whirred through the air. The balance of the blade felt familiar. Disappointingly so.

"Are you sure?" I asked.

Vigoren shrugged. "Here. Let me take another look."

I flipped the pommel toward him. The flat of the blade caught in my left hand. Chun Yi cut me in the crook of my thumb.

I grimaced. "Damn it."

Blood trickled onto the blade. Iridescence shimmered down the length of the steel, then ignited in a rush of magic. Chun Yi burned like an ember, glowing cherry red at the center, cooling to ash gray at the edges.

"Shit!" I nearly dropped the sword, though it burned without heat.

"Blood magic!"

I whistled low under my breath. "You were right."

Vigoren grinned. "Swordsmiths dream of discovering enchantments like this. Ancient, rare, and hidden in even the ugliest of blades."

Ugly? I decided not to argue the point.

The burning sword mesmerized me. I always found fire beautiful. "What is it?"

Vigoren rubbed his mustache. "The blade is bloodthirsty, very literally. The more blood it drinks, the more powerful it will become."

"Powerful? How?"

"Sharper. Stronger. Faster."

I moved through a few sword forms before sheathing the blade. The red glow died instantly. My hands still tingled. I drew Chun Yi halfway, watched the glow creep along the steel again, then let it fall back into the scabbard.

"Should I be extra careful with an enchantment?"

Vigoren waved his hand. "That sword has survived centuries of hacking and slashing."

I reached for my coin purse. "How much?"

"Ninety koronas."

"That sounds like a bargain." My blood smudged the gold. "Sorry."

"Don't worry about it." Vigoren smiled. "Just don't let your sword cut you again. It might get a taste for your blood."

"Never thought I would have a magic sword." I laughed in disbelief. "I borrowed some magic from a man's dagger once."

"What kind of magic?"

"It was like shadows. They crawled from his hand to mine and turned us all but invisible."

"I have never heard of such an enchantment. Was he an archmage?"

"No, a necromancer."

Vigoren's smile froze on his face. He swallowed, his throat bobbing. "Never trust a man who can raise the dead with his bare hands."

"I trust him with my life."

On the way back, after Vigoren had mended my sword and unveiled its magic, I lingered outside my favorite brewpub. The door swung open as a man wandered out, and the aroma of wiener schnitzel wafted to me. Laughter and a drinking song spilled into the golden afternoon.

I licked my dry lips, lured by the promise of ale.

At the bar, I ordered a pint of lager. The barmaid delivered a stein brimming with beer, deliciously cold and bitter. I propped my sore feet on the barstool, glanced around the brewpub, and sighed with growing contentment. Maybe this was what Austrians called *Gemütlichkeit*, the feeling of warm peace in good company.

I should ask Wendel if—

"Excuse me!" A big man sat on the stool next to me. He had thinning, greasy hair and a sloppy grin. "Didn't you hear me?"

I stared at him. "No."

The big man leaned down to my height, his breath damp in my ear. He fouled the air with his beer breath. Not to mention the remnants of his last meal clung to his beard. I pressed my lips together and tried not to gag.

"What's your name?" he asked. "I'm Dirk."

"Fuck off, Dirk."

He leaned back with mock surprise. "What's the matter? Just trying to be friendly."

Damn it, he had a sword. He must be some cut-rate mercenary or thug for hire.

I didn't want to start a brawl in my favorite brewpub and get banned for life. I drained my tankard, wiped my mouth on my sleeve, and barged outside. The door swung shut behind me but opened a moment later.

I glanced backward. Dirk was following me with rage in his eyes.

Just the wrong kind of drunk. Too drunk to keep his hands to himself, and too sober not to stay put in the brewpub.

My hand closed over the hilt of my sword. Adrenaline jolted my blood. I darted into the alley behind the brewpub.

A dead end.

Dirk stumbled to a halt and blocked my escape. Fuck, I had hoped to avoid violence on my day off, but he gave me no choice.

17

"Come on, sweetheart." Dirk grabbed his crotch. "I have a sword right here for you."

I challenged him with a stare. "Back off before I hurt you."

"Don't be such an uptight little bitch."

"Okay, now I *want* to hurt you."

With a grim smile, I freed Chun Yi. The blade smoldered with blood magic, and I saw surprise in Dirk's eyes.

He drew his own sword. The blade glinted in the late sunlight.

Was he stupid enough to attack me now? Apparently, he was.

I waited for him to charge, then swept past him and sliced his ribs just enough to hurt. Chun Yi crackled at the taste of blood.

With a shout, Dirk spun around. His sword whirled toward

my head, and I blocked his attack. The shock of it drove me backward and sent reverberations down my arm. I recovered my balance and pivoted away from him.

He was much stronger than I had thought. But I was smarter.

The thought steeled my muscles. When Dirk attacked again, I slid Chun Yi along the length of his blade and stabbed him in the shoulder. Dirk bellowed. Blood trickled down my sword's hilt and dripped hotly over my hand. When I yanked out Chun Yi, the blade sizzled and spat a trail of sparks into the air.

Dirk attacked again, his sword swinging wide. I dodged the blow with ease.

His stance left him vulnerable. In one swift movement, I crossed blades, reached under his sword's pommel, and grabbed his hilt. With a savage twist to his wrist, I wrenched his blade sideways and disarmed him.

Dirk bellowed again, trying to intimidate me. Idiot.

With a sword in each hand, I narrowed my eyes. His blade was dull and ugly, just like him. Chun Yi smoldered, on the verge of flames. An urge gripped me to slice his neck open and let his blood flow onto the dirt.

But there were always consequences for killing, everywhere but the battlefield.

"You lost," I said. "But I won't take your life. Not this time."

Dirk backed away, holding his head low like a wounded bull. His blood dripped down his shirt and plopped on the cobblestones. At the mouth of the alley, he groaned, swayed, then turned around and fled down the street.

After he ran away, I tossed his sword into the nearest garbage heap.

Rattled, I returned to the Hall of the Archmages. It was almost time to meet Wendel for dinner, but I wanted to talk to Margareta. As a mercenary, I couldn't go too long between missions, or I would run out of gold.

When I knocked on her office, she called out, "Enter."

I closed the door behind me. "Ma'am."

"Please, sit." Margareta steepled her hands on her desk. "I have an urgent job for you. You don't have much time to rest, I'm afraid. It's already Saturday, and you would need to arrive in Antwerp by Monday evening."

"Belgium?" I tilted my head. "That sounds better than Transylvania."

Transylvania would be forever linked to blood-soaked snow in my mind. Wendel would have bled to death there if I hadn't found him.

"Do you know of Dr. Rudolf Diesel?" Margareta asked.

"Of course."

"He's a brilliant man, one of Germany's finest engineers. However, he has been disloyal to his homeland."

I kept any judgment from my face. "Oh?"

Margareta thinned her lips as if her words tasted sour. "Diesel was a student at the Royal Bavarian Polytechnic of Munich, but he was born in Paris and spent some of his childhood in London. Now he plans to journey back to London for a crucial meeting of the Consolidated Diesel Engine Manufacturers."

That sounded reasonable to me, though I stayed quiet.

"Diesel's desire to help the British engineers has earned him the wrath of several powerful people within the German Empire. We suspect that there is a plot to...*convince* him of his loyalty to Germany, and it could end rather badly unless we protect him. The Archmages of Vienna have agreed that we should prevent this."

I glanced into her eyes. "You want me to be his bodyguard?"

Margareta smiled. "You always have a knack for stating things plainly. Diesel's steamer leaves from Antwerp on Monday evening."

"I'll do it."

"Good." She handed me an envelope. "Here are details about the mission. You may go."

I slipped the envelope into my jacket pocket. "Thank you, ma'am."

"And Ardis? Be careful with the necromancer."

I squared my shoulders. "Just to be clear, ma'am, what are you requesting?"

"Don't do anything that will jeopardize Project Lazarus."

"I don't know enough about Project Lazarus to know what will jeopardize it."

Her eyes hardened. "We need to keep the necromancer happy. He appears to trust you. Don't betray his trust."

For a moment, I thought she might forbid me from fucking him.

I exhaled. "Where can I find Wendel?"

"That's confidential."

"Well, that's inconvenient."

Margareta heaved a long-suffering sigh. "I will send word for him to meet you in the entrance hall. You are dismissed."

"Thank you."

When I returned to the entrance hall, Wendel met me only fifteen minutes later. That meant Project Lazarus had to be located nearby.

My heart skipped a beat at the sight of him. "Are you ready?"

"Very." He twisted his mouth. "Konstantin is addicted to work."

"I'm sure I'm not allowed to ask you about it."

"Definitely not." Wendel held the door for me. Together, we stepped into the evening. "Which is why I would love to tell you more over dinner."

I let out my breath in a rush. "Today has been a long fucking day."

"What happened?"

"Some asshole in a brewpub. He attacked me in the alley out back."

Wendel's hand caught my elbow. He stopped us both on the street. "Attacked?"

"I'm not hurt."

His jaw tightened. "Did he touch you?"

"He tried." I shuddered at the memory. "I beat him in a sword fight."

"Tell me his name."

"Just some random drunkard named Dirk."

"I will hunt him down and kill him for you."

Shivers crept down my spine. "You can't."

"I swore a vow to protect you. No one threatens you and lives." His words were as smooth and cold as ice.

His fierce devotion took my breath away. But I couldn't unleash the wrath of a necromancer upon my enemies.

"Promise me you won't hunt down Dirk?"

"I'm not sure I can make that promise."

I exhaled hard. "Wendel, you can't leave a trail of bodies behind."

"I beg to differ."

"We're in the middle of Vienna."

"And I already eliminated the assassins who tried to ambush us here."

Fuck, I couldn't argue with that.

"Dirk isn't worth your time. Please."

"As you wish." He brushed some of my hair from my eyes, a gesture that startled me with its thoughtfulness. "What did you have in mind for dinner? I'm famished."

I sighed. "This morning, I would have said my favorite brewpub, but now I don't want to run into any more trouble."

"I will keep you safe."

"You do know I can protect myself?"

"Undoubtedly, but you deserve a protector. Let me take care of you."

My tension melted at his words. "Why?"

"There is no question." He offered me his arm. "Come, walk with me. Show me the way to your favorite brewpub."

Evening fell on Vienna and turned the sky the color of sapphires. Stars glinted faintly above, all but lost in the glow of gas lamps. Lingering outside the brewpub for a moment, I breathed in deeply to steel my nerves.

Wendel held the door. "After you."

I stepped inside and scanned the area. No sign of Dirk, thank heavens. We settled at a quieter table in the corner.

Firelight played over the sharp angles of Wendel's face. God, he was gorgeous. The Prince of the Undying didn't belong here in this commonplace brewpub. It was surreal to bring him somewhere I had visited before.

"What's good here?" Wendel asked.

"The apricot dumplings are delicious. I love them in Vienna."

He traced the edge of the table with his finger, and wouldn't look me in the eye. "Will you be in Vienna long?"

I exhaled hard. "No," I admitted. "I'm leaving later tonight for Antwerp, Belgium. I have a mission to protect a target."

"Who?"

I lowered my voice. "Rudolf Diesel."

"Is it a dangerous mission?"

"Obviously."

"I wish I could come with you."

"Wendel, I'm a mercenary. It's my job."

"How long will you be gone?"

"I'm not sure. Less than a week. Will you be here when I return?"

His throat bobbed as he swallowed hard. "I don't know."

My stomach plummeted, my appetite vanishing into thin air. "Why?"

"The Order of the Asphodel won't stop until they have found me."

After dinner, Wendel walked me to the train station. As if the sky remembered, it began to rain again. I drew Chun Yi. Raindrops hissed and died on the blade. The steel remained cool and smooth under my fingertips.

How much blood did my sword want to devour?

"Enchanted?" Wendel said. "I didn't know."

"The swordsmith unlocked the enchantment."

"What kind?"

"Blood magic."

He arched his eyebrows. "Be careful with blood magic."

"I will."

Neither one of us wanted to keep talking, I could tell.

I bought a ticket for the next overnight train from Vienna to Frankfurt. From there, I could travel to Brussels, then Antwerp. I wasn't traveling first class this time, but of course Wendel wasn't coming with me.

Was this goodbye forever? I didn't dare speak the words out loud, afraid they would summon that conclusion.

A train's shrill whistle pierced the air.

"I can't miss my train." I turned away, ready to flee from our inevitable farewell.

"Ardis." Wendel caught me by the arm. "Wait."

He kissed me in the rain, a long, slow kiss as bittersweet as chocolate.

I clung to him, wanting to hold on until the last instant. When he broke the kiss, the depths of his eyes contained sorrow.

"This isn't goodbye," I said.

He said nothing. He had the grim look of a man resigned to kill or be killed.

Finally, I boarded the train alone.

I shared a couchette car with three German women in the white uniforms of nurses. They kept eyeing my sword, though they were very polite. I stashed Chun Yi in the luggage rack, kicked off my boots, and lay down on my berth.

What if I never saw Wendel again? What if one of us died before I returned?

Damn it, I wasn't going to cry, not in a couchette car with three strangers.

The overnight train clattered from Vienna and ventured into the deepening darkness. I closed my eyes and welcomed the oblivion of sleep.

I dreamed of blood, guns, and smoldering magic.

18

Frankfurt and Brussels passed by in a blur of gray skies as I sprinted through train stations to make my transfers. When I arrived in Antwerp on Monday morning, I hopped from the train and glanced around with bleary eyes.

So, this was the new Antwerp Central Station. I had heard about its impressive arches, ornate stonework, and immense windows that fanned like peacock tails. In America, you didn't get this kind of fairytale architecture.

I peered at a clock mounted above a gilded molding of Antwerp's coat of arms.

A quarter past eight.

Damn, I was late. Diesel's train arrived from Ghent at eight o'clock sharp, and I was supposed to meet him here.

I broke into a run and rushed down the platform. A conductor blew his whistle at me, signaling for me to slow down, but I ignored him. Staggered by the immensity of the entrance hall, I slowed to a jog. I reached into my jacket and took out a photograph of Diesel from the envelope Margareta had given me in Vienna. He wore spectacles over his dark eyes, and had a neatly trimmed white mustache.

Photograph in hand, I hunted for him in the entrance hall.

Diesel sat on a bench with his hands folded in his lap. He wore an understated suit that still looked costly. He had the same calm expression as his likeness in the photograph. When I walked up to him, he glanced into my eyes.

I squared my shoulders. "Dr. Rudolf Diesel?"

"Yes?"

"My name is Ardis. The Archmages of Vienna sent me to accompany you."

"Of course. Much as I would rather travel alone."

A subtle accent sharpened his soft voice. He had been born in Paris, then lived in London. He was a wanderer like me.

"Sir?" I asked. "Are you ready?"

Diesel bent to grab his luggage. I took his bag for him.

He cleared his throat and stepped back. "Please, let me. I don't require a porter as well as a bodyguard."

"I insist," I said, though his bag was heavy.

Diesel sighed. "Very well. Shall we?"

He strolled toward the doors. I matched his stride. It was awkward to carry the bag with Chun Yi sheathed at my waist, though I managed not to struggle. He shouldn't believe I was weak—or worse, extraneous.

"I had hoped for a bite to eat," Diesel said, "unless the arch-mages wish otherwise?"

"I go where you go, sir."

When my stomach rumbled, Diesel's mustache didn't quite hide his small smile. As we stepped from Antwerp Central, the early sunlight slanted down into our eyes. He winced and pinched the bridge of his nose.

"What is it?" I asked.

"Oh, it's nothing. Merely another migraine."

"Ah."

Something to watch out for. Headaches might distract him.

Diesel hailed a taxicab, then helped me load his luggage into the back. When the driver glanced at us in the rearview mirror, his blue eyes met mine. He stared at me for a moment too long, and I stared back without flinching.

Diesel pinched the knees of his trousers and tugged them straight as he sat in the taxi. "Driver, find us the finest nearby café."

The driver gave the taxi some gas. We accelerated smoothly away from Antwerp Central. Diesel gazed at the city, but I remained tense.

"Where are you from?" the driver asked, and again he glanced at me.

"Ghent," Diesel said. "I'm here on business."

"And your friend?"

He said the word like a synonym for *prostitute*. As if a lady of the night would ever dress so shabbily, or carry luggage for her client.

"I don't know," Diesel said, politely. "We have only just met."

"I'm from America," I said.

The driver shook his head. "What *are* you?"

"I'm a mercenary. And I'm here to make sure this man gets to where he needs to go as safely and quickly as possible. Understood?"

The driver gave the taxi more gas. I stared out the windshield until we stopped outside a café. After Diesel paid the driver, we exited the taxi.

I overheard the driver mutter, "Filthy Huns."

Was he trying to insult me for being half-Chinese, or Diesel for being German? Luckily, Diesel didn't seem to hear.

"Ardis, was it?" he asked, and I nodded. "I assume you will join me for breakfast?"

"Sure." I managed a smile.

I followed him into the café. It smelled strongly of coffee and toast inside, and the wood-paneled walls gleamed with newness. We sat by a window and ordered waffles, which were promptly delivered steaming hot, with heaps of whipped cream and syrupy canned strawberries on the side.

"Waffles are essential in Belgium," Diesel said.

I nodded in reply. I appreciated his friendly chit chat, though this was a mission. I wasn't here to entertain him.

Diesel shook more sugar over his waffle. "American?"

"Yes." I stabbed a strawberry with my fork.

"They seem more interested in beer than in inventions."

"Excuse me?"

"I sold the American rights to my engine to Adolphus Busch, but he has been too busy with his brewery to profit much from them."

I cocked my head. "Is there more profit in London?"

Diesel held out his hands as if weighing his options. "There is more opportunity there."

"Why not Germany?"

His spectacles flashed. "Are you loyal to America?"

He had a point.

At a riverside restaurant, Diesel's colleagues joined us—two Belgian men, Georges Carels and Alfred Luckmann. From what I could tell, Diesel and Carels were both directors of the Consolidated Diesel Engine Manufacturers. Carels ran a diesel engine factory in Ghent, where Luckmann worked as his chief engineer.

The men chatted in French, with a smattering of German, over cream of endive soup.

French wasn't a language that I had mastered, so I sat against the wall and tried to be inconspicuous. Carels kept glancing my way and then laughing to his companions. Luckmann sat farther from me, fidgeting when I looked at him, until finally I pretended he was invisible. Diesel merely ignored me.

Finally, at six o'clock, we left the restaurant and took a taxi to the docks.

We boarded the SS *Dresden*, a gleaming steel steamship, and followed the Scheldt River into the sea. Carels and Luckmann disappeared below deck, but Diesel stood at the railing and watched the sun bleed gold into the water.

The icy sea spray made my teeth chatter. I clenched my jaw. "It must be dinnertime. Your friends are waiting for you."

Diesel sighed. He looked tired, very tired, and older than I had thought.

"I suppose I should spend this one night with them," he said.

I frowned. "Aren't they traveling to London with you? For the meeting?"

"They are."

I edged closer to him, one hand on the hilt of my sword. The deck was nearly deserted at this instant, but soon we would sail outside of the influence of the Hex. Somewhere out on the English Channel, guns could kill again.

"You know why the archmages sent me," I said. "You aren't safe out here."

Diesel shrugged. "I am free to sell my patents to whomever I wish. Even if I sell them to the enemies of the German Empire."

"Is the profit worth your life?"

He laughed dryly. "Do you honestly think that they will act upon their threats? My inventions are far too valuable to them."

"Your inventions, but you are only their inventor."

"Only." He laughed again.

Diesel looked back to the horizon. After sunset, the water was the dark color of a bruise. He rubbed his forehead.

"My friends are waiting for me," he said in a distant voice, as if to convince himself.

I touched his elbow and walked with him down to the dining saloon. The saloon was a bit chilly, but cheery, with white paneling on the walls and electric lights in the chandeliers. Diesel found Carels and Luckmann and joined them at their table. I sat alone nearby, ignoring their curious glances.

I ordered a simple dinner—oxtail stew and boiled potatoes —and remained vigilant.

There were perhaps two hundred other passengers dining that evening. I didn't expect anyone to attack Diesel in such a public venue. If I had been hired to threaten a man into cooperation, I would do it in his cabin.

With that in mind, I waited. Diesel joked and laughed with his companions, the darkness outside forgotten. He ordered several courses from the menu, encouraged by the flirtatious blonde waitress. Diesel started with the French onion soup, worked his way through halibut in hollandaise sauce, and finished with a chocolate éclair and coffee. Everything looked delicious from where I sat. Glumly, I poked at my potatoes, wishing I hadn't spent so much money at the swordsmith.

Luckmann fingered a packet of cigarettes. "Shall we go for a stroll?"

Smiling, Diesel folded his napkin. "That sounds like a fine idea."

I abandoned my oxtail stew and followed them.

"Don't forget your shadow, Diesel," Carels teased.

Carels smiled at me, but he was also looking at me like I was an exotic spice to taste. Some men had that reaction to me.

We went above deck, where stars glittered in the sky like shattered glass.

"Cigarette?" Luckmann asked.

Diesel shook his head. "No, thank you."

Luckmann shielded his cigarette from the wind and shared a match with Carels. Diesel leaned against the railing and looked heavenward. They talked together, their voices boisterous. How much wine had they drunk?

"Well," Carels said, "I think it's time to be in bed."

Diesel nodded. "We have an important day ahead of us."

Carels leaned forward to clasp Diesel's arm, a whiff of wine on his breath. He caught my eye and winked.

"Good night!" he said.

Diesel lingered while his friends disappeared below deck. The *Dresden* plowed through a wave, and Diesel stumbled forward. He staggered against the steamship's railing. I caught him by the elbow before he could fall overboard.

"Careful!" I said.

"Thank you." He mopped his brow with his handkerchief.

"Too much wine to drink, sir?"

"I had no wine, only water and coffee."

My stomach plummeted. He didn't stink of alcohol like Carels, but he slurred his words. He gripped the railing, his knuckles tight, then lowered himself awkwardly to the deck. With unfocused eyes, he panted for air.

"Diesel, I need you to stay awake. Diesel!"

His eyelids closed before he slumped on the deck.

Poisoned.

19

"**F**uck!" I whispered.

I couldn't fight poison with a sword. A blonde woman in a uniform climbed onto the deck—the waitress from dinner.

"Get help!" I shouted. "He needs a doctor!"

The waitress ran toward us. *Wait.* My stomach flipped. Why was a waitress above deck so late? The sky was much too dark for her to be out, even if she was just sneaking a cigarette.

How easy would it have been to slip Diesel poison in his coffee?

My hand twitched to my sword. A second later, I unsheathed Chun Yi in a cascade of sparks. The blonde pulled a pistol from a holster on her thigh and sighted down the barrel. Cold determination steeled her eyes.

Sometimes I hated being right.

"Stop." I squared my shoulders. "The Hex might still reach this far."

"Want to risk it?" the blonde drawled.

"Who are you?"

"Really, darling?" The blonde scoffed. "I'm Natalya. Your superior."

I narrowed my eyes at the insult. "Superior? Doubtful."

"Go back downstairs. Nobody has to get hurt."

"You already poisoned Diesel."

"He's only unconscious."

I glanced down at Diesel while he wheezed for breath. Natalya slid her foot forward. Her gun gleamed in the starlight.

"Listen, darling," Natalya said. "You brought a sword to a gunfight."

Then why wasn't she firing?

I decided to find out. I feinted right and swung left at Natalya's neck. Natalya ducked—the blade whistled past her ear—and kicked me in the kneecap. My leg buckled before Natalya shoved me sprawling. I crashed onto the deck. The blonde aimed a kick at my face. I rolled away and sliced at her leg.

Natalya retreated. "Put down your pretty little sword."

This pretty little sword wanted to taste blood. Chun Yi's thirst pulsed in my hand.

Muscles bunching, I surged upright and lunged at Natalya. I judged the angle to hit a vital artery and swung Chun Yi.

But there was a blur of movement.

Pain exploded in my head. Pistol-whipped, I crashed onto the deck. Stars danced before my eyes and stole my breath away for a minute. I clamped down on my fear and pushed it far away. Fear could be fatal.

Blinking fast, I crawled to my knees. Where was Natalya?

I heard a grunt, followed by a scraping noise.

Head spinning, I staggered to my feet. Natalya dragged Diesel to the railing, hefted him onto the steel, and pushed him overboard. She watched him fall and waited until the splash. Then she glanced back at me.

"You saw nothing," Natalya said. "If you want to survive."

She vaulted over the railing. I rushed to the edge.

A long way down, the choppy waters of the English Channel unfurled.

Nausea washed over me and I retched. I stumbled to the stern, where the giant propellers of the steamship churned the waves. Out in the darkness, between tatters of fog, I saw a light bobbing in the waves.

A boat.

Shadowy figures dragged two people aboard—Diesel and Natalya. The light flickered out before the boat vanished into the night.

I slumped on a chair in the deserted dining saloon. The electric lights stabbed my eyes, and my stomach still churned.

The steamship captain scratched his mustache. "Diesel must have been drunk."

"I didn't see him drink any wine," Carels said. "Diesel was an abstemious man."

Nearby, Luckmann wrung his hands and kept quiet.

The captain bent down to my level. "You saw him fall overboard?"

When I nodded, the movement nearly made me vomit.

"There—there was a woman," I stammered. "A waitress. She was pretending to be a waitress. She gave him poisoned coffee."

"Poisoned coffee?" The captain folded his arms. "On my ship? Preposterous."

My memories kept drifting farther away. Carels and Luckmann shared a glance. Even though my eyes struggled to focus, the skepticism was plain on their faces. The captain pulled Carels aside and muttered to him.

"...she must be intoxicated..."

What if this was more than a concussion? What if I had been poisoned, too? Fear chilled my blood. When I tried to stand, I staggered to my knees. The men caught me by my elbows. Bitter bile crept into my mouth.

"I feel sick," I gasped.

They brought me a bucket just in time. I emptied the contents of my stomach. After vomiting, I shivered on the floor.

The captain touched my shoulder. "Bring this young woman to her room. She's unwell."

Crewmembers escorted me to my cabin and helped me lie down on the narrow bed. I squeezed my eyes shut against the spinning.

Listen, darling. You brought a knife to a gunfight.

Put down your pretty little sword.

I tried to summon the memory of Natalya's face, but I remembered Diesel falling over the railing into the churning dark water.

You saw nothing.

The steamship docked in Harwich at six o'clock in the morning.

Fog cloaked the coastline of England, and my mind felt equally obscured. I was steady on my feet, at least, and no longer nauseated. But I couldn't remember many of the particulars from last night with Diesel.

I had to tell the archmages, before I forgot all the details.

Quickly, I found the nearest telegraph office. It was a relief to hear English spoken at last. I dictated my message to the telegraph operator in English, as well, since I knew Margareta would understand it.

Diesel overboard still alive taken by mercenary reply at once

I waited for the reply.

Return by airship immediately

I had enough money to stay several nights—I had meant to book a room in Diesel's hotel upon arrival—but instead I caught a train from Harwich to London, and then a direct flight from London to Vienna.

The airship was a lumbering beast of a zeppelin, scheduled for a two-hour journey.

In the cramped seating, I rested Chun Yi across my knees and leaned my forehead against the cool glass of the porthole window. Below, England drifted away like a patchwork quilt of green fields and gray city. The zeppelin's shadow rippled over the English Channel, which looked almost insignificant from the air.

Diesel could be anywhere by now.

By the time I arrived in Vienna, I had a lingering headache. Gingerly, I touched the right side of my head. The pistol had left a painful lump. I stopped by a café for some ice, and wrapped the cubes in a napkin. Ignoring strangers staring at me, I held the ice to my head as I walked to the Hall of the Archmages.

I knocked on the door to Margareta's office.

"Come in."

I sat at Margareta's desk, the ice melting and dripping down my hair. "Ma'am."

"What happened?" Margareta said, without any proper greetings.

"We were attacked, after dinner, on the deck of the *Dresden*. This blonde dressed as a waitress—Natalya—she pistol-whipped me."

Margareta thinned her lips. "It looks rather painful."

"That's an understatement."

"And Diesel?"

"Gone. She…she poisoned him. I think. I'm having a hard time remembering."

"What *do* you remember?"

"Diesel fell overboard, and Natalya jumped after him. A

boat came from the fog and took them both aboard. I'm sure of that much."

Margareta said nothing for a long moment. "He was drunk, wasn't he?"

"No, ma'am, I don't think he was."

"He was drunk," she repeated, "wasn't he."

This time, I realized it wasn't a question. "Ma'am?"

"Diesel had too much to drink and fell overboard. An accident. You have no reason to believe otherwise. That is what you saw."

The sickening truth of it settled in my stomach. I dropped the ice in my hand on the carpet and watched the widening puddle.

My voice sounded hoarse. "This was staged?"

"Although it didn't go according to plan."

I pointed to the wound on my head. "Was *this* part of the plan?"

"Of course not. But we didn't anticipate that you would be so aggressive. Since when did you use an enchanted sword?"

"Why did you hire me at all?"

Margareta shrugged. "Backup. We had reason to believe that our enemies might try to make a move on Diesel before we could carry out our plan. Our other mercenary couldn't guard Diesel as well as carry out her mission."

"Drugging and abducting Diesel?"

Margareta's eyes glittered like frost. She slid open a desk drawer, grabbed a coin purse, and tossed it in my direction. "Your compensation."

I resisted the urge to slam my fist on Margareta's desk. "But I *failed*."

"There's no need for melodrama. You know now that our mission with Diesel was a success. You played your role."

"As your pawn."

Margareta's nostrils flared. "Perhaps you would like some time off from being a pawn? Three weeks sounds nice, doesn't it?"

My face on fire, I shoved my chair away from the desk and stood. "Yes, ma'am."

I turned to go, but Margareta cleared her throat. "Ardis?"

"Ma'am?"

"Don't forget your money."

Disgusting. I had been so stupid to think they trusted me with Diesel.

They didn't even trust me with the truth.

The thought of it burned in my throat. I stormed across the street to the Imperial Palace Hotel and returned to our room.

Wendel wasn't there.

The bed was neatly made. There was no sign of him anywhere. Fear clenched my throat in its iron fist.

Was he gone already?

Was he gone *forever*? The thought was too terrible to contemplate.

I tossed the coins from the archmages across the room.

They missed the bed, which was my target, and spilled on the carpet. Gold glinted temptingly in the shadows. The sick shame of failure burned in my throat.

I locked the door and stripped down to my skin. I needed a shower to scrub away the events of the past twenty-four hours. When the steaming hot water poured over me, it unlocked all the tension in my body.

Tears spilled from my eyes. Crying in the shower wasn't something I did often, and it had the feel of an indulgent luxury.

God, I missed Wendel.

His absence hurt with every heartbeat. I hoped he was still alive. I hoped he would return to me eventually.

I turned off the water and dried myself. Damn, these were the most luxurious towels I had ever touched before. I laughed despite myself, a broken kind of laugh.

With a shuddering sigh, I fell onto the bed.

My head sank into the pillow, and I began to feel better. Sleep would do me good.

Sunlight slanted across the wall, then faded into the cool light of dusk. My eyelids closed and I surrendered to sleep.

I woke to the click of the door opening. Startled, I hugged the sheets to myself. I had fallen asleep completely naked after my shower. Moonlight streamed through the open window. My heartbeat began to pound.

A man stood silhouetted in the doorway.

His honey-gravel voice invoked a shiver down my spine: "You came back."

20

"**W**endel." I whispered his name, as if any louder might wake me from a dream.

He glanced at the carpet. "Why are there coins scattered everywhere? Was there an attempt at a robbery?"

I couldn't tell if he was joking or not. My hands twisted in the sheets. "No."

"What happened?"

"I was angry." I swallowed hard. "I failed my mission."

He tilted his head. "Are you naked in bed?"

"Yes," I admitted.

He closed the door behind him and locked it. He kicked off his boots and tossed his coat onto the back of the couch.

When he stepped into the moonlight, his eyes looked intense. "I didn't know if I would ever see you again."

"Neither did I."

His throat worked as he swallowed hard. "The Order of the Asphodel hasn't sent any more assassins to Vienna yet, though it's inevitable that they will. They won't stop until they have captured me and dragged me back to Constantinople."

"Then we have no time to waste."

"What are you proposing?"

I let the sheet fall away from my naked body. "Come to bed with me."

He didn't need to be told twice.

He crossed the distance between us in a few long strides. He bent over the bed and kissed me. When he touched the wound on my head, I sucked in my breath.

"Have I hurt you?" he asked.

"Some bitch pistol-whipped me."

He cradled my face in his hands and looked at the injury. "I'm sorry."

"Just be careful."

"Of course."

He kissed me again, more gently this time, and I grabbed his shirt in both of my fists. I didn't want him to be *that* gentle. I dragged him into bed with me. He straddled me with his knees on either side of my hips.

When I unbuttoned his fly, his erection sprang free. His cock jutted from his princely black clothes like I had fantasized earlier on the train. I wrapped my fingers around him. God, his skin here was scalding hot. I pumped him in my fist until the head of his cock glistened with a hint of slippery arousal.

"Tell me you want me," I said.

"You can't tell?" he joked.

"I need to hear you say it out loud. I need...I need to feel wanted."

Sobering, he looked into my eyes. "Ardis."

"You're the only one here who cares if I live or die. Even the archmages see me as nothing more than a pawn."

He stroked his thumb over my cheekbone and brushed away a tear I hadn't even noticed falling. "I have never stopped wanting you. Sometimes, the want feels so sharp and deep inside me that it's frightening."

His confession stole my breath away. "Wendel..."

Was he falling in love with me?

No, he couldn't be. It was too soon, too fast, and lust wasn't the same as love.

Me. I'm the one falling.

"Fuck me." I grabbed his ass in both hands. "Please."

He leaned back long enough to roll a preventive over his cock. Anticipation fluttered through my belly. The blunt head of his cock pressed against my entrance before invading and dragging pleasure from my body.

My fingers tightened around his ass. "Harder," I demanded.

He slid out slowly, tormenting me, before slamming back into me. The movement knocked a moan from me. I arched from the bed. Except for his cock, he was still fully clothed, and I was naked beneath him. A delicious thrill shot through me.

"Pretend you broke into my room," I said, "and found me naked in bed."

"Oh?" Desire roughened his voice. "You want me to take advantage of you?"

"Fuck, yes."

His eyes narrowed, glittering in the narrow shard of moonlight. "Tell me more about this fantasy of yours first."

"Imagine that you want me so badly, you would do anything to have me." My cheeks heated. "You hold me down."

He pinned my wrists above my head. "Like this? Or is that too much?"

"Not enough."

"You want me to be rough?"

I let out a shaky breath. "Yes."

"Tell me to stop and I will."

"Don't stop."

Pinning me down to the bed, he started fucking me ruthlessly. His cock hammered into me and claimed my body again and again.

He had no mercy and I loved it.

"Don't stop, don't stop." It became a breathless chant, until I was begging him for release with every repetition.

He kissed me on the mouth, a hard kiss, with his teeth nipping my lower lip. The little shock of pain wound me even tighter. He brought his mouth to my neck, though he didn't bite me there like I hoped.

"You want me to defile you?" he murmured.

"Please."

His fingers tightened around my wrists. "Not until you come for me. Drench my cock with your pretty little pussy."

I whimpered. "I'm so close. God, please."

He released one of my wrists. His fingers found my clit. The same fingers that had killed men and raised the dead. This forbidden thought flitted through my mind like a shadow. His necromancy shivered over me, the cold fire of his magic igniting my nerves.

I couldn't escape him or the pleasure building inside me. I had no choice. My legs locked up and I cried out. My climax crashed through me. I drenched his cock, just the way he demanded from me.

"Fuck," he muttered through his teeth.

He lost control. He thrust wildly inside me, his face twisted with anguish. His cock thickened and throbbed as he came, his hips jerking in a primal way, like he wanted to drive his seed even deeper inside me.

His throbbing climax made me come again. Deeper, this time, until my legs were trembling. I clung to him and rode out the pleasure.

Breathing hard, I closed my eyes. My mind was an oblivion of bliss.

When he pulled out, I let out a soft noise of protest and tried to drag him back down to me. He escaped my clutches.

"Have to take care of this," he said.

Right. The preventive.

When he returned from the bathroom, he was unbuttoning his shirt. He tossed it aside before unbuckling his belt. Naked, he climbed into bed with me and tugged me closer. I craved the heat of his skin.

"Wendel?" I whispered.

"Yes?"

"Thank you."

"For defiling you?" He sounded amused.

"For indulging me."

"Trust me, I already wanted to fuck you. And I enjoyed your fantasy."

"Good." I laughed, still a little shy.

"I would do anything for you." His words were so soft and serious.

"I believe you."

21

Morning sunlight woke me, a golden glow streaming through the sheer white curtains. The Imperial Palace Hotel was a far cry from the battlefield tents and train berths I was so used to as a mercenary.

Wendel lay with his back to me, his breathing still slow with sleep. His hair spilled like ink across the pillow and glimmered blue-black. I stroked his hair in my fingers, wondering how he kept it so silky.

On his neck, just over his spine, he had a black tattoo of a double-headed eagle.

My breath caught in my throat.

After three years of looking, I had at last found the symbol my mother had seen tattooed on my father's neck.

Was it a symbol of Prussian royalty?

My heartbeat thudding, I traced the mark with my finger.

Strangely, the eagle's claws clutched a skull and a six-petaled flower.

Wendel tensed beneath my hand. "Ardis?" Sleep roughened his voice.

"I didn't mean to wake you. I saw the tattoo on the back of your neck."

He slid out of bed and bent for his clothes. "It wasn't my choice."

"Wendel."

He tugged on his trousers before grabbing his shirt. Why was he refusing to look at me? What did the tattoo mean to him?

I clutched the sheets to my naked body. "Wendel, what's wrong?"

With a hard exhalation, he sank back down on the bed and braced his elbows on his knees. His hair hid the eagle on his neck until he brushed it aside. "This was given to me by the Order of the Asphodel."

My stomach plummeted. Was my father one of them? An assassin?

"Against your will?" I asked.

"It's a hideous tattoo." He spoke with derision. "I have better taste than that."

"Is that why you let your hair grow long?"

"Yes." He glanced back at me. "Why so many questions?"

"Let me show you."

I leaned across the bed and took my brass locket from the nightstand. I slid my fingernail between the two halves of the locket. He tilted his head toward the tintype photographs. His gaze locked on my father.

Already pale, his face turned even whiter. "Where did you get this?"

"From my mother."

"Your mother? Are you serious?" His jaw hardened. "Is this some kind of sick joke?"

I stared at him. "No."

"Why is she with *him*?"

"Who is he? You know him?"

He grabbed his shirt and began buttoning it, though he couldn't hide how his hands were shaking. "I wish I never knew him."

"He's my father, Leo."

Wendel's throat bobbed as he swallowed hard. "His name isn't Leo." He glanced at me. "Your father? God, I don't know how I could have been so blind. I should have seen the resemblance the moment we met."

My hands twisted the sheets. "Who is he?"

"We both know the answer to that. Tell me the truth. Why did he send you?"

"He didn't send me. I've never met him!"

"Was this part of an elaborate plan to seduce me and lure me back?" He curled his lip in a sneer. "I must say, I'm impressed. You almost had me convinced."

My jaw dropped at his arrogance. "What's *wrong* with you?"

"Many things."

"Wendel, I swear I have never met my father. I don't even know who he is, or why you are so fucking afraid of him."

"Afraid?" His eyes glittered. "You would be a fool not to fear him yourself."

"Who *is* he?" The words exploded from me.

"Thorsten." His face froze into a mask. "Your father is Thorsten Magnusson, the Grandmaster of the Order of the Asphodel."

His answer hit me like a slap. I sank back onto the mattress. My stomach writhed with uncertainty and disbelief.

"The Grandmaster?" I repeated. "Your leader?"

"Yes." Bitterness saturated Wendel's voice. "My master, my tormentor."

The blood drained from my face. "No," I whispered.

"You fooled me, I admit. I can't believe I fucked you."

Rage roared to life inside me like a wildfire. I grabbed my scattered clothes from the floor and began tugging them on roughly. "I can't believe I fucked *you*. You're nothing more than a pretty boy with a fucked-up past."

Wendel jerked away from me like I had physically struck him. "You don't know me."

"You're a bastard." I glared at him while struggling with my boots.

"I'm flattered."

"Don't congratulate yourself. Whatever the Order of the Asphodel did to you, they broke any sense of decency you had."

Loathing burned in Wendel's eyes. The intensity of it took my breath away.

"Ardis." His voice cracked on my name. "Of course I'm

broken. They pushed me past my limits. I could blame them for everything I have become, but that would be a lie. I have done unforgivable things for them."

"Why the fuck did you vow loyalty to me?" My vision blurred.

"Because you saved my life."

Tears escaped from my eyes and rolled down my cheeks. They betrayed my emotions when I didn't want him to see me cry. I grabbed my sword. My fingers shaking, I fumbled to buckle the scabbard to my belt.

I needed to get away from him.

"Ardis," he said. "Wait."

I reached for the door. "Don't follow me."

"*Wait.*" He caught me by the wrist. "Where are you going?"

"Away."

"You aren't staying?"

"Why would I stay? That's right, to drag you back to Constantinople." I let out a scathing laugh. "You might have to murder me."

He dropped my wrist. "No."

Emotion burned in my throat like a hot coal. "You told me you would do anything for me. Was that an empty promise?"

"No," he repeated, in a hoarse whisper. When he bowed his head, his hair shadowed his face. "Ardis, I won't fight you. I swear that I don't want to hurt you."

"You already did, when you called me a liar."

"I apologize. I—I have been a bastard."

My teeth ached from clenching my jaw. I forced myself to exhale. "You still believe I might be an assassin?"

He hesitated. "Maybe."

"And you're still apologizing to me and refusing to fight me?"

"Yes."

"God, Wendel." I rubbed tears from my cheeks with the back of my hand. "You aren't making it easy to hate you."

"Even if you aren't an assassin, you are still Thorsten's daughter." He raked his hand through his hair. "It's difficult for me to accept. My memories of him are..."

"What?"

"Painful."

"I'm not my father. I've never met him."

He lifted his gaze, his eyes a luminous green. "Please forgive me."

I turned my back on him. It was too hard to look at him. He stepped behind me and wrapped his arms around my shoulders. My traitorous body melted against his. He bent so that his face rested in the curve between my shoulder and my neck. His lips lingered there like the hope of a kiss.

"I'm sorry," he said. "When I saw the locket, I panicked. Even now, it's hard for me to talk about this with fear throttling me. It feels like an iron fist around my throat."

I tried to face him, but his arms tightened around me. Maybe he found it easier to tell the truth without looking into my eyes.

"What happened to you?" I asked.

"More than I wish to admit."

My heart ached for him, imagining all the pain he must have endured over the years. "I'm sorry, too. I shouldn't have said some of the things that I did. You're not just a pretty boy with a fucked-up past."

"But you do think I'm pretty?"

"Devastatingly handsome."

"Good."

He was back to being sarcastic, though now I knew it was nothing more than a mask to hide the scars that ran so deep.

22

As part of his apology, Wendel invited me to breakfast at a café. We walked together through the morning streets of Vienna.

"Have you ever had poor knights?" he asked.

"Excuse me?"

"Poor knights."

"Never."

He arched an eyebrow. "Never? That's a crime."

He brought me to Café Amsel, a coffeehouse in a gleaming granite building, and held open the door for me. Warmth rushed out to meet us, the air scented by bitter coffee and sweet pastries. My mouth watered.

I had never been to Café Amsel before, since it was far outside of my budget. My boots rapped on parquet floors. Crystal chandeliers glittered over billiards tables. Wendel slid a chair from a small table and gestured for me to sit. He played the part of a gentleman well, when he wasn't being a bastard.

"Thank you," I said.

"My pleasure."

I traced the cool marble of the table. "It feels like I've been away from Vienna a lot longer than only a few days."

"Was your journey tiring?"

"Very." My mind drifted to faraway places. "When I left America, I came to Europe looking for my father. Would he be in Constantinople?"

Wendel tensed, a muscle in his jaw jumping. "I assume so."

"Was he there this whole time?"

"How long have you been here?"

"Three years."

He grimaced. "Then yes."

A waitress came to our table. "Good morning!" She smiled at Wendel, not even acknowledging my existence. "Are you ready to order?"

He brightened. "Poor knights for both of us."

"With cream?"

"Everything tastes better with cream." Wendel glanced at me.

Heat crept into my cheeks. Was I imagining the devilish glint in his eye? Or was he suggesting something indecent? Whenever I looked at him, it was impossible to forget all the filthy things we had done together.

"And can I get you some coffee?" asked the waitress.

"Please," he said.

She stopped mooning over him long enough to scribble

down our order. She smiled at him, and fucking *winked* before leaving.

I rolled my eyes. "You're too handsome for your own good."

"She doesn't know I'm a necromancer."

"Or a Prince of Prussia."

He snorted. "I'm not sure why anyone would want me."

I tilted my head. "Why *did* the archmages want you?"

"My necromancy."

"Yes, but for what reason?"

He smirked. "That's confidential."

"Your breakfast." The waitress slid two plates between us. "Enjoy!"

I stared at my food: two slices of bread, drenched in egg batter and fried until golden, with a dollop of cream on top.

"French toast!" I said.

"Gesundheit?" Wendel said.

I picked up my fork. "This is what we call French toast in America. I didn't know that you call it poor knights here."

"It isn't really French. I grew up eating it."

I sliced into the toast with my knife and took a bite. "God, this is delicious."

"Remind me," he said. "Weren't you protecting Rudolf Diesel?"

The toast turned into a hard lump in my throat. I swallowed with difficulty before replying. "That was the idea."

"What happened?"

I lowered my voice. "I don't know what you heard already, maybe about how Diesel drank too much on the steamship, then fell overboard and drowned? That's all lies. I only found out after the fact that this was all staged. They hired some other mercenary to drug Diesel and then smuggle him to a boat. But I still don't know why."

Wendel picked up his knife and stabbed his toast decisively. "It all makes perfect sense."

My jaw dropped. "They told *you* what happened to Diesel?"

"Hilarious." He waved his hand as if brushing away my words. "Do you think they trust me enough for that? But I have been collecting scraps of information here and there while I'm still valuable to them."

I shook my head. "And how exactly is your necromancy valuable to them?"

"Remember Konstantin's little project?"

"Project Lazarus? You never told me more."

"Oh, you couldn't guess?"

I glared at him. "Wendel. Just tell me. I might be the silent mercenary who stands outside doors, but don't treat me like I'm stupid."

"Sorry." He laid both of his hands flat on the table. "So. Project Lazarus."

"Like I said, I'm completely in the dark."

"Konstantin made me swear not to tell a soul." Wendel smirked. "Naturally, I'm happy to tell you everything."

Good God, was he always this shameless?

"Project Lazarus," he said, "started in 1912, when Kaiser Wilhelm II of Germany and King Joseph of Austria-Hungary convened the German Imperial War Council. Officially, they discussed the Hex in the Ottoman Empire."

I nodded. I remembered Konstantin returning from the Dodecanese.

"Unofficially," Wendel continued, "they discussed strengthening their army and developing superior military technology. That's the aim of Project Lazarus. The Hex was meant to be a diversion and buy them more time."

"Konstantin told you all this?"

He snorted. "The archmage talks too much. You ask him one question, and he prattles on for thirty minutes about his precious technomancy. I have no clue why he even trusts me, although of course he needs my expertise."

I suspected Konstantin was just naïve enough to be impressed by Wendel.

"What kind of military tech?" I asked.

"*Eisenkriegers.*" His eyes gleamed. "Imagine a soldier in a powered suit of armor that gives him superhuman strength. Thanks to some really clever magic, the man inside the machine can operate the metal arms and legs."

"Let me guess, you did the really clever magic?"

"Exactly." He spread his hands. "Though I can't take all the credit."

"How humble of you."

He tipped his head. "Konstantin thought of copying my necromancy so a soldier could control the Eisenkrieger. When I revive the dead, I can control them from a distance. I only need to touch them once. Together, the archmage and I mimicked that particular aspect of my magic. A feeble imitation, but it works."

I sat up straighter. "And they must want Diesel for the mechanical work."

"Correct."

"But Diesel wouldn't want to help the Germans, which is why they had to *encourage* him to join the team for Project Lazarus."

He smiled. "Exactly."

"Why the fuck did the archmages lie to me?" I rubbed my wounded head. "And that bitch didn't need to pistol-whip me."

He reached across the table and squeezed my hand. "If it still hurts—"

"I'm fine."

"You aren't a nurse, remember?"

"And you aren't a doctor."

"I *could* be." He smirked. "I would, of course, order you straight to bed."

"Wendel!"

I yanked my hand away and tried very hard not to laugh. He sliced his toast with enough innocence that he deserved a halo.

Joy whirred like a flight of birds through my chest.

"Wendel," I said, "I wish—I wish we could have more of this."

"Poor knights? Let me ask the—"

"No. *This.*"

Moments together where I couldn't stop looking at him, couldn't stop falling for him. But was this only a glimpse of a Wendel that could have been? Sorrow, beautiful and deep, ached inside my heart.

"This," he repeated.

He glanced out the window and scanned the street. Tension returned to the way he held his jaw. He folded his napkin, drank a slow swig of water, and dropped some coins onto the table for breakfast.

"It's a lovely day," he said. "Walk with me."

We left Café Amsel together. My heart pounded with uncertainty.

Wind tugged at my jacket and tossed his hair behind him in ribbons of black. With the sun lurking behind clouds, his skin looked white, his eyes almost as gray as the sky. He lingered outside the café.

"Have you seen the cathedral?" he asked.

"I have."

He hooked his fingers between mine, a little tighter than he needed, and tugged me on. "Let's go there together."

We walked down the Ringstrasse, an old road built over the memory of an even older wall that once circled the heart of Vienna. At the center of the city, the great Gothic tower of St. Stephen's soared heavenward. The cathedral's roof gleamed richly with a mosaic of twin black eagles—one for Vienna, one for Austria.

The bells of St. Stephen's began to ring. The heavenly clamor chimed over Vienna.

"The Angelus." Wendel quickened his pace. "It must be noon already."

"The Angelus?"

He shrugged. "It's a Catholic devotion. They ring the Angelus bell three times a day."

"I didn't think you were Catholic."

"I'm not, though I do love cathedrals."

We arrived on the steps of St. Stephen's, dwarfed by its Gothic immensity, and he held one of the iron-barred doors open for me. We stepped into the hush within. Incense and beeswax candles scented the air.

"Necromancers and cathedrals?" I asked. "You hardly seem holy."

He leaned close enough to me that his breath stirred my hair. "I love cathedrals," he murmured, "because they often have catacombs beneath them. Don't act startled, but someone has been following us."

23

My hand darted to my sword. "Who?"

"Keep walking toward the high altar." As we strolled through the rows of pews, Wendel whispered in my ear. "It's an assassin from the Order of the Asphodel." A muscle in his jaw twitched, though he smiled sardonically. "The bastard hasn't found the balls to come after me yet, though I suppose he *did* see what happened to the others."

"Others?" I whispered back.

"Six of them." He shrugged. "So far."

"You killed them all?"

"Not all at once," he said, modestly.

He turned toward the cathedral's north tower. I followed him. The muscles in my back tensed as if I expected a knife between my shoulder blades. Would the assassin dare attack us in the sanctuary of a cathedral?

"Are we safe here?" I asked.

"Safe?" He glanced sideways at me. "Don't worry, the assassins want me alive. I'm infinitely more valuable to them that way."

I grimaced. "I'm not infinitely valuable."

"You are to me." He touched his lips to my neck, earning us a glare from a passing priest. "Stay close. We can lure the assassin down to the catacombs and end this. I must say, it's so much easier when they come to me."

A shiver wracked my body. We had reached the entrance to the crypt.

We descended the stairs, each granite step worn smooth by centuries of footsteps. The glow from the candlelight and cathedral's windows dimmed as we walked into the lantern-lit darkness. The crypt twisted underground like a macabre rabbit's warren. I had never been down here before. Rumors spoke of royal innards kept in sarcophagi, and more common bones tossed in the catacombs.

"The catacombs are down this passageway." Wendel's voice sounded rougher than usual. He inhaled before letting out a shuddering breath. "I can feel them," he muttered. "Thousands. Tens of thousands."

"Who?"

He shut his eyes. "The dead."

The tiny hairs on my arms stood at attention. We hadn't even reached the catacombs yet, though clearly that didn't stop a necromancer from feeling bones through solid stone and earth. When I touched his wrist, the fire of his magic crawled onto my skin. I flinched away and rubbed my fingers together.

"Is there another way out of the catacombs?" I asked. "Or is it a dead end?"

He laughed. "A *dead* end?"

"I'm serious."

"There are two ways out. The way we came in, and stairs to the outside of the cathedral."

I nudged his elbow to get him walking again. "Let's leave the catacombs alive."

We strode down the shadowy tunnel, past mildew-slicked stone walls that glistened in the flickering lamplight. The weight of the entire cathedral aboveground flattened the air. I struggled to breathe evenly.

"It's claustrophobic in here," I whispered.

"If we are lucky, this will be quick." He guided me to the left. "Hurry, through here."

We pushed through an iron-barred door that creaked on rusty hinges. Beyond, there was no light. The door groaned shut behind us and plunged us into near complete darkness. A sliver of lamplight slithered underneath the door. Wendel took my hand and tugged me forward, but I dug my heels into the dirt.

"Wait," I whispered. "Step back."

"Why?"

"Don't want to cut you with my sword." I drew Chun Yi.

Smoldering fire rushed through the steel and banished the darkness. Skulls stared back at me with empty eye sockets. Bones, thousands of them, were stacked inside the catacombs like kindling for a bonfire in hell.

His stunned face looked ghostly by the glow of the blade. "Where did you—?"

"Same old sword. A swordsmith unlocked an enchantment."

He eyed the sword. "What sort of enchantment?"

"Blood magic," I said, as casually as I could manage.

He inhaled sharply. "Blood magic? Christ."

"You know a thing or two about it?"

"Enough." He wielded his black dagger, Amarant. "Take my hand."

Chun Yi crackled in my hand. Smoke unfurled from Amarant and spiraled down his hand, covering his skin with shadows. When the shadows ran from his hand to mine, fiery pain burned me in the shape of his fingerprints.

I gasped. "Let go!"

After I yanked away, I shook out my hand. My skin throbbed where he had touched me. The enchantments must have clashed.

Shadows dissolved from Wendel as he pocketed Amarant. "Did I hurt you?"

"No," I lied. "I'm fine."

"I don't trust your sword. Seems evil to me."

I glowered at him. "Evil? It must be *your* dagger—"

"Quiet!"

Outside the door to the catacombs, footsteps echoed down the tunnel. It sounded like only one person, though they weren't even trying to be stealthy.

"Get rid of it," Wendel muttered.

"What?"

"Your damn burning sword. Quickly!"

I sheathed Chun Yi and plunged us into darkness again. I edged toward Wendel, my arms outstretched like a blindfolded child playing a game. Sweat trickled down my back in the clammy air. My breathing sounded far too loud, like I was taking great ragged gulps of air, and I forced myself to calm down.

"I'm here," Wendel whispered.

He touched my shoulder. I felt my way along his arm and pressed myself close to him. His heartbeat thudded against my chest.

I lowered my voice until it was barely audible. "Your plan?"

He shrugged. "Kill the assassin?"

I shut my eyes, though it made no difference in this inky black. Why did he always have to be *so* arrogant?

The door creaked open.

Wendel stepped away from me, leaving me grasping air, and I heard a hissing that had to be Amarant cloaking him in shadows.

Footsteps.

I thought it was Wendel retreating deeper into the catacombs, but I couldn't be sure. What did he expect me to do? Stand by and watch? God damn it, I was going to kill him myself if we survived this assassin.

There was a scraping sound, a whoosh, and then a lantern flickered to life.

I flattened my back against the slimy wall, my fingers tight around Chun Yi, and held my breath. The light stung my eyes.

On the threshold of the catacombs, there was the silhouette of a sinewy man with a crossbow.

The crossbowman leaned over the threshold and loosed an earsplitting whistle. Was he summoning his allies? That meant he wasn't alone. If I moved fast enough, maybe I could disarm or disable him before—

A pungent aroma tickled my nostrils. I sniffed the air.

Naphtha.

My stomach clenched. You never wanted to smell naphtha in combat. And definitely never underground in some godforsaken catacombs. When the crossbowman stepped aside, my fears walked into the room.

Pyromechanics.

24

I had seconds to size up my opponents.

Two pyromechanics in gas masks and black-and-yellow asbestos armor. Salamanders. That's what people called them. They lumbered into the room, their backs burdened with tanks of naphtha—fuel for the flamethrowers that made them infamous.

I breathed in the stink of naphtha, my fingers frozen on my sword.

One of the salamanders squeezed the trigger of his flamethrower and jetted a lazy sweep of fire through the air. The inferno blackened bones and illuminated the catacombs with infernal light.

The shadows wouldn't hide me much longer. I backed into the darkness.

Where was Wendel? I had to warn him.

The crossbowman shouldered his weapon. "Don't move."

He spoke German with a thick accent that could have been Turkish.

"What do you want?" I bluffed.

"The necromancer."

I shook my head slowly. "Who?"

The crossbowman narrowed his eyes. I ducked as a crossbow bolt whirred over my head. It struck a skull behind me and knocked it clattering onto the floor.

Before he could reload, I fled into the catacombs. I sprinted down a long narrow tunnel, the light dimming, until I slammed against a rattling gate. Blindly, I groped in the darkness. I could go either left or right.

A hand clamped on my wrist and dragged me closer to the wall.

"It's me." Wendel remained cloaked by Amarant's shadows.

"Stealth won't work," I said, talking fast. "Your dagger is useless."

"Useless? It's still sharp."

"They have pyromechanics. Two of them."

"And?"

I growled. "Would you *stop* being so cocky? You can't hide in the shadows forever. They don't even have to find us, Wendel. You do realize that? They can burn all the oxygen and smother us into surrendering."

"Then let's not waste oxygen by talking."

Flames hissed down the tunnel as the salamanders swept the catacombs with fire. Silhouetted against the burning, the crossbowman stalked nearer. He had abandoned his lantern, but soon his targets would be bright enough.

"Where is the other exit?" I asked. "The one to the outside of the cathedral?"

"We passed it already," Wendel said.

"Fuck. Can you revive some skeletons?"

"No."

"Why not?"

He laughed grimly. "You have no idea how long it would take to sort these bones."

"Take out the crossbowman. I can distract him while you get closer."

"Yes, ma'am."

Wendel vanished into the darkness.

I flattened myself against the wall. My fingers clamped around Chun Yi's hilt. Smoke tickled my throat. I swallowed back a cough. The crossbowman edged nearer and entered the junction of the tunnels.

The muscles in my legs tightened before I lunged into an attack.

There wasn't enough time to draw my sword more than halfway. I bashed my pommel into his crossbow and knocked it askew, then kicked him in the knee and knocked him back. He found his footing and raised his bow. He still had a bolt loaded. For an eternity of an instant, we stared into each other's eyes.

Wendel stepped from the shadows.

He unceremoniously slit his enemy's throat.

Blood spurted from the crossbowman's severed artery. He fell to his knees and clutched his neck like he hoped to stop his life from pooling in the dirt beneath him.

Wendel crouched beside the dying man, a stance that

mimicked concern, though I knew he was waiting. His eyes couldn't be any colder. When the crossbowman finally collapsed, Wendel touched his neck.

"Is he dead?" I asked.

"Not yet."

My heartbeat pulsed in my throat, reminding me that I was still alive. On instinct, I backed away from the necromancer. When he looked at me, the coldness in his eyes melted into a strange distant sadness.

"Now," he murmured.

The undead man staggered to his feet. Wendel retreated, glanced at his blood-slicked hands, and grimaced as if the filth was all that bothered him. But his bravado didn't entirely hide the haunted look in his eyes.

"You can feel them die?" I asked.

He shuddered. "Yes."

I unsheathed Chun Yi. My sword looked pitiful by the light of naphtha-fire, as if technology trumped magic.

"Wendel," I said. "We have to run."

He took the crossbow and checked the quiver—only one bolt left. That gave him two shots. Two slim chances to kill.

"Run," he said. "They want me."

I stared at him. "I won't abandon you."

Singeing heat buffeted us as the salamanders advanced.

He glanced into my eyes. "You take the left tunnel. I will take the right. When they follow me, you attack them from behind."

"Okay."

He turned to his minion, the undead man. "Time for you to

say goodbye to your friends. Run to them. Bring them down."

The undead man swayed on his foot before obeying. Blood seeped from his neck and soaked his shirt. He shambled straight at the salamanders, who seemed confused enough that they stopped torching the air.

Wendel shouldered the crossbow. He squeezed the trigger. A bolt whirred down the tunnel and embedded itself in the eye of a salamander's gas mask. The pyromechanic toppled backwards. The other pyromechanic shouted, muffled by his mask.

I gripped my sword. "Time to run?"

"Not yet," Wendel said.

He hauled back the crossbow string and loaded another bolt. The undead man, with no sense of self-preservation, staggered in front of the remaining flamethrower. The salamander set him ablaze and left him to burn.

Black smoke choked the cramped space. I gagged at the smell of roasting meat.

When Wendel fired the crossbow, the bolt missed the salamander and clattered off the wall. "Run!" he shouted.

I lunged down the left tunnel. I ran headlong before I skidded to a halt. Sweat soaked under my arms. I whirled around just as the salamander lumbered into the junction.

Wendel fled down the right-hand tunnel. He hadn't bothered to hide himself. When the pyromechanic saw the necromancer, he pursued his prey. Flames licked the walls and blackened the stone.

I chased after them, my breathing ragged.

What if Wendel was trapped? What if I was already too late to save him?

25

The intense heat from the salamander's flamethrower sizzled over my unprotected skin. My eyes watered from naphtha and smoke. When the salamander heard me coming, he started to turn ponderously.

My legs aching, I summoned a burst of speed. My hand flew to Chun Yi.

I swung my sword. The blade sang through the air. Reflected fire gleamed in the eyes of the salamander's gas mask.

He hesitated, reminding me he was human, the instant before I beheaded him.

The momentum from my swing brought my blade clanging against the wall. Blood splattered me in the face. The salamander's corpse toppled at my feet, the flamethrower still sputtering in his hands.

Chun Yi burst into flames. Stone-cold fire crackled over the steel.

Gasping, I dragged my sleeve over my face to wipe away the gore. Blood magic thumped inside my bones. I tilted the blade sideways, my eyes narrowed, then thrust it into the scabbard. When I drew my sword halfway, the steel burst into flames again. I let it fall back and snuffed the fire inside the scabbard.

Should I be amazed or afraid?

"Ardis!"

Wendel ran from the darkness and embraced me. I closed my eyes and clung to him. Touching him unlocked a rush of emotion.

"You beheaded him," he said. I wasn't sure if he was impressed, disgusted, or both.

He backed away from the widening puddle of blood. Was Chun Yi still thirsty? My hand twitched to my sword before I stopped myself. What the hell was wrong with me?

I grimaced. "I want to get out of here."

Together, we strode down the tunnel until we encountered the charred corpse of the crossbowman. Had Wendel relinquished control of his necromancy? Or had his magic failed when flames burned the body?

I grimaced, not sure I wanted to know.

"Flamethrowers," Wendel said. "I never thought they would be so desperate."

The first salamander lay nearby, the crossbow bolt protruding from his eye socket. Wendel knelt beside the salamander and wrenched the bolt out of the gas mask, then peeled away the gas mask itself.

"What are you doing?" I asked.

He gave me a sliver of a smile. "I always kill first and ask questions later."

He touched the corpse's skin and closed his eyes. The undead man struggled to sit upright with the naphtha tank on his back.

"Stay down," Wendel said. "Answer carefully. How many assassins did the Grandmaster send to hunt me down?"

The Grandmaster. My stomach plummeted. My father.

"Nine of us, sir," said the undead man.

Sir. I swallowed down a sour taste. Was that some echo of the man's politeness?

"Nine?" Wendel asked. "You were the last?"

"No, sir. There are more of us."

The undead man stared sightlessly, waiting for a command. His face was still sweaty and red, not too far from alive yet.

Wendel clenched his jaw. "Is the Grandmaster coming?"

"I don't know, sir."

Grimacing, Wendel glanced at me. "The Order anticipated that I would question their assassins. Each of them knows only fragments of the truth."

I swallowed hard. "Smart."

He lifted his hand and let the dead man collapse once more. He glanced between the two corpses in the catacombs.

"Convenient." His voice was husky from the smoke. "Leave the bodies here."

His callous words failed to hide his emotions. He didn't relish killing in the slightest, unlike some mercenaries I knew.

"Do you always feel them die?" I asked.

"Every damn time."

Together, we abandoned the dead and climbed the stairs to the street.

"We should make ourselves look less like murderers," Wendel said.

He wasn't wrong. By the light of day, we both looked terrible. Blood crusted his hands and splattered my clothes.

I glanced skyward. "At least it started raining."

The gargoyles of St. Stephen's spat water from gutters onto the cobblestones. We held our hands under the mouth of a snarling stone lion. Blood swirled away into a drain. Long after I finished, he stood beneath the gargoyle, twisting his hands together under the water, his fingernails scraping his skin raw.

"Wendel," I said.

He shook the water from his hands. "Yes?"

"We shouldn't stay here."

He clenched his hands and glanced at the gargoyle again. Like he still wasn't clean. Like he would never be clean.

"Let's go back to the hotel," he said.

We walked through the rain together. Neither one of us spoke. His eyes looked distant, focused somewhere faraway.

Outside our room, I fumbled to unlock the door with my key. "My fingers are numb."

"Almost there. Then we can shower."

The lock clicked, at last, and we entered the room. He began stripping off his clothes before the door had even swung shut all the way. He tossed his waterlogged jacket on the floor. His wet shirt clung to his body.

Still on edge from the catacombs, I locked the door. It was impossible to relax.

"Damn," he muttered. "Another bloodstain."

He frowned at a spot of red on his sleeve. Maybe the bloodstain reminded him of the men he had killed. Maybe the blood held some lingering memory that he could sense with his necromancy. I shuddered.

Wendel stripped naked and stared out the window. The rain spilled down in sheets over the gray city of Vienna.

He looked lost. Alone.

"Are you all right?" I asked.

"I'm sorry." His voice had more gravel than honey. "I can't stop thinking of the catacombs."

"You don't have to apologize."

"We lured them down there to die."

"They were hunting you down. We had no choice but to kill them."

Rattling rain filled the silence between us.

"I need to shower." His throat worked as he swallowed hard. "Get this blood off me."

I followed him into the bathroom. He stepped into the shower. When the steaming hot water hit him, he closed his eyes and moaned out a sigh. He tilted back his head and let the water fall over his face.

I unbuckled my scabbard and kicked off my boots. A shower would do us both good.

Without looking at me, without saying a word, he rubbed the soap over his hands like they were still bloodstained. He stopped only to wash the rest of his skin, then returned to his hands, scrubbing under his fingernails to rid himself of imaginary dirt.

My clothes already wet, I walked up to him and wrapped my arms around his waist, resting my cheek against his back. He turned around and captured me in a kiss. It was a desperate kiss, filled with everything we wanted to say to each other. Everything we couldn't admit out loud.

He broke away. "Wait."

"What?"

"Why aren't you naked?"

I glanced at him through my wet eyelashes. "Can't you help me with that?"

He stripped off my clothes and tossed them out of the shower, though he still wouldn't look me in the eye. His body was trembling from lingering adrenaline.

"I can't stop remembering," he said.

"Remembering what?"

"What it felt like to be surrounded by the dead."

My throat clenched. I didn't know what to say to that.

He leaned against the wall. His fingers splayed on the marble of the shower. I lathered the soap, then ran my hands along his shoulders. He let me massage away the tension still tight in his muscles. My fingertips lingered on the scars crisscrossing his skin.

"Ardis," he said.

I froze. Had I touched a scar he didn't want to remember?

He turned to me and looked deeply into my eyes. "Help me forget."

26

I kissed him on the lips, on the cheekbones, and on the water that clung to his eyelashes. Wendel let out a shuddering sigh. He curled his arms around my waist and buried his face in the curve of my neck. He kissed me there, his lips lingering on my skin.

"I'm sorry," he murmured.

"Why?"

"There's something wrong with me."

My stomach plunged. "What do you mean?"

"I mean I can't stop thinking about death. About the things I've seen. About the things I've done."

I pulled away from him. "What are you saying?"

He stepped closer to me, his eyes locked on mine, water trickling down his face. "I'm saying I'm frightened of what I might do. Of what I might become."

"You're not a monster, Wendel."

He shook his head. "You don't understand. I feel like I'm losing control. I feel like..." He swallowed hard, his throat bobbing. "I feel like the dead are calling to me, whispering in the back of my skull."

I shivered. He was right. I didn't understand what he was going through. I didn't know what it felt like to have such a connection to death and darkness.

"You're more than just a necromancer."

"I...I'm afraid I can't be anything else."

I cupped his face in my hands. "I know who you are."

He searched my eyes for a long moment, then bent down to kiss me again. This time, the kiss was slow and deep, a promise of something more.

He let me wash him, running my soapy hands over his body, his scars. I followed the path of water trickling down. My hands hovered just above his cock. He wasn't hard, not yet, but he let out a soft moan.

I fell to my knees. "Maybe this will help you forget?"

When I kissed him there, he gasped. "Yes."

I licked his cock, then sucked it into my mouth. He leaned back against the shower.

His cock swelled inside my mouth while I lavished attention on him with my tongue, until he became so big that I struggled to take all of him. I tasted a hint of salty arousal. I swallowed it down.

My mouth slid off him with a wet pop. I stroked him in my hand to rest my aching jaw. His cock felt like silk over steel. Every inch of him was perfect.

"I didn't know it could feel this good," he muttered.

A thrill rushed down my spine. I wanted to make him feel good. I wanted to give him everything.

Determined, I licked the length of his cock and swirled my tongue around his crown. The muscles in his abdomen fluttered as his breathing turned ragged.

His hands tangled in my hair. I pleasured him until his hips started rocking. He moved with only the slightest thrusts, like he didn't want to choke me, but he couldn't stop himself from fucking my mouth.

"Ardis." He said my name like a curse. "I'm close."

In response, I sucked on him harder. My pussy ached with every heartbeat, demanding to be fucked, but I focused on his release instead. He needed this from me.

His fingers tightened in my hair, bringing little jolts of pleasure on the brink of pain. A deep, masculine groan escaped his throat.

"Fuck," he muttered.

Shuddering, he reached his climax. His cock jerked inside me while he unloaded spurt after spurt of release and flooded my mouth. I drank it all down.

Panting, trembling, he sagged against the marble.

He helped me to my feet and held me close. The tension in his body slowly unraveled. Lost in the steam of the shower, we embraced in our own intimate paradise. Nothing else mattered but the two of us together.

"Can we stay like this forever?" he asked.

"The water might get cold."

His laugh was husky. "True."

"Also," I added, "when you came in my mouth, it was very, very arousing."

He arched an eyebrow. "Was it?"

I slid my hand between my thighs. "Should I touch myself? Make myself come?"

With a feral gleam in his eyes, he growled. "No."

"Why not?"

"Your pleasure belongs to me."

He swept me off my feet and carried me out of the shower. Dripping wet, I clung to him with my hands hooked behind his neck. He stopped only to shut off the water, then carried me over to the bed.

He put me down on the edge of the mattress, then grabbed a fluffy towel from the bathroom. He dried me off slowly, his touch a tormenting caress. My nipples tightened under the soft cotton of the towel. I squirmed on the bed, my fingers gripping the sheets. I was aching between my legs, my body already begging for release.

He tossed aside the towel. "Lie back."

I obeyed his command. When he dropped to his knees, a shiver rushed down my spine. The Prince of the Undying was kneeling for me.

"I want to taste the nectar of your pussy," he said.

He parted my legs and devoured me with his gaze. When his tongue slid along me, I gasped at the raw pleasure. The stubble on his jaw rasped against my slick heat. He licked me like he couldn't get enough.

"Delicious," he murmured.

He savored the taste of me until I was shaking with unspent

desire. I curled my fingers in his hair and held on for dear life, desperate for more friction.

When he slid a finger inside me, my hips jerked.

"More," I begged. "Please, I need more."

He penetrated me with another finger and started fucking me with his hand. He sucked on my clit until I was almost sobbing with need. When he crooked his fingers, he hit a place deep inside me that unleashed a mind-blowing climax.

Heat gushed from me and drenched the sheets.

"Oh, fuck." I froze. "I'm sorry. I..."

Wendel groaned, a low rumble that vibrated through me. "Don't apologize." He lifted his head and wiped his mouth on the back of his hand.

"I didn't think this would happen."

"But it has happened before?"

"Only once or twice." Heat scorched my cheeks.

His eyes darkened with desire. "I'm flattered. And more than a little smug."

I laughed, some of my shyness vanishing. "Really?"

When he knelt over me on the bed, his hard cock throbbed. "I adore tasting your bliss."

I hooked my legs behind his ass. He thrust along me, not penetrating me, his unprotected cock a forbidden temptation. God, I needed him inside me. When I arched my hips, the tip of him slipped into my slick pussy.

He froze. Our eyes locked.

"Wait," he said. "We need to be careful."

"Right."

But neither one of us moved. His bare cock felt like absolute heaven inside me, even though it was just the blunt crown of him stretching my entrance.

"Just...just thrust inside me once?" I asked.

His pupils dilated. "That's dangerous."

"I know. I know, but I want to feel you. All of you."

"Ardis, if I come..."

"You might get me pregnant." My blunt words thrilled me.

He swallowed hard. "Are you willing to take that risk?"

"Yes," I whispered. "Are you?"

He hesitated. "Not yet."

Yet. My mind clung to the word. I wanted that future.

"That's okay," I said. "Thank you for telling me."

He pulled out of me. My pussy ached at the loss, but I respected his decision. He took the preventives from the nightstand and rolled one over his cock.

He lay back down, his arms caging me on the bed.

When he thrust into me, he felt so good I wanted to cry. He fucked me with a slow, powerful rhythm, driving me closer and closer to another climax.

Bliss exploded inside me. I cried out.

He was ruthless. He hammered into me and brought me to climax again and again. I lost count. Finally, he shuddered and pumped out his own release.

Afterwards, we lay tangled in the sheets together.

He stroked my hair, his eyes dark and unreadable. "You make me feel alive, when nothing else does in this world."

My heart ached at the raw emotion in his words. "Wendel."

"I'm utterly lost without you."

"What are you saying?"

"Stay with me. Please."

I blinked back tears. "Tonight, or forever?"

"We might not have forever."

Unspoken words choked my throat. I hugged him close. "After I saved your life, you promised to protect me. Let me also make that promise to you."

He swallowed hard. "You can't save me from them."

"Never tell me I can't do something. That just makes me want to prove you wrong."

"They would kill you to get to me." He sighed. "Can I stop you from protecting me? Convince you to save yourself?"

"Not a chance in the world."

27

When I woke, evening drenched the sky with violet. Shadows crept along the wall. I reached across the bed for Wendel, but he wasn't there. Blinking sleep from my eyes, I clutched the sheet and sat upright.

"Wendel?" I called.

No reply.

My heart started to pound. Had the assassins come for him again? Or had he abandoned me? Ugly doubts squirmed inside me like worms under a rock. I shoved them away and climbed out of bed.

On the nightstand, I spotted a paper with a handwritten note.

Ardis,

I will return soon. I suspect you will also be thirsty and hungry when you wake.

Wendel

Relief rushed over me. He wasn't gone, not for long.

Wendel had written the note in English. His handwriting had a sharp, precise quality to it, which suited him.

I showered, dressed in a bathrobe, and stood by the window. The glittering splendor of Vienna outshone the stars in the sky. Standing here in the hotel, looking down at the city, a curious sense of longing ached inside me.

I wished I belonged here.

A key clicked in the lock before the door swung open.

Wendel strode into the room with a bottle of green liquor. He held it high triumphantly. "I have returned victorious."

I took the bottle and stared at the ornate golden label. "Absinthe? How much was this? It looks like it cost a fortune."

He pinched the air between his fingers. "A tiny fortune."

I sloshed the absinthe in its bottle. "Let's not drink any on an empty stomach."

"I already ordered dinner for us both."

"Ordered? Where?"

"In the hotel restaurant," he said, as if this were obvious. "Don't worry, I asked the concierge if they could deliver it all to our room." He smiled. "Which means you don't even have to get dressed for dinner."

I rolled my eyes. "I'm keeping the bathrobe on."

His smile turned wicked. "You look your best in nothing."

I blushed at his flattery. "You're persistent, aren't you?"

Someone rapped on the door. "That should be dinner."

"Already?"

"Unless I missed a stray assassin."

How could he joke about such a thing? Though I supposed being hunted by assassins had become an everyday occurrence for him.

Wendel opened the door. "Yes?"

A waiter in a hotel uniform stood outside. "Your dinner, sir."

After Wendel swept open the door, the waiter wheeled in a trolley laden with covered platters and more than enough silverware and china for two. The waiter bowed stiffly and revealed each of the platters.

"We have lamb in mint sauce and grilled flounder in chervil butter. Followed by ragout of venison with butter dumplings, red cabbage with glazed chestnuts, and finally rhubarb cake with cream for dessert. Upon request, I took the liberty of bringing absinthe paraphernalia from the bar."

My mouth watered. It all looked delicious.

"Thank you." Wendel tipped the waiter with a generous handful of silver koronas.

"Most welcome, sir."

After the waiter bowed from the room, Wendel locked the door behind him. He took the bottle of absinthe from me.

"Did you order half the menu?" I asked.

"Possibly."

The luxurious food lured me over. "Are you rich?"

He shrugged. "Not very."

"I know you're a Prince of Prussia, but weren't you disinherited?"

"My dearest beloved family cut off all communication with me the day they banished me to Constantinople, but I found out later that they arranged for a monthly allowance in a bank account under my name."

"Why?"

"Guilt."

"How much?"

"Only a pitiful fraction of my inheritance, but enough to convince them I wasn't living in squalor." He curled his lip. "I hadn't touched a cent until the night I arrived in Vienna, when I promptly withdrew it all."

"All of it?"

"Before the Order could freeze the account." He tilted the bottle of absinthe and peered through the glass. "Though I'm not sure I will have the time to spend it all. There's enough for at least another week or two."

"What happens when you run out?"

He shrugged and waved away my question. "Please, eat."

We devoured the lamb in mint sauce, and demolished all but a sliver of flounder. I helped myself to a second bowl of ragout of venison, then took the last slice of rhubarb cake with a healthy dollop of cream.

"I'm finishing the cake," I said.

"Near-death experiences tend to whet the appetite."

When I licked cream from my fingers, he watched me with lust smoldering in his eyes.

"Don't look at me like that," I said.

"Like what?"

"Like you want to seduce me. I'm too full."

He tilted his head heavenward as if expecting a halo. "Your expectations amuse me."

I glanced at the forgotten bottle of absinthe. "You promised me you would show me how to serve absinthe properly."

"So I did."

Wendel guided me through the ritual of preparing absinthe. He stood behind me, his chest pressed against my back. Together, we poured a glass of the green liquor and balanced a sugar cube in a slotted spoon over the glass.

"Like this," he murmured. "Slowly."

His honey-gravel voice sent shivers down my spine. I tried hard to focus.

Ice clinked in the carafe of water as I tilted it over the glass of absinthe. The carafe chilled my fingers, but his steadying hand warmed mine. He angled the carafe to slow the water. It trickled onto the sugar cube, which melted and swirled into the absinthe below. Drop by drop, sweetness clouded the verdant green.

"This brings out the true essence of absinthe," he said. "Some call it *la fée verte,* or the green fairy, who visits them with waking dreams. Not that I have ever seen such things. I merely enjoy the taste."

"And this tastes better than drinking it straight?"

He laughed. "Try it yourself."

I took a long, slow sip of absinthe. The chilly water mellowed the fire of alcohol, and a strong licorice taste lingered on my tongue.

"You were right," I admitted.

He toasted me with his empty glass, then fixed himself a drink. He shrugged off his jacket, unbuttoned his shirt, and kicked off his boots. He dropped onto the couch, his glass in hand, and stretched out with a sigh.

My gaze wandered over his bare chest. He was beautiful.

I sipped my absinthe. "If you weren't a necromancer, what life would you have now?"

He sank deeper into the cushions, his eyelashes shadowing his cheeks. He lounged like a prince sitting on his throne. "I would be trying my hardest to ruin my reputation. Though that might not be enough to stop them from marrying me off to some duchess or princess to uphold the Hohenzollern honor."

I scoffed. "Duchess or princess?"

"Only the bluest blood." He had a shameless smile. "I am the eldest son, after all."

"Eldest son? So you have brothers?"

"One."

"Is he as horrible as you?" I teased.

"Hopefully." His smile faded. "I haven't seen him since I left home. Nor my sister."

I waited for him to say more, but his eyes looked distant. A little jittery, I swigged the rest of my absinthe and reached for the bottle.

"Let me refill your glass," I said.

He glanced sideways at me, then finished his drink and handed me the empty glass. He watched as I rested the absinthe spoon over his glass, balanced a sugar cube there, and twisted the cap off the absinthe bottle.

"Backwards," he said.

"Excuse me?"

"You did it backwards. Add the absinthe first, then the sugar, then the water."

"Oh."

He swung his legs over the couch and leaned against my back. He snaked his arms past my waist, reaching for the glass.

"Like so." His breath tickled the nape of my neck.

Distracted by the heat of his skin, I turned in his arms. He stared down at me with a glint in his eyes. It was impossible to ignore just how much taller he was, and just how masculine he felt against me. My heartbeat pounded as I explored his chest with my fingertips, feeling the scars crisscrossing his skin.

"Why so many scars?" I asked, with a shy glance into his eyes.

"I have been hurt many times." He leaned over my shoulder. Metal clinked on glass, followed by the gurgle of liquid pouring.

"You must be thirsty," I said. "You want the absinthe more than me."

His lips twitched. "I find you infinitely more charming. But I'm not seducing you, remember? My intentions are innocent."

"Innocent?" I glanced down at the bulge of his cock. "You look guilty to me."

He couldn't hide the shadows in his eyes when he smiled. "If only you knew."

A penny-sized scar puckered the skin above his collarbone. My fingers lingered there. "What is the story behind this scar?"

His laugh surprised me. "That particular scar was from a duel before the Hex."

"You were shot?"

"I lost the duel." He rubbed the scar absently. "I can't always be amazing."

"There must be more to that story."

"In the infinite wisdom of my youth, I provoked a spy from the Russian Empire and challenged him to a duel. I had been sent to interrogate and assassinate him. Rather than go to all the trouble of knifing him in a dark alleyway, I decided to take care of things in a duel. It sounded more sporting at the time."

"A duel to the death?"

"No. First blood. But that didn't stop the spy from trying to kill me."

I whistled. "Damn."

"He must have realized who I was, and that I didn't need him alive to ask my questions. But he was too slow." He poured ice water into the absinthe, his smile equally as cold. "Conveniently, the dead never lie."

He had a point. His necromancy could be brutally efficient.

Wendel retreated from me. "Shall we talk about something other than my scars?"

"What happens when your money runs out?" The question had been bothering me ever since he deflected it the first time.

He shrugged. "It won't matter."

"Why not?"

"If I'm dead, then I will have died happily bankrupt. If I'm alive, then I can loot what I need from Constantinople."

Shock crashed over me. "You're going back?"

28

He smirked like it didn't matter. "I can't avoid it forever. My fate is already written."

"You're leaving me?" My voice cracked.

The smirk on his face vanished like smoke. "I would never abandon you, Ardis, but I have no choice. I can't keep running forever. I have to go back."

"Why?"

"You don't understand." His eyes glittered. "I will never be free of them. They own my body, mind, and soul. Death is the only freedom."

Horror bloomed inside me like a bloodstain. "No."

"It's the only way."

"You don't think you're coming back, do you?"

He shook his head, his gaze haunted by shadows. "I don't know. Ironically, necromancers don't live very long. My great-

great-great-grandfather was a necromancer, but he also died an untimely death."

I glared at him. "You aren't allowed to die."

He walked away from me and stared out the window. "You can't determine my fate."

"I'm coming with you to Constantinople."

He turned back and stared at me. "You can't."

"I won't let you go alone."

"Why?" He seemed utterly confused by my reaction. "Why would you do this for me?"

"Because we swore to protect each other."

He narrowed his eyes as if he didn't believe me. "This isn't your fight."

I sank onto the couch and stared up at him. He turned his back on me and flexed his shoulders forward, his skin tightening. Stark white scars raked across his shoulder blades and ran down the length of his back.

"Look," he said. "See the scar below my left shoulder blade?"

"Which?"

"The thickest one. About as wide as a dagger."

"A...dagger?"

"Yes." He sipped his absinthe, then laughed hoarsely. "Stabbed me in the back."

I shrank back. "You survived?"

"Backstabbing is easier to survive than you might think."

"Who tried to kill you?"

His shoulders tensed like he was bracing himself for another dagger in the back. "The Grandmaster of the Order.

Your...your father." He hesitated to admit it out loud. "But he wasn't trying to kill me, he was trying to teach me a lesson."

My jaw dropped. "Why?"

"I defied him. He had a healer save me before I died."

"You almost died?"

"They had temporal magic readily available, like Konstantin's technomancy, so I wasn't in any real danger." Venom poisoned his voice. "To be honest, I have lost count of how many times I returned a little worse for the wear, and they patched me up and sent me right back out again."

I was stunned by the Grandmaster's cruelty. He had punished Wendel severely, stabbing his prize necromancer in the back as a warning to anyone else who dared disobey him. It was beyond barbaric.

"I can't even imagine how much that hurt," I said.

"You grow accustomed to pain." He drained his glass. "As I'm sure you know."

"They never should have done this to you."

"Done what? Twisted me into something evil?"

His words knocked me back. "You aren't evil."

"I'm not a good man. You should know that by now."

"How can you say that?"

"I'm a good necromancer." He let out a scornful laugh. His eyes glittered with loathing. "Better than good. What can I say? I have my pride."

"No." I shook my head. "Not pride. Wrath."

His eyes hardened. "I'm guilty of more than one of the seven deadly sins."

"Tell me. Tell me who you are."

Darkness filled his eyes. "Ardis, you are one of the few who has ever truly known me. And I would not want you to remember me that way."

"I would rather know the truth."

"The truth of my life will die with me, as it does with us all. And my memories will fade as my bones grow old, and I will live on only in the memories of those who cared that I should not be forgotten."

His words echoed deep inside my heart. I struggled not to drown in my emotions.

I couldn't stop staring at his back. The Grandmaster's dagger had left its mark, but most of his scars were far older, far deeper. They slanted across his back like a tiger had clawed his skin, though it couldn't be from an animal attack. The truth had to be far uglier.

"Whipping scars?" I asked.

"Obviously." He poured himself a shot of absinthe, knocked it back, and hissed through gritted teeth. The liquor must have burned his throat.

"What happened to you?"

"My disobedience went too far. Until that day, I had obeyed them. I practiced my necromancy on animals. On cats, at first, since they learned that was how I started. They killed the creatures for me."

"This was in Constantinople?"

"The city was beautiful. It gave me the best memories of my childhood." His voice sounded devoid of emotion, his eyes as cold as ice. "Can you believe I hoped animals would satisfy their morbid curiosity?"

Wendel grabbed the absinthe and drank straight from the bottle. Grimacing, he reached for his glass instead. His hands trembled as he poured himself yet another drink, and he spilled the liquor on the carpet.

"A bit too much absinthe," he muttered.

Tears stung my eyes. "Why did they hurt you?"

He stared into the distance. "Inevitably, they brought me to a dead man. He had been hanged." He rubbed his neck as if remembering bruises. "My magic was strong enough, at the time, but my mind... I blacked out. When I refused to revive the next dead man, I was whipped. Severely. They couldn't hold my hand to a cadaver's skin and force the necromancy out of me, but they could force me to obey them. I was sixteen."

"God, Wendel, you..." I pressed my knuckles to my mouth. "You were so young."

A muscle jumped in his jaw. "I was their prodigy."

I closed my eyes against brimming tears that threatened to overflow any second now. He dragged me into a tight embrace and stroked my hair.

"Ardis, Ardis, please don't cry."

"Promise me you won't die."

"I don't want to die." His voice rasped with raw emotion. "But I can't live like this any longer. I need to face the Order of the Asphodel."

Dread clamped around my throat like an iron fist. "No."

"I have to go."

"Don't go alone. I can't let them hurt you again. Let me come with you. Please."

He stared at me, his eyes glittering, before he squeezed

them shut. "No one..." He cleared his throat. "No one has ever wanted to help me before."

"Never?"

He was on the brink of tears, struggling not to cry.

"Never," he said. "Not until you. You're the only one who has ever truly cared for me."

My heart broke at his words. How could anyone not care for him? He was fiercely intelligent, brave, witty, and loyal. And yet he had been abandoned or betrayed by everyone important in his life.

He kissed me, his mouth bittersweet from lingering absinthe. When we parted, he looked deeply into my eyes. "Come with me to Constantinople."

"Did you think you could stop me?"

"No." His mouth twisted wryly.

"When do we leave?"

He swallowed hard. "Not tonight. We should sleep."

After I took off my bathrobe, he tucked me into bed. He undressed and lay beside me. I rested my head on his chest. His heartbeat thumped under my ear, a constant reminder that he was still alive, and he was still here with me. When I had almost fallen into the oblivion of sleep, he whispered something.

Quietly, so quietly I didn't understand him at first.

His words sank through my mind like stones in a pond.

"I love you."

29

Morning dawned in a gray the color of doves. Rain drizzled from the sky and hushed the sounds of the city. We sat in the restaurant of the Imperial Palace Hotel.

Wendel, who had a hangover, winced at the daylight like a vampire caught in the sun.

"That bad?" I asked.

He hunched over the table and sipped his coffee. "I would appreciate a convenient assassin right now. Put me out of my misery."

I hadn't been nearly as ambitious, and had only a slight headache from the absinthe.

I sipped my chamomile tea. "You look terrible."

"Thank you." He stirred his coffee. "Last night..."

"Yes?"

"I might have said too much. Blame it on the devil of drink."

"After that much absinthe, I'm amazed you stayed conscious for as long as you did."

He glanced into my eyes. "You asked about my scars."

My fingers tightened around my cup. "I did."

"And after I told you...?"

I realized what he meant. "You don't remember?"

"No."

My heartbeat pounded. He didn't remember saying he loved me last night?

He straightened the silverware to distract himself. I reached across the table and stilled his hand.

"Will I regret not remembering?" he asked.

Should I tell him what he said last night? But he was drunk. Maybe he didn't mean it. Maybe it was just the alcohol talking.

"We were naked in bed together, but it wasn't that scandalous. You fell asleep."

"So you need some more scandal tonight."

I rolled my eyes at his smirk. "You might still be too hungover for that."

"I apologize. I drank too much."

"You did...you did say something else."

"Did I?"

"I'm not sure you meant it."

His eyes narrowed. "What did I say?"

"You said you loved me."

He breathed out hard through his mouth. He drank from his

coffee until only dregs remained. "I shouldn't have told you while I wasn't sober."

My heartbeat raced. "Did you mean it?"

"I meant it." He reached across the table and took my hand. "And I still mean it this morning."

"Wendel, I..."

"I understand if you feel differently."

"I don't know what to say," I admitted, my voice barely above a whisper.

"You don't have to say anything." He squeezed my hand, his thumb stroking me. "I wanted to tell you before it was too late, even if my feelings are unrequited."

I pulled my hand away from his and leaned back in my chair. I didn't want to hurt him, but I couldn't deny my own tangled emotions. Was I falling in love with him?

"You don't even know my real name."

Surprise flickered through his eyes. "Your name isn't Ardis?"

"No." I stared into my teacup. "It's not."

"I would like to know, if you wish to tell me."

"Yu Lan." I hadn't spoken my name in years. "Jade Orchid. It means 'magnolia' in Chinese. I changed it when I left home."

"Where is home for you?"

"A long, long way away."

"Where in America?"

"San Francisco, California."

He poured himself another cup of coffee. "I've never been. Is it beautiful?"

"Some parts of the city. Like Chinatown. Although my

mother and I lived in what most people call a bad neigh-borhood."

He poured too much cream into his coffee, he was listening so intently to me, and it overflowed a little into his saucer. "Bad? Because it was dangerous?"

"I grew up in a red-light district."

He spluttered as he drank his coffee. Coughing, he set down the cup. "You did?"

"My mother ran a brothel." I shrugged, my face heating. "When my mother came from China, she trained some Chinese girls to be sophisticated courtesans. Skilled in the arts of music, dance, and seduction."

He stared at me. "Were you...?"

I put down the teacup with a decisive clink. "Are you asking if I worked as a whore?"

He cleared his throat and looked away, his cheeks flushed. "I meant no offense."

"None taken." I traced my cup with my fingernail. "I never did any whoring, though my mother wanted me to follow in her footsteps. You can make a lot of money as a courtesan who markets herself as exotic."

"Damn." He shook his head. "When did you leave?"

"When I killed that man at the brothel."

"That must have been...difficult."

I hadn't told anyone but my mother the whole story. Unspoken words crammed in my throat, choking me. I sucked in a slow breath, trying to calm myself.

"It's okay." Wendel never looked away from my eyes. "Take

your time. You don't need to tell me anything you would rather keep a secret."

"He mistook me for one of the brothel girls, no matter how many times I said no." My mouth tasted sour, and I swallowed hard. "He threw money at me. Literally. Like that paid for what he tried next. He didn't get very far before I grabbed a sword and cut his throat. That was the first time I killed a man."

"I'm sorry."

"Don't apologize. It wasn't your fault."

"I'm sorry you had to endure something so painful."

Anger still scalded my throat. "I hope his death was painful."

"I would have helped." He met my gaze, his green eyes almost gray in the clouded daylight. "Pity he's already dead. Men like that deserve to suffer."

"Sometimes I wish I could just forget."

"I understand perfectly."

Tears welled in my eyes, not from sorrow, but from the relief that crashed over me. He knew my darkest secrets, and yet he still accepted me for who I was.

"After what you told me," I said, "I don't doubt that."

"I will never let anyone hurt you again, for as long as I'm still breathing."

His fierce devotion took my breath away. "Why?"

"Because I love you, Yu Lan."

His words pierced my heart like arrows and brought a sweet ache. "Ardis. Just Ardis. I left Yu Lan behind a long time ago."

He nodded. "Of course."

I lifted my cup. When I sipped the tea, heat traveled down my throat and settled in my belly. The taste of chamomile grounded me.

"Thank you for listening to me," I said.

"Whenever you need me."

I bit into a slice of toast. "God, I hope nobody overheard our conversation. It was wildly inappropriate for breakfast. Hopefully, we won't get kicked out."

"Luckily, I'm a master of changing the subject." Wendel said it airily, then smirked.

"Oh really?"

He spotted a newspaper abandoned on the table next to us and snatched it, reading, "'Diesel Presumed Dead.'"

I cringed. "Please tell me they didn't mention me."

"You dodged that bullet." He frowned as he kept reading.

"What?"

He read another headline out loud: "'Balkan Powder Keg Ready to Blow.'"

I snorted. "Optimistic of them."

"Austria wants to investigate the Black Hand, but Serbia isn't cooperating."

"That's not good."

"An understatement. If Russia swoops in like Serbia's guardian angel—"

"Or bully of a big brother—"

"Hex or no Hex," he continued, "war is inevitable."

He wasn't wrong. I didn't disagree with him in the slightest. The Hex wouldn't stop the simmering tensions in Europe from boiling over eventually.

He tossed aside the newspaper. "What time is it?"

"Late in the morning?"

He flagged down a waiter. "The time?"

"Half past nine, sir," said the waiter.

Wendel frowned at his coffee like it had failed him somehow. "Damn, I'm late."

"For what?"

He shoved his chair from the table. Grimacing, he pinched the bridge of his nose, no doubt still fighting his headache. "I have an appointment."

"With who?"

His grimace deepened. "Konstantin."

"What does he want?"

"He wouldn't say. His attempts at secrecy are more obnoxious than anything else."

Excitement hopped inside me like a cricket. "Maybe it's about Diesel."

"Maybe."

I crammed the last bit of toast into my mouth and brushed crumbs from my hands. After Wendel paid the bill, I followed him into the street. Wind whirled down the street, scattering rain into our faces.

"I don't plan to be gone for long," he said.

"Wendel. It might be about Diesel. I'm coming."

He muttered what sounded like a German swearword still unfamiliar to me. "Fine."

"Thanks."

"Any idea where the Dirty Boar is?"

"The Dirty Boar? That's a brewpub."

"A brewpub? Fantastic. Konstantin is an idiot."

"Don't tell me you don't like beer."

"I don't like any alcohol. Too hungover to even think of it. Also, a brewpub is hardly a private location, if this really is a clandestine rendezvous."

I couldn't hide my curiosity. "For Project Lazarus?"

"Quite possibly."

We hurried through the rain, which chilled to hail and rattled on the rooftops. By the time we reached the Dirty Boar, we had to shake hailstones from our hair.

Wendel opened the door to the brewpub for me. "Let's make this quick."

30

Inside the Dirty Boar, I shrugged off my coat.

I hadn't spent much time in this brewpub before. It didn't hit that sweet spot between cheap beer and decent clientele. Their beer was a little too watery to cost so much, and the men drinking it always eyed me lecherously.

"Over half an hour late," Wendel said. "Hopefully Konstantin gave up and went home."

"You're out of luck." I pointed at the bar.

Konstantin perched on a barstool, splitting open hazelnuts with a nutcracker. He hadn't yet noticed we were here.

"Archmage." Wendel raised his voice over the hubbub. "Archmage!"

"Wendel?" Konstantin swiveled on his stool. "You're late. Ardis! I didn't expect you."

"Good morning." I could have sworn the archmage was tipsy, though he had no drink.

"Back from another mission?" he asked. "Margareta has been keeping you busy?"

"Not at the moment," I muttered.

"Pardon?"

"I'm on leave for three weeks. Margareta's suggestion."

He popped a hazelnut into his mouth. "Very nice!"

I started to correct him, then thought better of it. He must have thought my last mission was a success. There was no reason to relive my failures.

"If Margareta didn't send you, why are you here?"

"I'm with Wendel. Why would she send me?"

Konstantin fumbled with the nutcracker. "You know Margareta, always has a finger in every pot. Hard to cook up anything she doesn't know about. Especially if she doesn't approve of the ingredients."

I grunted in agreement. "I know what you mean."

Wendel sidled up to the bar and caught a barmaid's eye. "A shot of vodka, please."

"Sure thing, sweetheart." The barmaid leaned on the bar and bared her cleavage at Konstantin. "Sure you don't want anything with those hazelnuts?"

"No, thank you." Konstantin seemed oblivious of her impressive breasts. Maybe he wasn't interested in women? "I'm here on business."

"What kind of business?" Wendel asked.

The barmaid plunked down the vodka. Wendel knocked back the shot without hesitation.

Konstantin frowned at him. "Are you drinking this early?"

"Better drunk than hungover." Wendel smirked shamelessly.

"I would prefer it if you were conscious tonight."

"Tonight?"

"My apologies for asking on such short notice. But I'm missing the blueprints for a key component."

"Of?"

Konstantin hesitated and glanced at me. "Project Lazarus."

"Wendel told me," I admitted.

Konstantin heaved a sigh. "Wendel, how many times have I told you it was confidential?"

"I lost count, archmage."

"For heaven's sake. Admittedly, you might be interested in the job, Ardis."

"What kind of blueprints?" I asked.

"They're for a theoretical energy gun. I have been working on it for over a year now, but I keep hitting roadblock after roadblock. I'm afraid it will be impossible to meet Margareta's deadline without Lord Adler's blueprints."

"Lord Adler?" Wendel perked up. "The baron from Vienna?"

"He's quite an accomplished technomancer, but he's so damn eccentric." Konstantin raked his fingers through his already messy hair. "I spoke with him about buying his blueprints for Project Lazarus, but he refused. And the worst thing of all? Lord Adler bragged to me that he already has an interested buyer from America."

I propped my elbows on the bar. "Did the deal go through?"

"Not yet. He's meeting the American at a ball tonight."

"No doubt a Viennese ball." Wendel cocked his head. "Let

me guess. You expect me to sweet-talk my way inside without an invitation?"

"I do have an invitation," Konstantin said.

"Then why not do this yourself?"

"Because I already tried. Lord Adler won't bother with me for a second time, not when he has American dollars in sight. And then the energy gun will be the plaything of some tycoon with too much time on his hands."

Wendel frowned into his empty glass. "You believe the baron will sell them to me?"

"I have the money. And if the American has more, then..."

"Then what?"

"You will have to secure the blueprints another way."

"Steal them?" Wendel pretended to gasp. "Archmage, consider me shocked."

Konstantin scowled. "Lord Adler allows his greed to impede the innovation of technomancy. Did you know I helped him solve a very tricky problem with harmonic charms, and he didn't even give me a footnote in a journal?"

"Of course." Wendel laughed. "Revenge, I understand."

I leaned across the bar. "I'm also an American. Let me talk to the buyer and distract him while Wendel persuades Lord Adler to reconsider."

Konstantin stroked his beard thoughtfully. "The invitation does allow for a guest."

Wendel sized me up with a devilish smile. "It's a brilliant idea. The American will be more than distracted by a beautiful woman in a beautiful gown."

I scoffed. "Do I look like I own a ball gown?"

"They wouldn't let you inside in those clothes."

I glanced down at myself. "Point taken."

Konstantin cleared his throat. "I'm willing to pay you both. Name your price."

"Could you talk to Margareta for me?" I asked.

"About what?"

"I was the one who guarded Diesel on the steamship to England. I was the one who failed. Only I found out later that the mission—the real mission—had been a success, and I was no more than a dummy."

Recognition flickered on Konstantin's face. "Margareta never told me that."

"Why would she? She punished me when I complained."

"That's hardly fair. Help me with the blueprints, and let me have a talk with Margareta."

"I will." I squared my shoulders. "Thank you."

Wendel flicked a hazelnut with his finger. "And what could you possibly give me?"

Unease crossed over Konstantin's face. "I know you have unfinished business in Constantinople. I happened upon a secret that may be of interest to you."

Not even looking, Wendel toyed with his glass. "About?"

"The Grandmaster."

When Wendel lifted his head, his eyes gleamed. "Archmage, how could I refuse?"

Night tossed thousands of glittering stars like diamonds across the black velvet sky. I breathed shallowly, my ribs imprisoned by the boning in my corset. The silk sleeves of my ball gown fluttered in the winter wind.

When I shivered, Wendel said, "Take my jacket."

"I'm not that cold."

He looked stunning in a black tailcoat and ivory waistcoat, everything tailored to fit the lean muscles in his body. My gown wasn't half as practical, though it was gorgeous. A froth of golden lace spilled over emerald-green silk. As a mercenary, I spent too much time in leather and steel.

"I insist," he said. "Before you die of hypothermia."

"We're in Vienna. Nobody's dying of hypothermia. We're a thousand miles away from that snowy battlefield in the wilderness of Transylvania."

He arched an eyebrow. "Perhaps I should warm you up."

"What—?"

He backed me against a stone wall and captured me in a fierce kiss. In the shadows, we weren't completely hidden from the people on the street.

But I didn't care. Not when his mouth devoured mine, not when his hands explored my skin. Lust ached through my body. When he slid his knee between my legs, I groaned and gripped the lapels of his jacket.

If he fucked me against the wall, right here, right now, I wouldn't refuse him. I wanted him to lift my gown to my hips and stain the silk with his climax.

When he finally released me, we were both gasping for air.

"Still cold?" he asked, his eyes smoldering.

I shook my head, speechless with desire.

He leaned closer and whispered in my ear. "I can't resist you, even in public."

My heartbeat pounded between my legs. I wanted to feel him inside me again. I wanted to touch him all night long. But we had work to do tonight before we could indulge.

He offered his arm and escorted me through Vienna.

Ladies and gentlemen sashayed from gleaming autos and carriages. Horses snorted mist into the chilly night. Light spilled from the high windows of the Sofiensaal and illuminated the dance hall's ornate stucco façade.

A thrill fizzed inside me like champagne. "We're here."

31

Giddy, I wavered as we climbed the Sofiensaal's steps.

"Let me catch my breath." I clutched Wendel's arm.

He frowned. "What's wrong?"

My stomach clenched and the hair on my arms prickled, even though there was nothing to fear here. I glanced around the street, my eyes distracted by the resplendent display of women as bright as exotic birds.

"This corset," I lied.

"Don't worry." He squeezed my hand. "Follow my lead."

I masked my unease behind a smile. We stopped outside the grand entrance of the Sofiensaal.

"Good evening," said the doorman.

With a vaguely haughty expression, Wendel slipped the invitation from his coat pocket and handed it over. The doorman flipped open the invitation, gave it no more than a cursory glance, then let us inside.

Inside, the Sofiensaal glittered with chandeliers, gilding, and gemstone necklaces on many ladies. I touched my bare neck and hoped I didn't look like an impostor, though I certainly felt like one.

"What did the invitation say?" I murmured.

Wendel scanned the ballroom. "What do you mean?"

"Who are we supposed to be?"

"Oh, I didn't read the invitation," he said blithely.

"Wendel!"

"Neither did you, from the sound of it."

Damn it, I hated it when he was right.

I let him lead me around the outskirts of the ballroom. Dancers waltzed under the chandeliers to the music of Strauss. Beyond the orchestra, we climbed stairs to a dining area with luxurious buffet tables. Centerpieces of fruit and flowers towered above silver dishes offering a feast of opulent Viennese cuisine.

"Who are we?" I asked. "What's our cover story?"

He tilted his head, pondering the question. "I'm a penniless Prussian viscount. You can be a wealthy American heiress aiming for my title."

I snorted. "A viscount? I would aim higher than that."

"Would you?" He smirked. "I can't be a Prince of Prussia. Anything higher than a viscount, and we will have to answer too many questions."

"True."

He helped himself to champagne. "Any sign of Lord Adler?"

"Not yet." I meandered along the buffet. "I'm keeping my eye out for the American."

Not that Konstantin had done a good job of describing him. He had told me the man's name was Jesse Howland, and given me a newspaper clipping with a group photograph where Howland's face was a blurry smudge.

"Was Howland blond?" I asked. "Do you remember?"

Wendel didn't reply. Was he distracted by the champagne? Sighing, I turned around.

He was gone.

My heart leapt into my throat. I glanced around the ballroom, but the swirl of dancers blocked my way. I couldn't get a clear line of sight.

"Excuse me!" said a young man.

Barely older than a boy, he hadn't grown into his face yet. His black hair had been slicked back. Something about the sharpness of his cheekbones...

"That man with you," he said. "Where did he go?"

Fuck. Was this stranger with the Order of the Asphodel? I couldn't kill him first, ask questions later, unlike Wendel's strategy with necromancy.

I faked a smile. "Sorry?"

"He was with you a moment ago, but then he vanished—"

"Men often vanish at a ball," interrupted a lady, "when they tire of dancing."

She smiled at us. Her silk gown shimmered, a rose petal pink embroidered with ornate silver brocade, with long silver lacework sleeves in a fashion that evoked the Orient. The lady, too, looked like she had come from afar, with dark hair and eyes that reminded me of mine.

"Pardon me, but I couldn't help but overhear." She held out an elegantly gloved hand.

He kissed the air above her fingers. "Lady Maili."

"You might want to introduce yourself," Lady Maili said, "for her sake."

"My apologies." He dipped into a quick bow. "Prince Wolfram of Prussia."

I did a bad job of disguising the shock on my face. Another Prince of Prussia? What were the odds? And Wendel had mentioned having a brother.

I decided to mimic Lady Maili's charm. "A prince? This will sound very American, but I must say I'm surprised. I've never met a prince before."

Wolfram frowned. "But that man—I'm certain of it."

"Certain of what?"

"He was my brother."

My stomach plunged. Sometimes I hated being right.

"Another prince?" Lady Maili laughed. "This ball is turning out all right."

Wolfram's frown deepened. "I haven't seen my brother for years. He left home when I was no more than a child. Maybe I have my hopes up too high."

"How awful." Lady Maili had a sympathetic frown.

"What was his name?" I asked.

"Wendel."

I stared at him with an awful twisting in my stomach. I didn't know what to tell him.

"Sorry." He bowed again. "I should return to my sister."

Wendel's sister. A Princess of Prussia, no doubt.

I blinked fast. "Wait."

Wolfram hadn't heard me, so I grabbed him by the elbow. He gawked at me—commoners probably didn't touch princes—but I didn't let him go.

"Wendel came here with me," I said.

Wolfram's eyes lit up. "He did?"

"Yes."

"God, where is he? I thought he was dead."

I grimaced at the sad desperation in Wolfram's voice. Wendel must have abandoned me the moment he saw his brother. I hadn't thought of Wendel as a coward, but it seemed like such a cruel thing to—

"Ardis!" Wendel lunged from the crowd. "Time to go."

"Why? What happened?" My hand darted to where my sword should be, but of course I had left Chun Yi locked in our room at the hotel.

Wolfram stepped forward. "Wendel?"

The brothers locked gazes. A moment hung suspended in the air for an eternity. Neither one of them blinked, as if they were each waiting for the other to break first.

Wendel's jaw hardened. I could see him shutting his emotions off. "Wolfram," he said, with remarkable calm, "are you here with Juliana?"

"Yes."

"Find her and make sure she leaves. It isn't safe here."

Wolfram's face crumpled. "You can't—"

"What isn't safe?" Lady Maili fanned herself. "What are you talking about?"

"The Order?" I asked.

Wendel nodded. "Assassins."

Lady Maili dropped her fan. "You must be mad."

Wendel clenched his hands and glanced around the ballroom. "Ardis, I can't stay with you much longer. If they see me talking with you…"

"That would put me in danger," I finished.

"Don't leave." Wolfram straightened, not quite as tall as his brother. "I won't allow it."

"Wolfram. You can't stop me."

"I haven't seen you in years."

Wendel's shoulders sagged as if overburdened by the weight of reality. "Do as I say and keep Juliana safe."

"No."

"I outrank you."

"Not anymore."

Wendel glared at him. "I'm still your older brother."

Wolfram wouldn't back down. "My older brother is dead. That's what they told me."

"Did they?"

"I never believed them."

"Wolfram." Wendel softened his words. "Wolfie. Please."

No more than a flash of gray, a man ran along the edge of the ballroom. An assassin.

Wendel's stare locked on his enemy. "Run."

32

Wolfram reached for him, but Wendel stepped backward and slipped into the crowd. Lady Maili glanced at me, her mouth rounded with shock.

"Wolfram, where is your sister?" I asked. "Juliana?"

"I don't know," he admitted.

"Find her. We need to get out of here."

Wolfram frowned. "She should be dancing."

I scanned the ballroom. Near the back, Wendel stalked along the wall, but there weren't enough shadows for Amarant to hide him. As the music floated into its finale, the ladies and gentlemen halted their waltz.

"There!" Wolfram pointed. "I see Juliana."

An elegant brunette in silver silk laughed at her dancing companion. A tiara twinkled on her head. She certainly looked like a princess.

Hopefully this princess would take orders.

"Excuse me." I threaded through the crowd. "Milady?"

Juliana tilted her head at me with a faint sneer. "I'm afraid we haven't been introduced? And the correct form of address for a princess is 'Your Royal Highness.'"

Wonderful. She was even more arrogant than her brother.

When she turned away, I caught her hand. "I'm here to escort you from the premises."

"Escort?" Juliana grimaced at me touching her, even though she was wearing silk gloves. "Wolfram, who is she?"

He stepped forward. "She's with Wendel."

Juliana's nostrils flared. "That's a cruel joke."

"It's no joke." Wolfram shook his head, his dark eyes serious. "He's here. He's being hunted."

"Hunted? By whom?"

"Assassins."

Juliana curled her lip. "What nonsense."

"We have to trust him."

"I will trust him after I have spoken to him."

She swept through the ballroom, her head held high, in search of her long-lost brother.

But she was oblivious of the advancing danger.

Assassins crept through the ballroom, their gray cloaks not quite disguising the unmistakable glimmer of chainmail. They had invincible armor next to my ball gown. When an assassin's cloak rippled, it bared his scimitar and the knives strapped to his belt.

"Why do they want to kill Wendel?" Wolfram sounded more like a boy than a man.

I dragged him through the crowd. "They won't kill him."

Unless Wendel fought to the death.

An assassin strode past me, so close that his cloak brushed my arm. Fear gripped my throat, but my gown disguised me. I zigzagged through the crowd to Juliana. When the orchestra launched into another Strauss melody, I dodged dancers as they began to waltz.

"Juliana!" Wolfram called.

Sneering, the princess glared at us. "Wendel isn't here. If you're lying—"

A fantastic crash deafened us. I whirled in time to see Wendel shove a second crystal decanter off the buffet table. It shattered into a thousand shards. Liquor sprayed onto the ladies and gentlemen nearby.

He had given away his position to the assassins.

"What the hell is he doing?" I muttered.

Juliana teetered on her heels. She stared at him like he had returned from the dead.

To them, he had.

Wendel hefted a candelabra and hurled it over the table. The candelabra wheeled through the air, rolled into the spilled liquor, and torched the alcohol. Fire rushed along the parquet floor. Screams punctuated the music.

The waltz turned into a stampede.

In the churning panic, the assassins held their ground. Ladies fled from flames licking at their skirts. Gentlemen forgot chivalry and elbowed through the crowd toward the exits of the Sofiensaal.

Still holding Wolfram's hand, I grabbed Juliana's wrist and hauled her forward.

We struggled against the jostling crush of people, then burst through the doors into the street. Juliana wrenched free and slapped me across the face.

"Don't you dare touch me," she snapped.

I clenched my jaw and resisted the urge to hit her back.

"Juliana!" Wolfram shouted. "She was trying to help."

"Who is she? Why is she here with Wendel?"

"I don't know." Wolfram caught her arm. "You can't go back in there."

She glared at him, her earrings quivering with barely restrained anger. "But Wendel."

Smoke billowed from the burning ballroom as people stumbled out. I sprinted toward the chaos, even though every instinct screamed for me to run away.

The flames had spread fast. They crawled along curtains and devoured gilded chairs.

"Wendel?" I shouted.

"Get out of here!"

I whirled toward his voice.

Blood splattered his face and drenched his shirt. He was breathing hard, though he didn't look hurt. He wielded his black dagger in his left hand and a scimitar in his right. A dozen assassins pursued him doggedly.

Wendel baited an assassin, letting his enemy come close enough to swing, then parried the scimitar and lunged down the length of the blade. He drove his dagger into the assassin's neck, splitting chainmail.

The assassin fell. Blood spurted from his severed artery.

"Wendel!" I walked through fire for him. "Come with me!"

"No." Smoke roughened his voice. "I have to kill them all."

"You can't "

"It's the only way to stop them." He bared his teeth. "I won't let them hunt you down."

I knew what he meant. They had seen me with him.

Wendel slashed at an assassin, but his scimitar glanced off the assassin's chainmail. He couldn't hold them off forever.

I sprinted to grab a fallen scimitar from the ground. My hand touched the hilt.

Steel caressed the back of my neck.

An assassin was behind me. Ready to behead me.

"Wendel," I rasped.

The flames in the ballroom soared into an inferno. Heat stole my breath away.

A dead assassin crumpled against a burning table. Wendel lunged and touched the man's face, then vaulted onto the table. The undead assassin staggered upright, his hand clamped around a scimitar. He didn't even have time to attack before a living assassin cut off his head.

"Wendel!" I couldn't speak above a croak.

The scimitar stung my skin. Blood mingled with the sweat trickling down my neck.

Wendel rose from the table with menace. He kicked an enormous centerpiece of fruit onto the ground. Apples and pears rained down and rolled underfoot. The assassins stumbled back. Wendel lunged, his blades flashing. Blood splattered across the ruined feast.

The scimitar bit deeper into my neck. The assassin who had captured me shouted, "We will kill her!"

Wendel froze. His eyes found mine.

An assassin leapt onto the table behind him.

I sucked in air to scream a warning, but it was too late. The assassin bludgeoned Wendel's skull with the blunt end of his sword. Wendel toppled from the table. Kneeling, dazed, he shook his head hard. He staggered to his feet, still armed with a dagger and a scimitar.

"Wendel!" I cried. "You can't win. Not like this."

"No." He snarled the word.

The assassin behind me grabbed a fistful of my hair. He yanked back my head and bared my neck. On the ceiling, flames spread above like the glorious destruction of the heavens. A chandelier plummeted only yards away and shattered into thousands of broken crystals. Time fragmented into shards of clarity.

This was how I would die.

Like this, in a gown, in a ballroom. How humiliating.

I didn't want to die on my knees. I didn't want to die without a fight.

The assassin lifted the scimitar above my neck.

Twisting, I ripped my hair from his fist. I tackled his legs, knocked him down, and clawed at his eyes with my fingernails. When he covered his face with his hands, his scimitar clattered on the floor.

I lunged, my fingers straining to reach it.

"Ardis!"

Gasping, I scrambled to my feet.

Wendel stretched out his empty hands. Surrendering. He never looked away from me as he fell to his knees and let the assassins capture him.

Chunks of the plasterwork ceiling fell. The backbone of the Sofiensaal groaned, then broke. Fire plunged from above and roared across the ballroom. I stumbled back and shielded myself from the heat. Smoke stung my eyes. Blinking back tears, I tore the skirt of my gown and pressed the silk to my mouth.

When the smoke drifted away, Wendel had vanished.

33

I fled from the burning ballroom.

Coughing, I sucked in a lungful of cold, sweet air. When I stumbled upon a horse hitched to an ambulance, it whinnied and shied away with flattened ears. Firefighters scrambled to pump water onto the flames.

"Thank goodness you're all right!"

Lady Maili touched my arm. The sleeves of her beautiful silk gown looked a bit singed, and her eyes were bloodshot from the smoke.

I cleared my throat. "Have you seen Wendel?"

"I'm afraid not," Lady Maili said. "Are you alone? Why don't you come with me?"

"Thank you, but I can't."

Lady Maili pursed her lips and let me go.

I wandered into the street.

The night whirled around me like a merry-go-round that

wouldn't stop. Konstantin. He could help. Flames still bright in my eyes, I plodded through Vienna.

Wind raked its fingers through my hair and scraped the heat from my skin. Shivering, I hugged myself. My lungs burned with every breath.

Why did I feel like I was drowning?

Smoke. It had to be the smoke.

Shadows smothered me. Not much farther to the Hall of the Archmages. Not much farther before I was off the streets. What if the assassins were already hunting me? I walked faster, my teeth chattering.

Across the street, a tall man stalked with purpose. His pale hair glinted in the lamplight. I had seen him before, in the photograph inside my locket.

My father.

The Grandmaster.

Between one blink and the next, he disappeared. Was he no more than a hallucination?

I staggered to the Hall of the Archmages. Gasping, I leaned against the doors until they groaned open. The room tilted. I landed on my knees. I clawed my way standing again, only to sprawl out onto the floor. The chilly marble beneath my cheek soothed the burning of my skin.

I splayed my fingers against the stone and clung to the sensation of reality.

Then I fell into darkness.

"Ardis?"

I blinked open my eyes. I was lying on my back, somewhere strange but familiar.

"Where am I?" I croaked, my throat raw.

Konstantin leaned over me. "The Hall of the Archmages."

"I remember. I walked here, then..."

"You fainted." He clenched his jaw, his eyes dark with concern. "Carbon monoxide poisoning, to hazard a guess, judging by your singed clothes."

The fire.

Wendel.

"God, no." I struggled to sit.

Konstantin caught me by the shoulder. "Lie down. Please, you only just woke up."

I obeyed. Shivers wracked my body. I was resting on a couch in an office. Bookshelves reached to the ceilings, crammed with haphazardly stacked books. Sunlight crept through a lone curtained window.

Where was I?

Konstantin tilted his head. "Can you breathe better now? We were worried when we found you. I have oxygen in my laboratory, and a pressurized chamber. It was built to test deep-sea diving suits, but—"

"I'm fine," I whispered.

He furrowed his brow. "Are you sure?"

I nodded.

"What do you remember, Ardis?"

"Wendel." I swallowed hard. "Wendel is gone."

Konstantin's shoulders sagged in defeat. "Gone."

A tear snuck from my eye and slid down my cheek. I rubbed it away. He knelt beside me and draped a blanket over me. Blinking, I clutched it closer.

"We failed the mission," I said. "Spectacularly."

"What happened?"

A sick ache lodged in the pit of my stomach. "The Order of the Asphodel came for Wendel. There were too many of them, too many assassins, and he couldn't fight them all. I tried to escape with him, but he wouldn't retreat. He surrendered only when they threatened to kill me. God, Konstantin, he let the Order take him."

He stared at me solemnly. "I know."

My heartbeat stumbled. "How—?"

"Ardis, that was last night."

I stared at him. "I was out that long?"

Konstantin strode to the window and yanked open the curtains. The amber light of afternoon poured into the office. "We sent for a doctor. He told us to wait."

"You stayed up with me all night?"

His mouth bent in a crooked smile. "I had quite a lot of rather boring paperwork to catch up on, so the all-nighter was prearranged."

I met his eyes. "I don't know how to thank you."

"I couldn't sleep. Not after what happened."

"But how did you know?"

He laughed bleakly. "The Sofiensaal burned for hours. Word travels fast in Vienna."

"Margareta must know."

"Obviously." He toyed with a tassel on the curtain. "Though

she doesn't care about Lord Adler's blueprints. She has bigger fish to fry, as you Americans say."

"Bigger fish?"

"The Grandmaster."

The blood drained from my face. "He's here?" I whispered.

"He caught the first train from Constantinople to Vienna, after he learned his necromancer was helping with Project Lazarus. Margareta is meeting with him tonight."

Dread filled my stomach like lead. "What will he do?"

Konstantin looked away. "I don't know."

"We have to stop them."

"Wendel belongs with the Order."

"Wendel belongs *to* the Order. Konstantin, he was running from them. He was terrified."

He frowned. "Terrified?"

"They tortured Wendel when he disobeyed them." I touched behind my shoulder. "His back is covered with scars. They whipped him when he was sixteen, because he refused to raise his second dead man, after he passed out the first time."

Konstantin stared at me. "He showed you his scars?"

"Yes." My voice shook with vehemence. "He wasn't lying. He has no one else."

"Ardis…"

"We have to save him."

He sank onto a chair opposite me. "We can't."

"No." I swung my legs over the edge of the couch. The tattered skirt of my ball gown slid to my ankles. I gritted my teeth. "I need my sword. It's locked in a hotel room."

"Ardis! You aren't in a condition to rescue anyone."

"I'm not sitting here while they torture him."

When I moved toward the door, Konstantin blocked me. I glared into his eyes.

"Let me go," I said.

"I can't let you do this alone."

"Konstantin. You—you won't stop me?"

"On the contrary, I can help you." He smiled lopsidedly.

"How?"

"Officially, since I'm one of the Archmages of Vienna, I can't interfere with the Order of the Asphodel. Unofficially, we could orchestrate an escape."

I hugged him. He startled, then patted me on the shoulder.

"You should rest. Carbon monoxide poisoning is a serious—"

"Konstantin." I withdrew. "Not without my sword."

"How very mercenary of you." But he was smiling. He handed me a black coat that must have belonged to him. "Wear this so you stay warm."

I shrugged on the borrowed coat. Konstantin was so much taller than me that it looked like I was wearing robes. "Thank you. For everything."

"Come back with that sword of yours and we can scheme. I'm good at scheming."

I laughed hoarsely. "I don't doubt that."

"And, Ardis? Stay alive."

My stomach clenched. "I'll try."

34

Shadows slanted long in the late sun. Twilight would fall in less than an hour.

Cold lingered deep in my bones. My teeth chattering, I walked to the Imperial Palace Hotel. It looked no less grand than it had the night Wendel brought me there, but its magnificence seemed foreboding now.

On the stairs to my room, I clung to the railing, my lungs burning for air. Konstantin had called this carbon monoxide poisoning. How much longer would it last?

I didn't have the luxury of time.

Panting, I hauled myself upstairs. The key to our room bit into my hand, I was clenching it so hard. I reached the right floor and leaned against the wall. A maid tsked as she strode past, her eyes full of judgment.

Maybe she thought I was drunk.

I turned the key in the lock, but the lock didn't click.

The door was already unlocked.

My heartbeat galloping, I gripped the doorknob. What if Wendel had escaped already and returned to the hotel? This hope giddied me like alcohol. I turned the knob and swung open the door.

A pale-haired man stared out the window.

Fear hit me like a punch in the gut. A visceral sense of dread radiated from this stranger. Holding my breath, I backed away from him. The stranger wasn't alone. Two men in gray cloaks flanked him.

"Stop," the man said quietly.

Chun Yi lay carelessly on the couch—not where I had left it, or ever would—and I gritted my teeth. I couldn't abandon my sword, but I doubted I was quicker than the assassins, especially after being poisoned.

The stranger turned around.

His gunmetal-gray eyes gleamed with fierce intelligence. He had cropped hair and a beard like the devil's. His tanned, battered face looked like it had been sculpted by years of hard weather and harder fighting.

My father.

The Grandmaster.

My knees threatened to betray me by buckling. I clutched the doorframe and tried not to seem so helpless.

The Grandmaster raised one scarred eyebrow. "Have we met?"

"No," I whispered.

"You look familiar."

I looked like my mother. Maybe he remembered her.

One of the assassins stepped forward. "Sir?"

The Grandmaster raised his hand to halt him. "Not yet." He narrowed his eyes at me. "What's wrong with you?"

"I was in a fire last night. Breathed in too much smoke."

His eyes glinted. "You were there? At the Sofiensaal?"

"I was."

He glanced at the assassins. "Leave us."

"Yes, sir."

The assassins left without a word, closing the door behind them. The Grandmaster stepped forward, his gaze traveling down the length of my body. I was breathing too fast, the rhythm ragged with fear.

"Who are you?" he asked, his voice low and dangerous.

"I'm...I'm no one," I stammered.

"Don't lie to me. You were there with him, weren't you? The Prince of the Undying? He tried to protect you."

My heart thundered in my chest. He knew.

What was the point of lying?

"Yes, I was there with Wendel."

The Grandmaster's eyes narrowed. "You may prove valuable."

Valuable? My stomach clenched. I had walked right into his trap. Would he capture me? Torture me?

"Please sit," he said, surprising me.

I chose a chair by the window. The Grandmaster dropped onto the couch. His stance gave me the impression of a tiger who had returned from a successful hunt, and was now feeling indulgent toward his prey.

He had, after all, caught Wendel.

"Do you know who I am?" he asked.

"Thorsten Magnusson. The Grandmaster of the Order of the Asphodel. And..."

"And?"

I swallowed hard, my mouth dry. *And you're my father.*

But the words died in my throat. Instead, I tried another angle of attack. I shook my head and clutched the locket at my neck.

"I have this," I said.

"Have what?"

"This...this photograph of you."

He froze, a muscle in his jaw ticking. "Who sent you?"

"No one sent me."

I lifted the chain over my neck. When he took the locket from me, the chain looked tiny in his hand. With his fingernail, he pried the locket open.

"Who gave you this?" he asked.

I clenched my shaking hands into fists. "My mother."

He curled his fingers around the locket. "I will ask you once again. Who sent you?"

"No one sent me. I came here myself from America."

He had an expression of sharp scrutiny in his eyes, and it hid his emotions well. "Why?"

"To find my father."

"The father you never knew," he said, still studying me like a puzzle to be solved.

I nodded.

Silence thickened the air between us, burdened by unspoken words. The Grandmaster still held my locket, and I couldn't bring myself to ask for it back.

"Tell me your name," he said. It wasn't a request.

"Ardis." He didn't deserve my birth name.

"Does death thrill you, Ardis?"

A chill ran down my spine. "Why would you ask me that?"

"Because you chose to be with Wendel." His gaze flicked over to my sword. "Because you must have brought that blade with you when you left America."

"How did you know?"

"It's a Chinese sword. And I have a faint recollection of it belonging to your mother."

My stomach knotted. "How long were you together?"

"Long enough."

The Grandmaster reached across the distance between us and placed his hand over mine. It felt rough and warm. Like I had imagined my father's touch would feel, back when I was nothing more than a lonely child.

I bit the inside of my cheek. I wasn't small and helpless.

Not anymore.

"Who are you, Ardis?" he asked, his voice gentler than I would have thought possible.

"Your daughter," I said, still not wanting to believe it.

"Then you belong with me." His eyes darkened. "With us."

"With the Order of the Asphodel?"

"Of course."

I tried to jerk my hand away from him, but he tightened his grip until my bones ached. "Let go of me."

"I'm not done with you yet."

Fear hammered inside my ribs with every heartbeat. "Will you hurt me like you hurt Wendel?"

He tilted his head. "Why do you say that?"

"He has the scars to prove it."

"Wendel is one of our best assassins. By his own hand, he's killed perhaps ninety. With his undead minions, the number is more like nine hundred."

The ice in his voice chilled me to the bone.

"Why are you telling me this?" I asked.

The Grandmaster's face could have been carved from stone. His eyes gleamed with keen intelligence, as if he were calculating the best response.

"Wendel has been lying to you," he said.

"Why would he lie to me?"

"To bend you to his will."

"I don't believe you."

"He's a dangerous man, Ardis."

I twisted my hand, struggling to break free from his grasp. "You're hurting me."

He released me so suddenly I jerked back against my chair. My hand still ached from his crushing grip. He watched me with an unreadable expression.

"Why do you even want me in your ranks?" I asked.

"Because I have no other progeny but you."

I leapt up, pushing the chair back, and bared my teeth. "You can't lay claim to me. Not after abandoning my mother before I was even born."

When he stood, he towered over me. "She never told me she was pregnant with you."

His words sliced through me like a knife. "Why wouldn't she tell you?"

"Because she knew I was dangerous."

Chun Yi lay on the couch. Almost within reach.

"Take it," the Grandmaster said.

Was that a threat?

The muscles in my legs tensed, but I held my ground. He handed me Chun Yi in its scabbard, his face blank and his eyes gleaming. When my fingers closed around the pommel, he didn't let go of the sword.

"Come with me," he said.

I clenched my jaw until my teeth ached. "No."

"You remind me of myself when I was your age. Full of pride and righteous anger."

"I'm nothing like you."

The locket dangled, glimmering, in his other hand. He pressed it into my palm. Instinct urged me to fling it away, but it was all I had from my mother.

"Take it," he said. "And think about my offer. I will not linger in Vienna much longer."

I needed to know where he was taking Wendel. "Where will you go?"

"Tomorrow, I will return to Constantinople, and I will see if you are ready."

I swallowed down the sour taste rising in my throat. Tomorrow? Time was running out. I could lose Wendel forever.

The Grandmaster paused, his hand on the doorknob. "One more thing."

"What?"

"Be careful, Ardis. Fate does not favor those who reject their destiny."

35

Evening fell in Vienna. The dying sun slid down the sky. Walking through the streets alone filled me with a vague paranoia. Wind tossed my hair into my eyes, and I tugged my borrowed coat tighter around myself.

Dusk softened the hard angles of the Hall of the Archmages. I leaned against the doors and slipped into the cool silence. My footsteps echoed through the halls. Each step reminded me I was alone.

What was Wendel enduring without me?

When I rapped on the door to Konstantin's office, he answered it at once, blinking like someone who had spent too much time in the dark. His curly hair had been mussed to a spectacular degree, and a pair of aviator goggles were pushed up over his head.

He smiled. "You got your sword."

"I did," I said flatly.

His smile faded. "Is something the matter?"

"I'm a little tired."

I didn't know Konstantin well enough to tell him the whole story about my father.

He cocked his head. "Better come inside. I have something to tell you."

When I sat on the couch, he shut the door behind me.

"Wendel is still in Vienna." His voice was hushed in the shadowy stillness of the office. "I don't know where, not the precise location, but I know how to find him."

"How?"

He brightened. "The Eisenkriegers."

"The Eisenkriegers in Project Lazarus?"

He dragged a chair closer to me and sat. "The technomancy involved in the Eisenkriegers' control systems was inspired by Wendel's necromancy. Specifically, his ability to control the dead remotely."

"Wendel told me. Called it really clever magic."

"It's brilliant! Though we have a lot of work ahead of us. We're still getting problems with interference. The technomancy is, at best, only a crude approximation of Wendel's magic."

Frowning, I cocked my head. "In what way?"

"A necromancer can control an army of the dead as a legion, or command each man independently. We still don't have the level of precision required to pilot more than one Eisenkrieger. Commands sent to one interfere with the others."

"I don't see how this helps us find Wendel."

"Ardis, we can use the interference. Each of the

Eisenkriegers responds to Wendel's necromancy. We can rewire the control systems to find him."

"Like a compass?"

He broke into a smile. "Exactly."

My mind floated from a dark place. We had a chance to save Wendel.

"How long will it take?" I asked.

"I already started! There's only one problem."

I dug my nails into my palms. "What?"

"I need a pilot."

The way he was looking at me, with that glint in his eyes, made my mouth go dry.

"Me?" I asked.

"I need your help."

I tugged my jacket straight. "I can't say no."

Konstantin sprang to his feet. "Excellent."

I hoped I wouldn't regret this, but I had to cling to any scraps of hope at all.

The Academy of Technomancy resided in a monumental brick building that looked as if it might house something as mundane as a bank, if the place didn't always smell peculiarly like a thunderstorm. Some evenings, the windows flickered with tiny wisps of escaped magic.

The archmages weren't officially part of the University of Vienna, but they had the political clout to treat the campus like a playground. It wasn't so shocking, then, that the Academy of Technomancy had burned to the ground after a magical containment issue a few years back. The laboratories had just been rebuilt.

"Project Lazarus is here?" I asked.

Konstantin held a finger to his lips. He veered from the main entrance to the Academy and walked down an alleyway. He stopped outside an unmarked door and fumbled in his pocket before finding a key ring.

He unlocked the door and stepped inside. I followed him into a dimly lit concrete stairwell that spiraled down. The rapping of our shoes echoed off the concrete walls. It smelled like mildew and stale air, the walls slicked with something damp. At the bottom of the stairwell, Konstantin unlocked another door and held it open.

"Ladies first," he said with a quick smile.

I walked into an underground laboratory. The length of the room stretched out of sight, and the height of the ceiling reached at least ten feet. Rows upon rows of stark electric lights stretched overhead. A dozen men and women in white coats bustled around the laboratory, tinkering with a menagerie of technomancy gadgets.

"Damn!" I muttered. "This is Project Lazarus?"

"Impressed?" Konstantin startled me with his proximity.

I paced along the wall, trying to orient myself in the laboratory. I felt completely out of my element around so much mysterious technology and magic.

"Careful! There's a lot of voltage over there."

My hand clamped on Chun Yi, though I was pretty sure a

sword wouldn't be any good against high-voltage electricity. We walked deeper into the laboratory.

Then I saw the reason for the high ceiling.

The Eisenkrieger.

It stood against the wall, seven feet tall, its steel carapace gleaming like a suit of plate armor for a giant. The Eisenkrieger had no face, and inside the hollow head there was what could only be a cockpit.

I whistled low under my breath. "Damn, that's big."

"Ardis!"

Diesel? I spun around. He stood near the Eisenkrieger, wearing a white coat like everyone else. He dabbed the sweat from his brow with a handkerchief.

"Dr. Rudolf Diesel." I shook my head. "I never thought I would see you again."

His mustache twitched with a smile. "We parted under unusual circumstances."

"Circumstances I regret." That night wasn't my fault, but guilt still wormed inside my gut at my failure to protect him.

Diesel touched my elbow and glanced at me. "I'm worried."

I stared at him. "About what?"

"Project Lazarus is powerful. I shudder to think of that power in the wrong hands."

A shiver crawled down my spine. I hadn't even seen these Eisenkriegers in action yet.

Konstantin stepped forward, his hands clasped behind his back. "Sorry to interrupt, Dr. Diesel, but we're rather pressed for time. Do you know who has the second prototype?"

Diesel glanced between us. His eyes glinted with curiosity.

"Archmage Carol. We discovered yet another flaw in the Eisenkrieger's leg pneumatics, though she should be finishing the repairs presently."

"I had hoped we might borrow both of them."

"Borrow?" Diesel asked. "Both?"

Konstantin cocked his head. "We can't operate more than one at a time, not with the interference, but we can power up two to triangulate his position. Otherwise, we will be working with much less accuracy."

Diesel studied him with shrewd eyes. "May I ask who you want to find? And why did you rewire the control systems for both of the Eisenkriegers?"

"Ah." Konstantin cleared his throat. "Well..."

I interrupted. "Unusual circumstances."

Diesel stepped back and held up his hands. "Understood."

"Thank you." Konstantin linked his fingers behind his back. "Would you find Archmage Carol for us?"

Diesel nodded. "Might as well stretch my legs."

He tucked his handkerchief in his pocket and trudged down the length of the laboratory.

Konstantin glanced back at me. "Ready?"

"Ready for what?"

He smiled like I might be joking. "To pilot the Eisenkrieger, of course."

36

The muscles in my legs locked. I stared into the machine's hollow metal head.

"Why can't you pilot the Eisenkrieger?" I asked.

Konstantin clapped me on the shoulder and steered me closer. "Because I need your help. And I'm a bit too tall for the prototype. My legs cramp if I stay in there for too long. It's uncomfortable and unproductive. Though the final Eisenkriegers will be much bigger."

Much bigger? Seven feet tall wasn't tall enough?

"Ardis?" Konstantin waited for my answer.

"Technically, I have to take orders from you."

"Excellent!"

He rubbed his hands together. Humming, he hurried to the Eisenkrieger and unlatched a metal door in the chest, revealing the pilot's chair inside the cockpit. I unbuckled Chun Yi's scabbard from my belt. Touching the sword brought a boost of courage.

"Let me give you a hand," Konstantin said.

"Thanks."

He grasped me at the waist and boosted me into the cockpit. I twisted around and lowered myself into the seat. I found boots for my feet to slide inside, and articulated metal gloves for my hands.

"Now for power," Konstantin said. "The ignition should be near your left shoulder."

"Inside the Eisenkrieger?"

"Yes. Twist the key."

I peered inside the cockpit. Right over my heart, I found a slot with a key. I slipped my right hand from the metal glove. The key turned with a click, and the Eisenkrieger shuddered to life. Deep rumbling vibrated through the steel and reverberated through my chest.

Konstantin danced back. "Carefully, now!"

When I flexed my fingers, the Eisenkrieger's metal fingers clinked together. I raised my arm and the Eisenkrieger's arm swung upward. Power hummed through the giant metal body. I had never felt so strong before.

I waved at him. "How is this?"

"Impressive!" He laughed. "You have a knack for it."

Another archmage came running down the laboratory, her white coat billowing behind her in the wind of her speed. She had the lean look of someone who never stopped moving, and she glanced between us with a grin.

Konstantin greeted her with a smile. "Archmage Carol!"

"Found a better test pilot?" Carol asked.

Better? Hopefully the last pilot hadn't died.

Konstantin nodded. "Ardis will be helping us today. Is the other prototype ready?"

She waved us onward. "Come and see for yourself."

Archmage Carol jogged deeper into the laboratory. Konstantin hurried to follow her. She easily outpaced even his long strides.

Konstantin glanced back. "Ardis?"

Clenching my jaw, I took one step. The Eisenkrieger's massive metal foot swung forward and clunked on the floor. I tensed, worrying it would be unsteady, but it seemed to borrow my sense of balance. Another step. Then another. After only three lumbering strides, I had already caught up with Archmage Carol.

"That's it," Carol said. "Nice and slow."

"Slow?" I laughed. "How fast is this thing when it runs?"

"The prototype is twice as fast as your average soldier."

"Damn."

"The technomancy in our Eisenkriegers combines the speed and strength of the machine with the skill of the pilot. The pneumatics aren't always flawless, though. That's what happened to the second prototype."

We reached the far end of the laboratory. The second Eisenkrieger lay on its back on a massive flatbed trolley. The metal plate on its shin had been removed, revealing the gleaming oiled innards of its leg.

"Konstantin?" Carol asked. "When do you need this up and running?"

Out of breath, he caught up with us. "Not literally up and running. Powered should be sufficient."

Carol leaned over the trolley. She turned the key in the ignition, and the Eisenkrieger rumbled to life. Lying flat on its back, the machine purred with a low hum that echoed inside my chest and sent a thrill down my spine.

I needed to spend more time in this secret laboratory.

"Wait!" Konstantin jumped back. "Did you disconnect the control systems from the pneumatics?"

"Obviously." Carol looked sideways at him. "Otherwise I would never run both prototypes at once."

"I'm guessing the interference is bad?" I asked.

Carol nodded with a grim smile. "Nearly lost one of our pilots before we figured out why. We need to get that necromancer of yours back to help."

Konstantin clambered onto the trolley and scooted into the cockpit of the Eisenkrieger. He fiddled with something inside the second prototype, then crawled back out and leapt down from the trolley. From a workbench, he grabbed a notepad and a brass instrument that resembled a pocket watch, though the dial clearly didn't measure minutes.

Konstantin smiled. "Today interference will be our friend!"

After he pried open a panel in the Eisenkrieger's chest, he clipped the instrument to a wire inside and stared at the dial. His pencil scratched furiously as he jotted notes.

"Archmage Carol?" he asked. "How far is it to the other end of the laboratory?"

She shrugged. "Two hundred meters, if you start at that mark on the floor."

"Exactly?"

Carol laughed. "Exactly. They wouldn't build me a track for testing, so I measured one out myself."

Konstantin stared at her like she had given him all his Christmas presents early. "Perfect! Ardis? Walk to the other end of the laboratory."

"Yes, sir."

I clomped down the laboratory. The archmages followed in my footsteps. Konstantin clipped the pocket watch lookalike to a wire within the guts of my Eisenkrieger and took notes on the reading. Hunching over a table, he scribbled a page of mathematical computations, frowned at the numbers, and scratched his head with his pencil.

"Never liked trigonometry," he muttered.

Carol leaned over his shoulder. "Need help?"

He curled his arm around the paper and dragged it closer protectively. "According to my initial reading, we should be looking about seven kilometers southwest of here. So with a baseline this small, our triangulation will be primitive. But it should be better than nothing."

Carol stood watching with crossed arms. "What's next?"

"I need a map of Vienna."

Archmage Carol nodded and sprinted away. She returned a few minutes later with a rolled map.

"Thank you."

Konstantin spread the map on the table. With his tongue poking from his mouth, he sketched out a few points over the city. He circled one of them, then lifted the map and jabbed the paper with his pencil.

"There! He's south of Vienna, in the town of Liesing."

I had never been. "What's Liesing like?"

"It's an industrial area." He frowned at the map. "A lot of factories. Abandoned, under construction. They could be keeping Wendel anywhere."

My hands curled into fists, and the Eisenkrieger mimicked my movement. Dread pounded with my heartbeat. "We need to find him, even if we have to tear it all down."

37

Under cover of darkness, we drove from the Academy of Technomancy with a questionably borrowed truck and an even more questionably borrowed Eisenkrieger. With Konstantin behind the wheel, I sat shotgun with my sword across my knees. I kept glancing in the side mirror at the bulk in the back of the truck.

"Are you sure you tied down the tarp?" I asked.

"Ardis," he said, "for the thousandth time, I'm sure. They won't see us coming."

I dug my fingernails into the scabbard. "The Grandmaster is meeting with Margareta tonight. This is it, Konstantin. We don't have time for mistakes."

"I don't intend to make mistakes."

"Then you might want to double-check the tarp."

He softened his voice. "We won't let them take Wendel."

I bottled up my emotions and stared straight out of the windshield. "How much farther?"

"Twenty minutes. Just twenty minutes."

I nodded and counted down in silence.

"And remember," he added, "be extremely careful with the Eisenkrieger. We only have two prototypes, and we have to bring this one back in one piece. I don't want a single dent or scratch on it. Do you swear?"

"I swear, I won't scratch your precious Eisenkrieger."

A corner of his mouth tugged into a crooked smile.

We left behind the glittering lights of Vienna and drove into the darkness. One by one, the night swallowed the buildings around us. The humming of tires on the road lulled me into a trance. My mind circled through the same thoughts again and again.

He loved me, and I couldn't save him.

A hollow hurt lingered inside me. I hugged myself, pretending I was just cold. I waited without speaking until Konstantin pulled into an empty weed-choked lot. Brick factories loomed in the shadows.

"Are we here?" I asked.

Konstantin nodded at the truck's odometer. "That's about seven kilometers."

When he killed the engine, it was deathly quiet, broken only by the sound of rain.

"Can you pilot the Eisenkrieger while I take some readings?"

"That's why I'm here."

I opened the door of the truck and grabbed my sword on

the way out. I craned my neck to look at the black sky. Wind scattered rain onto my face.

Konstantin flicked on a flashlight and yanked off the tarp from the Eisenkrieger. "Get in."

I blew out my breath, fogging the air, and climbed into the back of the truck. Biting my lip, I handed him Chun Yi. I had been holding it so tight, the scabbard's sharkskin left its pattern on my hands.

He held the sword gingerly. "What do you want me to do with this?"

"Hold onto it for me."

"I could leave it in the truck?"

I shook my head. "We're not leaving my sword."

Konstantin sighed, but he tucked the scabbard under his arm. I lifted myself into the cockpit of the Eisenkrieger. In the darkness, I fumbled for the ignition before I turned the key. The Eisenkrieger hummed to life.

"Let me take the first measurement," he said.

He opened the front panel of the Eisenkrieger and hooked up the pocket watch lookalike. He bent over the dial and rubbed rainwater from the glass with his sleeve, then squinted at whatever the numbers told him.

"Not far from here." He unhooked the device and pointed his flashlight about forty-five degrees to our left. "The interference is strongest that way."

I jumped from the back of the truck and landed in a crouch. I pressed the Eisenkrieger's knuckles into the dirt and pushed myself to my feet. The pneumatics of the metal limbs pumped with smooth power.

"Follow me," Konstantin said.

I lumbered alongside him. The Eisenkrieger left deep footprints in the mud from the rain. We crossed half of the empty lot, and he held up his hand to stop me. He took another reading on the device.

"Turn clockwise. More. Less. Stop." He unhooked the device. "Walk."

I did as he said. We walked for a few hundred meters, stopped, took another reading, turned right and kept walking. Rain silvered the air like scratches on glass.

"Somewhere," he murmured. "Wendel has to be here somewhere."

I scanned our surroundings. The nearest factory looked out at me with shattered and empty windows. Deep within the darkness, a light flickered for no more than a second before it vanished. I froze and stared at the factory. Faded white letters had been painted over the doors, but I struggled to read the German.

"Konstantin," I said. "Look. I saw a light over there."

He ran the beam of his flashlight over the lettering. "Sargfabrik," he read. "Coffin factory."

We shared a glance. Unease slithered through me.

"Should we go in?"

"It looks abandoned. Are you sure you saw a light?"

"Yes."

He took another reading. "The interference is off the charts. He has to be here."

"I'm going in."

I left him behind in three giant steps and stood at the

threshold of the factory. A padlocked chain hung across the doors. I wrapped the chain in my metal fist and snapped it like it was no more than a thread.

"Ardis!" Konstantin hissed my name. "Stop! You can't go in there with the Eisenkrieger."

"Isn't it fully functional?"

"Yes, but it's only a prototype."

I shrugged. "Prototypes are made to be tested."

"We can't risk it."

I tried to smile. "I won't scratch it, I promise."

"We would jeopardize Project Lazarus."

"More than we already have?"

He squared his shoulders. "Get out of the Eisenkrieger."

Damn it, that sounded like an order. I unlatched the cockpit door and hopped out.

"Can I at least have my sword?" I asked.

His sigh clouded the air. He held out Chun Yi, and I buckled the scabbard to my waist. He caught me by the wrist and glanced into my eyes.

"Wait," he said. "We can't rush in."

I stared at the factory doors, zeal burning in my chest, and drew Chun Yi. Flames shivered over the blade and hissed in the rain. Squinting, he retreated from my sword. I wondered if he mistrusted blood magic.

"We should assess the situation first," he said.

"Fine. I'll start."

The doors squealed open on rusty hinges, and the mustiness of decay rolled over me. I stepped into the gloom, tense and ready to fight.

The coffin factory's ceiling, spiderwebbed with mildew, floated high overhead. Decrepit iron machinery hulked like the black bones of giants. The floorboards creaked under my feet. I glanced at a machine with a press in the shape of a cross, meant for a coffin lid. Clearly, this factory hadn't profited enough from the dead.

Rain drummed on the roof. Wait, that couldn't be the roof. There should be a second story above me, judging by the number of windows I had seen outside. I followed a zigzagging steel staircase upstairs.

Half of the roof had collapsed. Rain splattered on the splintered furniture and floorboards. There must have once been offices here. The faint glow of distant streetlamps leaked through the jagged chasm in the ceiling. In the shadows beyond, I could barely make out the opposite wall and the jumble of dark shapes there.

One of the dark shapes moved.

I slid my feet forward, wary of rotten floorboards. Chun Yi burned brightly enough to light my way. Slowly, the darkness yielded to my sword's fire.

Horror hit me like a blow to the stomach.

38

Wendel slumped against the wall with his hands shackled above him. He lifted his head. Blood stained his mouth and trickled down his jaw. His long hair had been hacked away, the ragged remnants falling to his chin.

My heart broke into a thousand pieces.

I ran across the rain-streaked darkness to him.

"Wendel! Wendel. I'm here."

When he opened his mouth, more blood trickled down his chin.

I knelt beside him. "Are you alone?"

He shook his head.

Pain glittered in his eyes. No, it wasn't only pain. Fear. Shame. I swallowed past the fierce ache in my throat. The chain on his handcuffs looped through the iron frame of a window with shattered glass.

"Wait here," I said. "Let me get Konstantin."

Wendel yanked against his handcuffs. The chains rattled. He shook his head again, harder this time. The incessant rush of rain filled the silence.

Why wasn't he speaking? What was he trying to tell me?

The tiny hairs on my arms prickled. When I stood, Wendel lunged against the chains, the muscles in his arms straining. He didn't want me to go. But I wanted to break him free, and I needed the Eisenkrieger for that.

A floorboard creaked behind me.

Armored hands closed around my neck.

I barely had time to suck in a breath before darkness constricted my vision. The pressure on my arteries was relentless. I struggled against my unseen attacker, but it was too late, I was losing consciousness already.

My cheek hit the floorboards. Rain splattered my face.

The sensation faded as I sank into oblivion.

Blood whooshed through my ears.

I blinked open my eyes. Where the fuck was I?

I was sitting in a chair, my arms pinned down with rope twisted tight around my wrists. Something was wrong with my head, or something was wrong with the world. Time stuttered and sped forward like a bad movie reel.

Disoriented, I squeezed my eyes shut.

"Look at me," said a man.

Adrenaline jolted my nerves. I peeked through my eyelashes. Rain fell through the chasm in the roof of the coffin factory.

A man stepped into my line of sight. An assassin. His blood-splattered white cloak flowed to his feet. Engraved gauntlets armored his hands. Although he had a grizzled beard, his dark eyes glinted with vitality.

"Temporal magic often does strange things to the mind."

No wonder I had blacked out so fast. The chokehold had been accelerated.

"Who are you?" I asked.

He pondered my question. "A technomancer. You may call me Hieronymus. And you?"

I narrowed my eyes. What did he already know?

"He knows your name, doesn't he?" Hieronymus dragged my chair around.

Wendel.

He fought his handcuffs, his wrists raw and bloody, and knocked shards of glass from the window. His eyes glittered with powerless fury.

My throat clenched. "Why can't he speak?"

Hieronymus leaned over my shoulder and smiled indulgently as if I were a stupid child.

"Because he wouldn't."

The blood on his white robes had to be Wendel's blood.

Rage exploded inside me like a firework. I snarled at him. "You never should have touched him."

"Why?" Hieronymus stared at me. "Do you care about him?"

Fuck. The icy fist of fear clenched my gut. There was no right way to answer that.

I forced my face to be blank. "Why do you care?"

"Curiosity." When Hieronymus tapped my shoulder, I flinched. "Tell me your name."

"Ardis."

"Ardis," he murmured in my ear, his breath hot and rank. "I'm afraid that pain has lost its meaning for Wendel. Hurting him has become pointless."

Out of the corner of my eye, a black blade glinted. Fuck, he had stolen Amarant. My heartbeat thundering, I stared straight at the floor.

Hieronymus circled me and traced the razor edge of the dagger along my forearm. "You cared enough to find him. Is the feeling mutual?"

My mouth went bone dry. "I'm a mercenary with the Arch-mages of Vienna. I was hired to find the necromancer and bring him back to them." None of that was a lie, though it omitted much of the truth.

I prayed that Konstantin had realized something had gone terribly wrong. I hadn't returned from the coffin factory. I didn't know how long it had been.

"Ardis?" Hieronymus sighed. "You are a pitiful liar."

"I'm telling the truth."

"I see the truth in Wendel's eyes."

Hieronymus twisted my left arm and exposed the veins in my wrist. Oh, fuck, oh, fuck. I curled my fingers into a fist and forced myself to look away.

I had never been tortured before. I had to be strong—

Hot liquid spilled over my skin, chased by a blinding bolt of pain. I gasped and glanced at my wrist. Blood trickled down and pattered on the floor.

He cut my wrist. That fucker cut my wrist.

Hieronymus grabbed my right wrist. Amarant sliced my skin like a razor through silk, so mercifully sharp I felt nothing until my nerves responded a second later.

"Jesus fucking Christ," I muttered.

With every heartbeat, a searing hurt pulsed along the length of my arms. I clenched the muscles in my legs and moaned through clenched teeth. An alarming amount of my blood pooled on the floor by my feet.

When I looked at Wendel, he had a perfectly blank face, but he was shaking badly. If he couldn't keep it together, then this whole ruse was useless.

They would know we cared about each other.

"How do you feel?" Hieronymus asked me.

I bared my teeth. "Like I want to kill you."

Hieronymus inspected his handiwork. When he cupped his hands, his gauntlets crackled with a green glow. Temporal magic. I had seen it before when Konstantin healed Wendel, and I remembered Wendel's agony. My heart raced so fast the beats became uncountable.

"Too much blood," Hieronymus said, "too quickly."

He grabbed my wrists and squeezed the magic into my wounds. Pain roared through me and obliterated all thought. I doubled over, my muscles in spasms. A scream ripped through my throat and left it raw.

"There," he said. "Better."

I blinked back tears. The technomancer's gauntlets still bruised my flesh. Blood seeped between his fingers. He lifted his hands and revealed pink scars running the length of my arms.

He had healed me, but he would only hurt me again.

"Thanks," I rasped.

Hieronymus hardly seemed amused by my sarcasm. He strode over to Wendel, who slumped with his head bowed, his ragged hair shadowing his face.

Hieronymus lifted his chin. "Disappointing."

Wendel stared at him, blankly, his eyes ice cold.

Hieronymus smeared my blood on his jaw. "Perhaps I'm wasting my time." He brought the dagger back to me. "I may have to simply kill her."

39

Cold seeped into my skin. My emotions floated higher than I could reach. Hieronymus lifted Amarant and tilted the blade. A drop of blood rolled to the ground.

"Wait," I bluffed. "You don't want to do that."

"Why not?"

I took a deep breath, stalling for time, and—

The window nearest us shattered. An iron beam flew through the air and crashed against the opposite wall. Shards of glass chimed on the floor.

Swearing, Hieronymus ran to the window.

When Wendel glanced at me, I mouthed, "Konstantin."

Downstairs, a massive crash shuddered the walls of the coffin factory. The rain-soaked floorboards groaned. The Eisenkrieger's footsteps thudded below us and shook the building. Christ, that thing was loud. Startled shouts betrayed the presence of assassins somewhere on the ground floor of the coffin factory.

Hieronymus backed away from the window and whirled around. He curled his lip in a snarl. He grabbed me by my chin, his hand bruising, and held the dagger at my neck. When I swallowed, the blade nicked my skin.

"Ardis," he said, "tell me who—"

An excruciating screech, like metal on metal, interrupted him. Silence.

The floor exploded.

A hunk of iron machinery splintered the rotten wood. The force of it flung Hieronymus and me against the wall. I hit the bricks hard; he hit them harder. He collapsed on the ground while the machinery skidded to a halt.

The chair cracked beneath me, loosening the ropes around my wrists. I wrenched my hands free, elbowed the chair away, and jumped to my feet.

The black dagger spun to a stop. It teetered on the brink of falling through the chasm.

Gritting my teeth, I lunged. Hieronymus seized my ankle.

I kicked him in the face.

Time around me slowed to a crawl. Sweat dripped from the technomancer's cheek and hung, suspended, in midair. Wendel stared at me in silent horror, caught between one blink and the next. My skin prickled with the wrongness of it.

I had broken the technomancer's temporal magic.

My heartbeat thundered in the uncanny silence. How long did I have before my luck ran out? Seconds? A key glinted on a chain at Hieronymus's neck. It had to be for the handcuffs. Fingers shaking, I snapped the chain.

When I whirled around, my vision flickered. The magic had to be fading fast.

The black dagger tumbled infinitesimally to the ground floor, barely within reach, and I snatched it from the air. Clutching the key, I ran to Wendel. As I unlocked his handcuffs, his eyes flicked toward mine.

Time lurched back on track.

My hand tightened around the black dagger just as Hieronymus straightened. He glanced down at his gauntlets, as if surprised they had failed him. Wendel staggered into the light. Blood dripped from his mouth before he wiped it on his sleeve.

Hieronymus eyed the black dagger in my hand. "Amarant's magic won't obey you. It's a necromancer's dagger."

I lifted the blade. "I don't want to hide in the shadows."

Wordlessly, Wendel stood by my side. Ready to fight. Ready to defend me.

Blood trickling from his nose, Hieronymus shuffled backward unsteadily and leaned onto a battered desk. He tugged away a cloth and revealed Chun Yi. My sword looked dull and dark without its fire.

"Where did you steal this sword?" Hieronymus asked.

"Steal?" I spat. "What makes you think I stole it?"

His fingers slipped around Chun Yi's hilt, caressing it, and brilliant flames whispered down the length of the blade. "It's far too powerful for a girl like you."

Wendel's hand found mine. His necromancy skittered like

icy fire over my skin. It jolted down the length of my arm, electrifying my nerves, and traveled into the hilt of Amarant. Darkness unfurled from the dagger.

I gasped as shadows swept over us both.

Wendel squeezed my hand, but I didn't know what he meant when he couldn't speak. He dragged me away from our enemy and pressed us both against the wall. His heartbeat pounded against my chest.

"We need to get the hell out of here," I whispered.

He shook his head and pried Amarant from my hand.

Shadows rushed from me like a wave retreating into the ocean. I stood illuminated in the dim light. Hieronymus spun my sword and traced a burning figure eight in the air. I fucking hated theatrics.

The floor shuddered. I glanced at my feet.

Hieronymus closed the distance between us in a few long strides. One more step, and he could strike. If he swung high enough, I could catch the blade with my hands. Painful, but it might deflect the blow. I edged along the wall and searched for an impromptu weapon.

"Pity." Hieronymus lifted my sword. "It would have been a pleasure to kill you slowly."

A boot ever so softly scraped the floorboards.

Hieronymus turned to look, though he only made it halfway.

Wendel stepped from the darkness like an avenging angel. He drove his dagger into the technomancer's eye. Savagely, he twisted the blade before wrenching it out.

Hieronymus screamed. Wendel kicked him in the back and

knocked him down, then crushed his sword hand beneath his boot. The sword clattered on the floor, flames sputtering out, and I lunged to grab it.

Hieronymus clawed his way forward. Wendel grabbed a fistful of his beard, wrenching his head up, and slit his neck. He left him to drown in his own blood.

My body shook uncontrollably. "Is he dead?"

Wendel's gaze locked with mine, his eyes bleak and soulless. He wiped his dagger on the man's robes, pocketed the blade, and took both of my hands.

He bared my wrists, every movement careful, though I couldn't stop myself from flinching at the memory of pain. His fingers traced my scars delicately, and the emotionless mask of his face cracked.

He dragged me closer and held me like he never wanted to let me go.

When my hand found the nape of his neck, he shuddered beneath my touch. I escaped his embrace, though I couldn't stop staring at the blood on his hands. The corpse's foot twitched in the corner of my vision.

Downstairs, a quaking thump shook the building.

"Konstantin." My stomach plunged. "We have to help him."

40

I skirted the splintered floorboards and crept downstairs.

In the dimness of the factory, the assassins clung to the shadows. Konstantin, in the Eisenkrieger, wasn't nearly so subtle. He swung a massive arm and swatted an assassin. The man flew clear across the room, slammed against the wall, and crumpled on the floor.

Konstantin powered the Eisenkrieger into a sprint. He swung at another assassin, who rolled out of the way. The machine punched the wall with bone-shattering force.

I counted the bodies. Six assassins.

But six more of them had Konstantin cornered. Worse, he was limping. The pneumatics in the Eisenkrieger's leg had been damaged by a blade. If the assassins crippled the other leg, it wouldn't take much to drag the machine down and pry him from the cockpit like crabmeat.

Time for a distraction.

My fingers closed around Chun Yi's hilt. Sharkskin pressed its pattern into my skin. Sword blazing, I leapt from the stairs and charged the assassins.

The nearest assassin barely had time to turn before I feinted and swung at his face. He dodged. I veered and slashed his arm instead. Chun Yi gouged flesh and carved bone like a knife through butter. The assassin screamed and clutched his half-severed arm.

"Ardis!" Konstantin called out. "Thank heavens."

I flashed him a smile. "Here to help."

He limped forward a few steps, the floor shuddering under the Eisenkrieger's weight, then swung his arm and smacked the assassin I had just wounded. The man flew through the air and slammed on the bricks.

Five more assassins to go.

A flash of steel sliced the darkness—a throwing knife. I dove to the bricks, tucked into a roll, and slid behind a machine. The knife ricocheted off the iron above my head. I flattened myself to the floor. My fingers grazed the arm of a dead assassin who had been tossed aside like a broken doll.

No, not dead yet. The man moaned and opened his eyes.

I should kill him. Now, before he alerted the others. But we locked eyes with each other, and his fear and pain riveted me.

Wendel stepped from the darkness. Amarant's shadows still clung to his skin.

The wounded man crawled on his stomach, struggling to drag himself upright. Wendel grabbed the man's hair and drove his dagger into his neck. He severed his spine and lingered only long enough to raise the dead.

Cold chills ran down my spine. "Wendel."

He looked at me with hollow eyes, then turned to another wounded man and slaughtered him. The dead man climbed to his feet and awaited his command.

Metal clanged on metal.

I peeked over the machine and saw an assassin hacking at the Eisenkrieger's undamaged knee.

"Is that another scratch?" Konstantin said.

Maybe he should be more worried about dying instead.

Konstantin grabbed the assassin by his cloak, dangling him so his feet kicked. Disgusted, he flung him away. I tracked the man's arc through the air. I didn't see where he landed, but I heard a sickening crunch.

Only four assassins were still alive.

Wendel's undead minions shambled breathlessly behind us. I snuck closer to the Eisenkrieger. An assassin lingered nearby, searching the darkness. My sword's flames dimmed like it knew I needed stealth.

Wendel waved his minions onward.

The undead men dragged their scimitars along the floor. I winced at the screeching. The assassin narrowed his eyes, holstered the throwing knife, and unsheathed his scimitar instead. Backing away, he held his blade at a high angle, ready to behead the dead men.

I crept around the machine and circled the assassin.

He never saw me coming.

I aimed for his heart and stabbed him between the ribs. Chun Yi cleaved his flesh and sank to the hilt with stunning ease. The assassin died almost instantly. Wendel raised him from the dead an instant later.

I yanked out Chun Yi, my sword blazing even brighter.

"Three more," I said.

Wendel commanded his tiny army of the dead with a wave. The undead ran almost as fast as the living, their muscles not yet stiff, and left bloody footprints. The assassins retreated to the center of the room. They stood back-to-back and brandished their scimitars.

Wary of more throwing knives, I kept to the shadows.

The dead men threw themselves onto the blades without hesitation. Impaled with a scimitar, a dead man clawed at an assassin. The second assassin hacked at the dead man's neck and swore when the blade stuck. The third faced two undead at once, struggling to shove them back.

Konstantin limped closer and loomed over the fight.

I tensed, ready to duck flying machinery, but he balled the Eisenkrieger's hands into fists. He reared back before charging the assassins. He knocked two out of three flying and clobbered an undead man on the way.

Bones cracked loud enough that I flinched.

I ran to finish off the last assassin, who dropped his scimitar and held up his hands.

"I surrender," he said. "I surrender!"

I started to lower my sword.

The assassin stiffened as darkness descended behind him. A blade sliced his throat. The assassin went limp, like a marionette with its strings cut, then straightened as he was puppeted by Wendel's necromancy.

"He surrendered!" Konstantin stammered.

Assassins lay scattered across the factory, silent or moaning, many with limbs at awkward angles. Wendel walked from assassin to assassin like an efficient reaper, slitting their throats and severing their spines.

He killed them all without hesitation.

"Wendel," I said.

He said nothing. He looked...lost.

"We have to go. He's here. The Grandmaster."

Wendel stared at me with such concentrated fury that I retreated a step.

"I saw him," I said. "He's in Vienna."

He shook his head, though I didn't understand why.

Konstantin limped over to us. "What happened to him?"

"I don't know. We have to get him out of here."

Konstantin had to duck to fit through the doors of the coffin factory. I followed close behind him, counting on the Eisenkrieger's bulk as a shield. The steel reflected the flames of my sword. Wendel lingered near one of the windows, staring intently into the darkness.

I turned back. "Wendel?"

Blinking, he followed me into the light.

Outside the factory, it was still and silent. Any number of assassins could be lurking.

"See anything?" I asked Konstantin.

From the height of the Eisenkrieger, he scanned our surroundings. "No."

"There could be more. Stay hidden."

Konstantin laughed nervously. "How? I'm huge."

I led the way from the coffin factory and across the empty lot. Rain weighted down my hair and trickled down my clothes. I wished I were inside the Eisenkrieger. It was drier, and safer, inside the machine.

That's when I realized Wendel wasn't with us.

I turned back and found him lingering in the shadows again. He stared into the darkness like he belonged there. He had a distant, empty look in his eyes.

What was wrong with him?

41

I backtracked to meet him. He opened his mouth, as if he wanted to speak, but blood trickled down his chin. Grimacing, he wiped it on the back of his hand.

Dread froze in my belly like ice. Had the Order done something irrevocable to him?

"Are you okay?" I asked.

He shook his head. I had never seen him look so lifeless.

"How did they hurt you?"

He curled his lip as if annoyed by the simplicity of my question. Even bleeding and mute, he had a hint of arrogance that reminded me of the Wendel I knew, the Prince of the Undying. There was hope for him yet.

"We need to go," I said.

He shook his head again. He worked his jaw back and forth.

"We can't stay here. Believe me, Wendel, I know you want to hunt down every last assassin in Vienna. I do, too. But now really isn't the time for revenge. Especially brutal soulless revenge that will get you killed."

Grimacing, he spat blood on the ground.

"Besides, you owe me," I said. "I saved your life again."

He dropped to one knee in parody of the time he swore undying loyalty to me. He arched an eyebrow with wordless sarcasm, his eyes glittering.

I held out my hand. "Wendel."

Never looking away, he clasped my hand and let me help him to his feet. His necromancy rushed over my skin, and I couldn't help but shudder. Even now, the full force of his magic was an overpowering sensation.

I glanced at his minions. "Let them go."

When he snapped his fingers, the dead men fell to the dirt.

Still in the Eisenkrieger, Konstantin climbed into the back of the truck. He lowered the machine to its knees, tucked in its arms, then killed the engine. He jumped from the cockpit and bent over the Eisenkrieger's knee.

"For heaven's sake," he muttered. "That scratch won't buff out. And the pneumatics—"

"Konstantin," I said.

"Right."

Wendel and I had far more scars than the Eisenkrieger—not that the archmage seemed to notice. I helped Konstantin drag the tarp over the Eisenkrieger. He slid behind the wheel. Wendel and I climbed in beside him.

Konstantin twisted the key in the ignition. The truck coughed to life. "We can't return to the Hall of the Archmages. Not tonight."

"Why?"

"The Grandmaster is meeting with Margareta."

Wendel tensed beside me, his shoulder pressing into mine.

"Where should we go instead?" I asked.

"My laboratory." Konstantin shifted into drive. "I have a first aid kit and my temporal magic, so I should be able to patch up both of you."

Pain panged through the scars along my arms. I wasn't sure if I could ever look at temporal magic the same way again, after being tortured with it.

How had Wendel endured years of this agony?

"Do me a favor?" Konstantin asked.

"What?"

"Pray that Margareta doesn't go looking for the prototype."

I laughed bleakly. "At least we left no witnesses."

Wendel had stopped bleeding, but he still hadn't spoken. When he leaned against the window, it bared the double-headed eagle tattooed on his neck. Impossible to hide, now that his hair had been hacked off.

They had done this to shame him.

Tears blurred my eyes. God, he had suffered so much.

I rested my hand on his knee. A shudder traveled through his body. Even from the slightest comfort, he seemed to be on the verge of breaking down. He linked his fingers with mine. I squeezed his hand and tried to lend him my strength through our connection. We had almost escaped. All he had to do was hold on.

Night shrouded Vienna. In an alley behind the Academy of Technomancy, Konstantin maneuvered the Eisenkrieger from the back of the truck and limped it to the freight elevator. I hit the call button and waited.

"Fucking hell," I said. "We made it."

Wendel touched my arm. Exhaustion shadowed his eyes, but he managed half a smile. The elevator arrived with a ding. Konstantin entered first, still inside the Eisenkrieger. It was a miracle it fit in the elevator. Wendel and I wedged in beside the Eisenkrieger, which had to be too big to press the buttons.

"Which floor?" I asked.

"Basement." After I hit the button, Konstantin cleared his throat. "If anyone asks, we were testing the Eisenkrieger."

"We were. Unofficially."

He coughed. "Nobody but students and interns should be up this late. Midterms, you know. And if they value their grades, they won't interfere."

Wendel smirked. What joke did he wish he could say?

The doors to the elevator clunked open, and we entered a dull concrete hallway. When Konstantin waved us onward, the knuckles of the Eisenkrieger accidentally scraped the ceiling. He winced at the noise.

Luckily, nobody seemed to notice, and we reached the laboratory without incident.

It was dark inside, so I hit the switch. Bank after bank of lights blinked on above. Konstantin hobbled to a flatbed trolley and hoisted himself onto it. Slowly, he lowered the Eisenkrieger onto its back. After scooting from the cockpit, he hopped down and staggered on his own stiff legs. Wendel caught his arm to steady him.

"Thank you," Konstantin said, his cheeks pink. "Ardis? Help me hide the Eisenkrieger."

I raised my eyebrows. "Hide?"

"Until I can fix it. Or explain why it needs to be fixed."

Konstantin grabbed a tarp and unrolled it over the battered Eisenkrieger. I took the opposite corner and helped him.

"What happened to Wendel?" Konstantin whispered.

My stomach clenched. I couldn't even guess what they had done to Wendel. I had once seen a criminal with his tongue cut out, but that had been much bloodier. And that hadn't silenced him so completely.

"I don't know," I admitted.

Wendel leaned against the wall and raked his fingers through his ragged hair. Slowly, he slid down to the floor and huddled there.

Worry jolted my nerves. "Wendel?"

He tried and failed to speak again. Obviously, it hurt him greatly to do so, but why? I found a pen and notepad and slid them across the floor to him. He started to write, his words wavering as his hand shook.

Clever of you. Thank you.

"Can you tell us what happened?" I asked.

When Wendel staggered upright, Konstantin wheeled out a chair. "Sit, please."

Wendel sat down and hunched over a table. He tugged the

notepad straight, then hesitated, the tip of his pen digging into the paper. His throat worked as he swallowed hard. Wincing, he motioned to his mouth.

This is their curse. To punish me.

"A curse?" I asked. "What kind of curse? What do you...?"

Wendel put down his pen. He opened his mouth wide. His tongue had been inked with black symbols I couldn't read. They cut deep enough to bleed.

I gasped. It hurt just to look at him.

He had endured such a cruel punishment, one that had robbed him of his voice. Was it permanent? Would I never hear his honey-gravel voice again?

I wanted to help him, but I didn't know how.

Konstantin pressed his knuckles to his mouth. "This is worse than I thought."

I closed my eyes for a moment, trying not to be over-whelmed. "Why?"

"I would recognize those runes anywhere. It's a silencing curse."

Wendel swallowed hard before he picked up the pen.

Is there a countercurse?

Konstantin grimaced. "Curses aren't my specialty, but I do know one thing. Only the technomancer who cursed you can remove the curse."

The light in Wendel's eyes dimmed. He stared at the paper.

That man is dead.

42

endel leaned over the table, his head propped on his hand, and touched the pen to the paper. I waited for him to write more, but instead he sketched line after line across the corner of the paper.

Dread filled my stomach like rocks. "Who did this to you?"

He kept blackening the paper.

I placed my hand on his. "Was it Hieronymus?"

He nodded.

I grimaced at Konstantin. "Hieronymus was a technomancer at the coffin factory."

"There was a technomancer there?"

"Yes." I rubbed my scarred wrists. "Wendel killed him."

Wendel shoved back his chair from the table and stood. He swayed on his feet, his face deathly pale, and sat back down hard. The chair screeched against the floor.

"Wendel?" My heart pounded. "Are you okay?"

He shook his head.

"Konstantin, help me. Don't let him fall."

Wendel shook his head, though he didn't fight the arch-mage when he grabbed his arm. He slumped between the two of us. We kept him steady.

"Have you slept since the assassins found you?" I asked.

He shook his head again.

Konstantin looked nearly as pale as Wendel. "He can't stay here. But my apartment isn't more than two blocks from the laboratory."

"Can you walk, Wendel?" I asked.

He nodded. We helped him to his feet. After a few paces, he no longer looked so frighteningly pale. He shrugged off our hands. Konstantin still hovered nearby, glancing at him, until Wendel managed a glare.

"We can take the freight elevator," Konstantin said.

That was smart. I wasn't sure Wendel had the strength left in him for the stairs. Predictably, Wendel grimaced at this acknowledgment of his weakness, but I didn't give a damn about his pride at the moment.

We ascended to the city above.

I tilted my head skyward. "It's snowing."

Snowflakes fell like goose feathers from the clouds and hushed the nighttime sounds of the city. Beautiful. I appreciated it in a detached way, since I still felt so dead inside. Shivering, I followed close behind Konstantin. Wendel trudged alongside me without even looking up from his boots.

We walked for two blocks before stopping outside a tidy apartment building. From the lobby, we took the stairs to the second level. Wendel clung to the railing with his head bowed. Every step betrayed the depths of his exhaustion.

Konstantin unlocked the door. "Let me get the lights."

He flicked on a switch, and electric lamps blinked awake. Curious, I looked around the archmage's apartment. Small and cluttered, it had overflowing bookcases and glowing technomancy apparatuses that looked like they belonged in the laboratory. The corner of my mouth curled in a smile. How much luggage had he brought to Vienna, and how chaotic had it been when he unpacked? Wendel lingered by the door, like he didn't trust so much technomancy in such a little space.

Konstantin patted the back of a couch. "Please, make yourselves at home."

"Wendel," I said. "Sit down before you fall down."

He looked mildly insulted, though my comment motivated him enough to walk to the couch. Konstantin bustled off to the kitchen. While the archmage was out of sight, Wendel dropped onto the couch and sank into the cushions. He closed his eyes, some of the tension leaving his muscles.

"Tea?" Konstantin called from the kitchen.

Wendel nodded without opening his eyes.

"Yes, please." I settled in a battered old chair. "For two."

A clock with gleaming naked gears caught my eye. This was bizarre—teatime at two o'clock in the morning with a necromancer and an archmage. I laughed, feeling the drunkenness of extreme fatigue.

Wendel cracked open an eye and tried to speak, then thought better of it.

"Are you hungry?" Konstantin asked.

"A little," I admitted.

"Good!" He sounded happy to have guests.

Konstantin returned to the living room, balancing a platter piled with sausage, half a loaf of dark bread, a stick of butter, and a little jar of mustard. He delivered it all to the coffee table, ducked back into the kitchen, and brought mismatched plates and silverware. He arranged everything precisely in front of us.

"Here you are," Konstantin said. "Now you can refuel."

I glanced heavenward. Of course he would think of it that way.

Konstantin sat on the couch beside Wendel without touching him. He cleared his throat and shifted his weight. Wendel pantomimed writing in the air. Konstantin jumped to his feet and fetched a notebook.

I tilted my head so I could read his words.

Wendel wrote, *Thank you for saving me.*

Konstantin blushed to the roots of his hair. "We couldn't leave you there in the laboratory. Or in the coffin factory, for that matter."

Wendel arched one eyebrow. *You could have.*

"Please," I scoffed. "Who do you think we are?"

A smile shadowed Wendel's mouth.

"And thank you for inviting us here, Konstantin," I said. "It was very kind of you."

"You're most welcome."

We ate together in a companionable silence. I helped myself to a second sausage and liberally applied mustard. I was famished.

"This is good," I said.

Konstantin shrugged. "I scrounged it up in my kitchen. It's hardly fit for a prince."

Too late, Wendel wrote. *Disinherited a long time ago.*

"You're still the Prince of the Undying."

You flatter me, archmage.

Konstantin leaned closer to Wendel to read what he had written. Their elbows bumped on accident. Still blushing spectacularly, he fumbled with the bread he was buttering. "You're welcome, necromancer."

Wendel's eyes glinted, but he cringed and rubbed his mouth. He couldn't even laugh. Worry wormed in my stomach. When I looked at Konstantin, his eyes betrayed his own unease. The mood in the room darkened.

Wendel tapped his pen on the paper. *How did you find me?*

Konstantin straightened. "I rewired the control systems in the Eisenkriegers, then used the interference to triangulate your location in the coffin factory." If he was waiting for a compliment, he wasn't going to get one.

I see. Wendel clenched his jaw. *The Eisenkriegers were not what I expected.*

"What do you mean?" Konstantin asked.

Wendel hunched over the paper as he wrote. *You killed those assassins like insects.*

Konstantin's eyes flickered as he read and reread the words.

"Killing efficiently?" I asked. "That bothered you, Wendel?"

Wendel locked gazes with me. His eyes burned with intensity. He touched a napkin to his mouth, and it came away red with blood. He wanted to speak so badly that pain wouldn't stop him from trying.

"The Hex will not last forever," Konstantin said. "We need Project Lazarus."

"Not even the archmages believe in the architecture of their peace?"

Konstantin pressed his mouth into a grim line. "I may be the youngest archmage in Vienna, but I'm not the most naïve. Removing gunpowder from the equation might buy us another year, two at most, but that hasn't stopped Romanian rebels from fighting Austria-Hungary for control of Transylvania."

"Agreed," I said. "We have been on the brink of war for months."

Wendel's pen scratched quickly. *How will an army of Eisenkriegers help with peace?*

Konstantin frowned. "Austria-Hungary's safety depends on the strength of her army."

An army of metal men. You don't intend to give your enemies a fighting chance.

"Isn't that the point?" I said. "We need to win this war as fast as possible."

His eyes shadowed, Wendel looked away. He tore the page from the notebook, crumpled it in his fist, and tossed it into the fireplace.

The teakettle shrieked. Konstantin leapt to his feet.

"Wendel," I murmured. "Now isn't the time to argue with the archmages."

He locked stares with me, and I tried to decipher his emotions. Desperation battled with hope in his eyes. God, I knew that feeling all too well. He had hit rock bottom, when the only way out was up.

Konstantin returned with a chipped teapot. He poured us each a cup.

"Enough about the Hex," he said. "I have been thinking about Wendel's curse."

Wendel cupped his teacup in both hands, listening intently.

"It might be impossible." Konstantin paced around the table. "It might even be too late. But theoretically, if we can work out all the technicalities, Wendel should be able to resurrect Hieronymus and countercurse himself."

Wendel straightened, the fire in his eyes rekindled, and reached for the notebook.

Constantinople, he wrote. *The Order will send his body there for a funeral.*

"When?" I said.

Wendel frowned. *Hieronymus was Greek. They never bury the dead on Sundays. His funeral will be Monday, at the earliest.*

Of course a necromancer would know so much about funerals.

"Monday," I repeated. "The day after tomorrow. Is that enough time, Konstantin?"

Lost in thought, Konstantin gazed at his overflowing bookshelves. "If we hurry."

43

agic remained a mystery to me. I tried my hardest to decipher the thick books on curses and countercurses, but after only half an hour, the symbols swam through my head in a soup of nonsense.

"Sorry," I said. "I'm better with swords than sorcery."

Konstantin leaned back on the couch and stretched until his spine cracked. "We may need to take a more practical approach to the countercurse."

"Meaning?"

"We won't know until we try it."

"Are you coming? To Constantinople?"

He shook his head. "I'm afraid not. I can't abandon Project Lazarus."

I stifled a yawn. "Understood."

"You look exhausted," he said, as if he weren't himself.

I glanced at Wendel, who had to be infinitely more tired.

"We shouldn't go back to the hotel. Not the Imperial Palace Hotel, anyway."

"Why not?" Konstantin asked.

"The Grandmaster broke into our room."

Wendel's jaw clenched, the muscles in his neck taut. *Did he hurt you?*

"No." My heart ached at his concern.

He had been chained and tortured in the abandoned coffin factory for much longer than I had been, but he was still worried about me.

His pen dug into the paper. *What did he want?*

"The Grandmaster wanted me to join him."

Konstantin jerked back, blinking. "Why?"

There was no easy way to explain this, but I had to try. "He's my father." I grimaced. "No, he's the man who got my mother pregnant and abandoned her. I didn't know his true identity until Wendel told me."

Konstantin whispered, "My God," under his breath.

Wendel wrote fast, the pen scratching across the paper. *Why did he let you go?*

"I refused him." I shuddered. "But I doubt he's letting me walk away forever. He told me that fate does not favor those who reject their destiny."

Wendel rubbed his hand over his eyes like he wanted to erase his memories.

"Stay here tonight," Konstantin said.

"What if assassins track us down?" I asked.

He waved away my question. "I have measures in place to keep us safe. Just trust me."

The knot of fear loosened in my chest. Konstantin was a powerful technomancer and an Archmage of Vienna. We were in the middle of Vienna itself, at the heart of their empire. If anyone could protect us, it was him.

Standing, Konstantin put down the book he had been reading. Gold letters glinted on the spine: *The Art of Blood Magic.*

"Blood magic?" I asked.

Konstantin glanced into my eyes. "It's a forbidden art. One that only a few dare learn."

"Why is it forbidden?"

"Because it requires sacrifice. Blood must be spilled to work the magic."

I swallowed hard. "Like the silencing curse."

"Indeed."

Wendel wrote, *Forbidden like necromancy?*

Konstantin locked his fingers together and hesitated before responding. "Less so than necromancy. In the hierarchy of magic, death magic is considered the darkest, and necromancers an abomination."

When Wendel put down his pen, it clicked on the table with finality. He leaned back on the couch and crossed his arms with a cold, arrogant sneer on his face. I could tell he wasn't at all surprised by the archmage's answer.

When we first met, even I believed necromancers to be an abomination. But Wendel had no choice. He had been born with necromancy. His magic ran bone deep. He couldn't deny his power over death without denying a part of himself.

"Do the Archmages of Vienna still consider necromancy an abomination?" I asked.

Konstantin swallowed hard. "Admittedly, yes."

"Even though you can't do Project Lazarus without it?"

His blue eyes looked dark, like a storm gathering in the sky. "Sometimes, in order to defeat evil, we must embrace the forbidden."

"Blood and death magic," I said grimly.

But I couldn't shake off the feeling that we were playing a dangerous game of chess, and we were running out of moves.

Konstantin slipped *The Art of Blood Magic* back onto a bookshelf. He glanced at the clock. "It's late. Nearly three o'clock."

"Where should we sleep?" I asked.

"Would you prefer the couch or the floor? I have a bed roll. It was quite comfortable during my work on the Hex in the Dodecanese Islands."

"The floor sounds good to me."

Wendel touched my elbow before he shook his head.

"You're hurt worse than me," I said. "No need to be a gentleman."

He scribbled on the notebook. *It's the least I can do.*

"Are you sure?"

He nodded, and I sighed at his persistence.

Konstantin brought out the bed roll. "Good night."

"Night," I yawned.

Konstantin turned off the lights and left us alone.

I stretched out on the couch and rested my aching bones. Wendel lay down on the bed roll and closed his eyes, though tension stiffened the muscles in his body. He was still ready to run or fight in a heartbeat.

I knew the feeling all too well.

Darkness invaded my dreams.

I couldn't escape the coffin factory. This time, I was chained to the wall. Blood slicked my mouth and spilled from my wrists. I snapped my chains, but the Grandmaster blocked my way. He held out his hand to me, beckoning me. Time tortured me with its slowness, favoring my enemies, and left me helpless as they advanced.

I jolted awake with a pounding heartbeat.

It was still night. Wendel was sleeping on the floor. His hands clenched around fistfuls of a blanket, and he jerked like someone had hit him.

I stared at him. Was he also having a nightmare?

He doubled over and shuddered. I shook his arm. He flinched, but didn't wake up.

"Wendel," I said.

At the sound of my voice, his eyes snapped open.

He lunged from the bed roll and grabbed me by the arm, driving me back. My shoulders slapped the wall. The shock of it flooded my blood with adrenaline, but I refused to fight back. He was only sleeping—

The black dagger glinted in his hand by my throat.

"Wendel!" I gasped. "Wake up!"

He was breathing hard, his hand bruising my arm. Then he let me go and staggered back. Awareness sharpened his eyes.

"You were having a nightmare," I said.

Wendel dropped the dagger. It fell with a dull thud on the

carpet. His eyes flickered as he searched my face. He took my arms with cautious gentleness. I flinched when he touched the bruises from his fingers.

"I shouldn't have woken you," I whispered.

He recoiled from me, stumbling into a bookshelf, before he sank to his knees on the carpet. He dug his knuckles into his temples. My instincts urged me to put more distance between us. When I backed away, his head jerked up at the sound of my footsteps. Our gazes locked across the room.

Tears overflowed from his eyes. His sobs never made a sound.

My fear twisted into anguish. I dropped beside him and dragged him into my arms. He buried his face against my shoulder, his whole body shaking, his ragged breaths muffled against me. His tears wet my shirt.

"It's okay," I whispered, though it was a lie. "It's okay."

He pulled away from me, clenched the pen in his fist, and stared at the notebook with unfocused eyes. Without a doubt, he was struggling not to fall apart. Ink dripped from the nib, a black blotch staining the paper.

I don't belong here. I don't deserve you.

44

y throat clenched. "That's not true."

I can't escape them. His fallen tears blurred the ink on the paper. *I belong to them.*

"I refuse to believe that."

He bared his teeth. *You don't understand.*

"Then tell me." I cringed at my words. "Fuck, I'm sorry, I didn't mean it like that."

I've done terrible things for them. This pain is so deep, I'm drowning in it.

His words stabbed me through my heart. His pain echoed inside me. I caught his gaze. "You don't have to do this alone."

I hurt you. I almost—

He stopped writing, as if he couldn't admit such a terrible truth, but we both stared at the black dagger on the carpet. He snatched up his dagger, stared at the blade for a moment, then hid it high on a bookshelf.

He wrote, *Forgive me.*

"I'm still afraid of your nightmares," I admitted.

When I rubbed my bruised arms, he looked tormented by what he had done. *Please don't touch me when I'm having a nightmare. I'm not myself.*

"I won't." I swallowed hard. "But I want to help you."

You can't.

Two words, and yet they were enough to knock all the air out of my lungs.

"No." I glared at him. "I won't abandon you now, not when you're in so much pain, when you're hurting too much to see a way out."

He stared at the paper until he tore it from the notebook and crumpled it in his fist. He tossed it into the embers of the fire and watched it burn.

"We don't have to go," I said. "Fuck the Order of the Asphodel."

His eyebrows descending, he stared sideways at me in disbelief.

"Instead of Constantinople, we can take a train to Switzerland. They don't want anything to do with this war. We can find some little cottage in the mountains and learn how to make cheese." I shrugged. "Actually, I'm pretty bad at cooking. We might have to raise cows, or do whatever else it is the Swiss do."

His mouth twitched. Was he amused by my idea?

Chocolate, he wrote. *I like Swiss chocolate better than Swiss cheese.*

"I'm not sure I trust your skills in the kitchen. Princes aren't exactly known for cooking. Neither are necromancers."

He smiled, but it faded fast. *I can't—* He crossed it out. *I would love more than anything to run away with you. To Switzerland or America or anywhere else.* He tapped the nib of the pen on the paper. *But I can't put you in danger.*

I breathed in through my nose. "I'm willing to take that risk."

Ardis, I am dangerous.

"Really?" I deadpanned. "I had no fucking idea."

He smiled again, and this time it touched his eyes.

"But you're more than that." Emotion rasped my throat and turned my words husky. "You're more than a necromancer, more than the Prince of the Undying. Don't let the darkness inside you swallow you whole."

He stared into my eyes before he reached out to me. He touched his fingertips to my wrist, cautiously, as if afraid I might recoil from him. Instead, I embraced him. He let out a shuddering sigh and kissed me. The intensity of it rushed through me. I hooked my hands behind his neck and melted in his arms.

"I forgive you," I whispered against his lips.

He kissed me back, harder, letting his body speak for him.

Finally, we broke apart. He placed me on the couch and tucked the blanket over me. He kissed me on the cheek, a sweet gesture that surprised me. It had to be his silent way of wishing me good night.

I stared into the darkness while he lay back down on the bed roll.

After counting a hundred heartbeats, I heard his breathing settle into a gentle rhythm. Only then did I sleep.

I woke at the first light of dawn.

Wendel was gone.

On his bed roll, he had left an envelope. It contained a folded piece of paper. When I opened it, something fluttered out and landed on the carpet. A tram ticket? I frowned at it before returning to the paper.

He had written me a letter. I read it with a pounding heart.

Ardis,

This letter must be my apology, and my goodbye.

Wendel had blacked out a sentence or two. I skipped to the next legible line.

It was always too late for me to promise you anything forever. It would be cruel of me to pretend to be the man you deserve. I must face the Order of the Asphodel alone. Until they die, or I die, you will never truly be safe.

I'm sorry for hurting you.

I vowed to protect you. I'm saving you from myself.

I am not sure how to end this letter. I hate endings.

Wendel

· · ·

I stared at the letter until the words blurred. I traced my fingers over his handwriting.

"Fuck!" I muttered.

Wendel wanted to say goodbye like this? Abandoning me in the middle of the night? We had already agreed that I would go with him to Constantinople. We had already agreed that we would protect each other.

"Ardis?" Blinking owlishly, Konstantin shuffled into the room. "What is it?"

"Sorry, did I wake you?"

"No. I noticed one of my technomancy wards was triggered. Someone must have opened the door of the apartment."

I let out a shuddering sigh. "Wendel. He's gone."

"He must have left moments ago."

Moments? My legs tensed with an urge to run after him, but he had his black dagger, Amarant, and could hide in the shadows.

I handed the tram ticket to Konstantin.

"The 71 tramline," he said. "But it's an old ticket."

"Wendel gave it to me."

The color drained from his cheeks. "Did he?"

"Yes."

He studied the ticket. "Ardis, have you heard anyone talk about taking the 71?"

I shook my head. "Never."

"It's a euphemism for death. The 71 line has a terminus in the Zentralfriedhof. The grandest cemetery in Vienna."

My blood chilled. "Was the ticket a threat or a promise?"

"I don't know." He rubbed his beard. "Wendel may intend to lure out the Grandmaster."

"But why would he give me this ticket?"

His face tightened with a curious mix of hope and despair. "I would interpret this as a warning. He's telling you to stay away from him and his fight with the Order."

"I won't stay away. I refuse to abandon him."

"I understand your loyalty to him. But the Grandmaster and his assassins might kill you. Consider that carefully before you do anything regrettable."

"You know what I would regret more than anything? Leaving Wendel to die, knowing I could have saved him. I wouldn't be able to live with myself."

He nodded with quiet resignation. "I know."

All the air left my lungs. "Thank you, Konstantin."

"For what?"

"For being my friend."

"No need to thank me." He smiled. "And what I said earlier still stands."

"What was that?"

"Stay alive."

My laugh sounded reckless, even to my own ears. "I wouldn't dream of dying."

45

Vienna floated in mist, the highest of its towers and spires lost to the walkers below. Snow sifted from the sky. It was a day closer to Christmas. I sat near the back of the 71 tram, swaying as it clattered along the tracks. I hadn't slept since my nightmare in the apartment, but a cold clarity sharpened my senses.

The 71 whined to a halt at its terminus.

I leapt out on stiff legs and looked around. Just shy of six hundred acres of land sprawled before me, populated with the dead. More dead than any other cemetery in all of Europe. This was the Zentralfriedhof.

"I hope you're here," I muttered to myself. "I hope you're waiting for me."

And I hoped the Grandmaster wouldn't find him first.

Starkly black trees veined the sky. Gravestones reached from the snow and tried to touch the heavens. The sun arced in its short-lived flight above the earth. I knew the sunlight would die at four o'clock. I had only a short day to find Wendel before the darkness overtook us. My sigh fogged the frigid air.

A crow flew overhead with a rowdy caw. A second crow, and a third, rushed above me on the rustling of wings. Crows foreshadowed necromancers, didn't they? I chased the birds deeper into the cemetery.

Snowfall erased angels and monuments, white on white, but couldn't diminish an ancient gnarled oak. Crows perched in its branches, blinking at me with their black glittering eyes. I circled the tree and tried not to hope.

A man in black left the shadow of a mausoleum and walked down a row of graves.

Wendel.

"You bastard," I whispered, shaking my head.

When he strode through the snow, the crows fled from the tree. They scattered across the sky like ragged scraps of black. He mouthed my name before wiping blood from his lips. He was still cursed, still unable to speak.

My heartbeat pounded. "I'm always finding you alone and bleeding in the snow."

He shrugged, his smile brittle with pain, and stepped closer to me. I could have reached out and touched him, but I didn't.

I took his letter from my pocket. "You wrote this?"

He nodded.

I ripped the letter down the middle, sighing in destructive satisfaction, and watched his words drift into the snow.

I glared at him. "This isn't goodbye."

In the low angle of light, his green eyes looked luminous

and betrayed the depths of his emotions. He still loved me, even though he thought he would lose me. My heart hurt so savagely that tears stung my eyes.

"Why would you leave me like this?" I asked.

He closed his eyes for a long moment, then fell to his knees. He bent over his ruined letter, reading it again, before he ripped out a smaller piece of paper: *I vowed to protect you. I'm saving you from myself.*

"We agreed to protect each other," I said.

Wendel straightened. He kissed my forehead, then my mouth. I tasted his blood on his lips, bitter with iron. He turned away; his face twisted. He might have been ashamed to be bleeding from the curse on his tongue.

I caught his face in my hands and kissed him again. The tension melted from his body. My own anger and fear faded away like mist in the sun. He touched me with all the love he couldn't speak out loud.

I opened my eyes. "Wendel, promise me you will stay with me until the end. No matter how dark things get. Promise me."

His lips parted as he stared deeply into my eyes. The armor of his arrogance fell away, and he looked soft and vulnerable. Slowly, he nodded.

My sigh fogged the air. "Thank you."

His eyes hardened, his armor snapping back into place, his hand locked on my arm.

"What is it?" I asked.

He yanked on my arm to swing me around.

Natalya, the mercenary who had abducted Diesel, stood in the snow. Her blonde hair gleamed in the late sun. She had a rapier in one hand, a dagger in the other, and a smile that said we had just walked into her trap.

I glared at her. "Natalya."

"Thank you, sweetheart." She twirled her dagger. "I can take it from here."

Wendel raised an eyebrow, clearly disdainful. Maybe he had put two and two together, and knew this was the blonde mercenary who had defeated me.

I reached for my sword. "Why the fuck are you here?"

Her smile widened. "You just kissed a wanted man."

"Wanted? Are you stupid? I already brought Wendel to the Archmages of Vienna."

She scoffed. "Sweetheart, the Grandmaster pays triple. You could have delivered Wendel to him on a silver platter and earned a hefty purse of gold."

The facts clicked together in my head.

She was working for the Grandmaster.

She was a double agent.

Natalya tilted her head. "You let him fuck you, didn't you?" She laughed scornfully. "I'm surprised he went for a woman while she was still warm."

Wendel bared his teeth at her, his eyes dark.

"Don't make him mad," I said. "He might order your corpse to walk into a cesspit."

Natalya laughed again, like this didn't scare her in the slightest. "The necromancer is mine. Just walk away, and I won't have to hurt you."

I scoffed. "That was my line."

With an impatient sigh, Wendel drew his dagger.

I stopped him with my hand. "Let me do it. I have a vendetta against this bitch."

He stepped back and waved me forward. Of course, he understood revenge.

Natalya let the tip of her rapier rest on the snow. I eyed the dagger in her left hand. If she wasn't stupid, she wouldn't hunt a powerful necromancer with ordinary blades. The dagger was probably enchanted.

There was only one way to find out.

When I unsheathed Chun Yi, flames rippled down its length. Natalya's shoulders tightened, almost imperceptibly.

Was she afraid? Good.

I charged and swung Chun Yi high. Natalya deflected the blade with her dagger. Counterattacking, I drove the dagger away and hacked at her neck. The mercenary dodged it and backed against the mausoleum.

"Beheadings are too flashy," Natalya said.

"Always worked for me."

I pressed my advantage, swinging at her shoulder, forcing Natalya to defend herself with her dagger. She kicked me in the stomach. I staggered back, winded, and her rapier whipped through the air.

The blade cut my cheek. It burned like a wasp's sting.

"Don't toy with me." Strangely, my words were slurred.

After I retreated, I touched the wound on my cheek. My skin went numb. A strange kind of numbness, one I had encountered once before.

The dagger wasn't enchanted, but the rapier was, with paralysis magic.

46

My heartbeat thundered. The numbing poison pulsed through my blood.

Strength or skill wouldn't win this fight. But deception was the special of the day.

With exaggerated clumsiness, I stumbled to my knees and clutched Chun Yi. Natalya edged nearer. Out of the corner of my eye, I glimpsed Wendel striding into the fight. Natalya's attention shifted to him.

Perfect.

I surged to my feet and swung Chun Yi. The magic in my sword rushed through my arm and steeled my muscles. I chopped Natalya's rapier in half, jerked my sword backward, and bashed the pommel into her face. Blood gushed from Natalya's nose. She staggered back, trying to escape, but I caught her arm, wrenched it hard, and stabbed the broken rapier into her chest.

Shock froze in her eyes. She tottered into the snow.

I stared down at Natalya. She lay like a bug pinned to a wall. Her lips had frozen in a silent gasp, her breath misting the air. Blood trickled past the rapier's blade, still embedded to its hilt between her ribs.

"Fuck you," I said. "And honestly? A necrophilia joke is so unoriginal."

My tongue didn't feel so fat in my mouth. I rubbed my cheek again. The numbness seemed to be fading away, bit by bit.

Thank God the magic wasn't stronger.

Crouching, Wendel held his dagger over Natalya.

"Don't." I caught his wrist. "Someone will find her eventually."

He had the audacity to look innocent, like he had never killed in cold blood before, but he shrugged and pocketed his dagger.

I wiped my sword in the snow. "We overstayed our welcome in Vienna."

He straightened, his gaze on the horizon. The wind stirred his butchered hair, the tattoo of the black eagle bare on his neck.

"Constantinople?" I asked.

Wendel nodded, his eyes still focused on his destiny.

The Orient Express Airways zeppelin floated, anchored to a steel mooring mast, over the grass of Aspern Airfield in Vienna. Sunset angled through the haze of clouds, shimmering over the airship's silvery skin.

We waited in line to board the zeppelin. Wendel gazed at the airship with a faint smile shadowing his face. Anticipation buzzed in my stomach. In my hand, I clutched two first-class tickets. We hadn't booked a round trip flight, but then again, who knew how long we would spend in Constantinople.

Or if we were ever coming back.

A page ushered us into an electric elevator at the bottom of the mooring mast. We climbed to the height of the zeppelin. Whistling wind stung our eyes. We hurried over the swaying gangway and stepped inside the zeppelin's nose, where we were greeted by smartly dressed officers of the Orient Express Airways.

I wanted to glance around the luxurious foyer, but Wendel slipped his hand into mine. He led me to the left-hand prome-nade deck. Windows ran along the wall, tilted so that passen-gers could lean against the railing and see the ground below. He found us a spot by the windows just as the airship began to glide away from the mooring mast. Below us, people waved handkerchiefs and hollered goodbyes.

I watched the world drift away beneath me. In another life, we could have been newlyweds traveling on our honeymoon, with hope instead of dread for our future. The impossibility of that idea tasted bittersweet.

"I wonder when we will see Vienna again," I said. "Or if we will."

His fingers tightened around mine, though he kept his stare on the ground.

We departed at five o'clock. By six o'clock, Vienna had disappeared in the distance, and the cathedral of Budapest towered over the city. By seven o'clock, the moon had risen, and the zeppelin sailed over Serbia.

We went to dinner together in the airship's dining room. I gazed through the windows at the glittering lights, so far beneath us. My breath clouded the air. The interior of the zeppelin had no heat, and it was a chilly night. Around us, passengers wore furs while they sipped wine and ate their dinner.

Wendel had liberated some stationary from our cabin, and he slid it toward me now. *I hope the waiter brings our food while I'm still awake.*

"Tired?" I asked.

He nodded, then scribbled his reply. *I feel like the walking dead.*

"You should know."

His mouth twisted into a wry smile.

The waiter served us sea bass with almonds. I rubbed my thumb over my fork, concentrating on the silverware's ornate engravings. A thought had haunted me for hours now, but I hadn't had the courage to ask.

"Wendel?" I said.

He glanced into my eyes, only for a moment, still focused on cutting his fish.

"Should we sleep in the same bed tonight?"

He relinquished his knife for a pen. *I have fewer nightmares when I'm with you. Are you comfortable with this?*

I reached across the table and squeezed his hand. "Yes."

After dinner, we went to our cabin together.

Our berth was lightweight, like everything on the zeppelin, with linen sheets and a featherdown comforter. I undressed down to my underwear and climbed into the berth. Wendel stripped totally naked before sliding under the sheets.

I rolled over to face him. "Do you always sleep naked?"

He tightened his arms around me. Our bodies fit together like puzzle pieces. He couldn't get any closer to me without being inside me.

Desire curled in my belly, but I didn't know if he wanted more than this. He had been through so much trauma recently.

"Are you okay?" I murmured.

He nodded. When he looked down, his eyelashes shadowed his cheeks like black crescents. He was achingly beautiful.

"Can I touch your hair?"

He nodded again.

I stroked my fingers through his ragged hair. I couldn't help but mourn his long locks, which had been stolen from him, though the shorter cut highlighted the razor-sharp angles of his cheekbones and jaw.

"You're still far too handsome for your own good," I said.

A smile shadowed his mouth, and his eyebrows jumped upward.

"I still want you," I murmured.

Between my thighs, his cock hardened. His hands moved over me, evoking shivers of magic on my skin. I shuddered beneath his touch. He slipped his fingers between my legs and tugged my underwear aside. The blunt head of his cock nudged the wet heat of my pussy. The urgency of his desire excited me.

I wanted to erase his pain with pleasure.

"Fuck me," I whispered.

He glanced into my eyes as if requesting permission, but of course he still couldn't ask me what I meant. I needed to talk dirtier to help him understand my consent.

"I want you to slide your cock into me and find out how wet I am for you. I want to feel you with nothing in the way."

It was a dangerous request, and we both knew it. His pupils dilated. His heart pounded hard against my chest. Slowly, he dragged my underwear past my hips. He pressed against my pussy before invading me in one thrust.

A groan escaped me. "Fuck, you feel good."

Scalding hot, his cock was like silk over steel. He shivered, the muscles in his ass tensing, before he slid all the way out. He questioned me with his eyes, no doubt wondering how many risks we should take.

I wanted more. I wanted to feel him lose control.

"More," I said.

He thrust back into me. I clung to him as he moved faster, harder, deeper. Our bodies communicated all the passion and longing between us.

His hand slipped down, his fingers stroking my clit in slow circles. I rocked my hips, desperate tension building inside me. The magic of his necromancy skittered through me and intensified my pleasure.

White-hot bliss scorched through me. I shattered around him, clenching hard.

Suddenly, he pulled out. His cock jerked as he spilled his release across my belly.

Holy fuck, that was hot. My empty pussy ached. I grabbed his hand, urging him on, and he stroked my clit with godly mastery. My back arched off the bed as another climax obliterated me with ecstasy.

Breathing hard, he braced himself over me. He left for a moment and returned with a handkerchief. He wiped his seed from my skin, every touch a caress, before he lay behind me and kissed my neck.

I floated between the earth and the sky.

Outside, the world was cold and distant, but here, together, we had found peace.

When I woke in the darkness, I had lost all sense of time. The zeppelin soared so soundlessly that we could have been moving or moored at a faraway city.

My stomach plunged. Wendel had left in the middle of the night? Maybe it didn't mean anything significant, but it was hard not to worry.

I dressed, left the cabin, and discovered it was dawn. The night's chill still lingered in the sky. On the promenade deck, I peered through the tilted windows.

The first blush of sunlight gilded a carpet of amber fields.

We flew not more than five hundred feet above the red-tiled roof of a farmhouse, and laughing children chased the zeppelin's shadow.

We had to be flying over the Ottoman Empire already.

In the dining room, relief crashed over me. Wendel stood by the windows, his hands clasped behind his back. He looked over his shoulder at me and smiled. Sleep had smoothed much of the worry from his face.

"Good morning," I said.

When I stood by him, he tugged me into the crook of his arm. I rested my cheek against his chest. His steady heartbeat thumped beneath my ear. The sound comforted me, telling me he was here with me, and he was alive.

A city shimmered in the distance. The spires of the mosque Hagia Sophia soared heavenward. I had seen the Hagia Sophia once before, but only in a book, and it looked so much more vibrant and real than the gray, crosshatched engraving in those pages. Anticipation bubbled up inside me like champagne.

Constantinople.

The city where it would all end.

47

We wandered through the Grand Bazaar of Constantinople.

Wendel had bought a black cloak, and he wore it with the hood shadowing his face. I tugged my scarf straight over my hair and clutched a golden Ottoman lira in my hand. The covered streets of the Grand Bazaar no doubt swarmed with pickpockets.

The kaleidoscope of sights dazzled my eyes. On my left, men praised rich Turkish rugs. On my right, glowing glass lamps like fairytale baubles hung from the vaulted ceilings. They hawked opium beside dates and pistachios. Rare and exotic spices perfumed the air—sandalwood, ginger, nutmegs, cinnamon.

Even I blended into this city's crowds, with so many faces from faraway lands. No one looked twice at me.

A woman with birdlike eyes beckoned me with toy scarab

beetles that flicked open their iridescent shells and flew on mechanical wings. I couldn't tell where the magic ended and the clockwork began.

We found an even more wondrous clockwork beast: a griffin crafted from ivory and brass. When it blinked, its eyes clicked like a camera shutter. A lion's growl rumbled from its mechanical throat and made me shiver.

Wendel lingered at the edge of the street, waiting.

I hurried to meet him. "I wish we had more time. I would love to get lost here."

His mouth bent in a smile. Perhaps he had before.

I followed him down a street that echoed with the hammerings of coppersmiths. We rounded the corner and came upon a newsstand. Wendel bought a newspaper. He flipped through it, then tapped a page. I glanced at the text, recognizing it as Turkish. Honestly, it was impressive that he understood so many languages.

I only recognized one word: *Hieronymus*.

"His obituary?" I asked.

Wendel pointed to his wrist where a watch would be. I knew that we didn't have much time. We abandoned the Grand Bazaar. He flagged down a hackney carriage and showed the driver the obituary. The driver replied in Turkish before waving us both inside.

We rattled through the crowded streets of Constantinople. Wind corrugated the steely waters of the Bosporus. The hackney stopped outside a small church with a stark white façade. Wendel leapt from the carriage, helped me to the street, and tossed the driver a coin. Then he flipped back the hood of his cloak and strode inside.

The velvety smoke of frankincense sweetened the gloom. At the far end of the nave, an intricate gilded screen glimmered by candlelight and dwarfed a simple wooden casket. Mourners shuffled toward the casket.

Wendel held his finger to his lips and slipped into the procession. I followed in his footsteps, my heart pounding in my ribs, and prayed that nobody would recognize us. I bowed my head, hiding my face. We inched closer to the casket, until only a gray-haired woman stood between us and the dead.

Hieronymus lay in eternal sleep. But soon he would be woken.

The gray-haired woman bent over the casket, weeping, and kissed a cross placed on Hieronymus's chest. His widow? When she walked away from the casket, she was comforted by others. My chest tightened, and I backed out of the procession. No one questioned my behavior. Perhaps they mistook it for grief.

Wendel strode to the casket and bent over the body as if paying his respects.

Hieronymus sat upright.

His widow glanced back, looked into his dead eyes, and collapsed in a faint. Screams and gasps punctuated the silence. I gripped my sword, ready for a fight.

One word echoed in the church. "Necromancer!"

Wendel offered his dagger to the corpse. Hieronymus seized the dagger and grabbed him by the jaw. He shoved Wendel's head back, yanked open his mouth, and carved an X across his tongue.

It looked like he was crossing out the curse.

Wendel broke away from Hieronymus, doubled over, and spat what looked like black ink onto the carpet. The corpse collapsed in the casket.

Wendel wiped his mouth on his sleeve and raked his hair from his eyes with a shaking hand. After taking back his dagger, he faced the horrified crowd.

To them, he was a sinister man cloaked in black, his pale face devoid of emotion.

"You can bury the body now," he said, his voice unbelievably hoarse.

A priest darted toward the necromancer and tossed a whole flask of holy water into his face. Wendel curled his lip and dried himself on his cloak, then flipped up his hood and strode down the aisle to the doors.

When the priest tried to follow, I blocked his path. "No."

Even if he didn't understand English, he understood my hand on my sword.

Quickly, I exited the church. Wendel waited for me outside. Bending with his hands on his knees, he spat more of what looked like ink.

"This curse tastes horrible," he rasped.

"Are you bleeding?" I asked.

When he dabbed his tongue with a handkerchief, it was stained black. "I don't think so. And it definitely doesn't hurt so damn much."

The priest ran from the church, brandishing a cross, followed by a mob of mourners.

We shared a glance. "We should go," I said.

"Before they bring pitchforks."

I shot him a glare for the wisecrack.

We didn't stop running until we had reached the banks of the Bosporus, where we slowed to a walk. Our breathing clouded the salty air.

Wendel flung back his head. "Finally!" he shouted.

I grimaced at him. "We should keep quiet. We just desecrated a funeral."

"Desecrated?" He laughed, and it was only a little rusty. "Did I do anything to the body? Believe me, I thought about it, but even I have morals."

"You do?" I deadpanned.

He gave me a look. "Ardis. Please."

Shivers ran down my spine. "I thought I might never hear you say my name again."

Closing his eyes, he leaned down and rested his forehead against mine. He may have had his voice back, but he didn't seem to know what to say.

"Ardis, I—"

I interrupted him with a kiss, still trembling from the adrenaline in my blood. He grabbed me by the hips, pulling me closer like he couldn't get enough of me. The bitter taste of the curse lingered on his tongue.

We broke apart, breathing hard.

"Walk with me," he said. "I want to show you something."

I followed him across the slick stones. He halted at the edge of the strait, his eyes narrowed against the wind. The Bosporus spat saltwater onto his boots. He pointed across the water to a lighthouse on an island.

"The Maiden's Tower," he said. "Long ago, an oracle foretold that a beloved princess would die by snakebite on her eighteenth birthday. Her father, the sultan, built the tower to keep her safe. When she turned eighteen, the sultan gave her a basket of fruits. And of course, the story ends tragically, like all fairy tales."

"What kind of fairy tales have you heard?"

"The old ones they tell to scare children at night." His smile didn't touch his eyes. "When the princess ate the first fruit, she startled an asp hiding in the basket. One snakebite was enough. And she died in that very tower."

I shivered. "How morbid."

"There's another tower."

He curled his arm around my shoulders and turned me to the left. The heat of his body on mine accelerated my heartbeat. Wind buffeted us, a perfect excuse to press against him and shut my eyes.

"Look." His breath warmed my neck.

I opened my eyes. He pointed to a second, bigger island in the Bosporus. This island also had a tower, but it wasn't a lighthouse. It jutted from a fortress that braved the waves like a stone battleship.

"The Serpent's Tower," he said.

I shivered. "For the asp that killed the princess?"

"So the story goes, though you won't find any asps there. Only assassins."

Dread clenched my stomach. "The Order of the Asphodel?"

"Yes."

I turned in his arms. When the wind blew his hair across

319

his face, I smoothed it away, but his expression remained unreadable. My fingers traced his cheekbones. He was beautiful in such a heartbreaking way.

"You have me until nightfall," he murmured.

My stomach dropped. "Nightfall?"

"Yes." His throat worked as he swallowed hard. "I can't escape my destiny forever."

48

endel took me to the Grand Constantinople, a luxurious hotel which overlooked the Bosporus. Our boots rapped on the lobby's black marble floor. Gilded flourishes decorated the wallpaper in art nouveau style. White lilies perfumed the air with sweet spice. Porters bustled through with luggage, the Orient Express Airways label marking some of the suitcases.

Wendel booked us a room for one night. He slid an ungodly amount of money across the front desk to the concierge. Just how expensive was this place?

Wendel strolled away with the key. "Good news. I'm nearly bankrupt."

"You spent all your money?"

He brushed away my comment with his hand. "Remember? I wasn't planning on taking a cent to my grave."

I glared at him. "Don't joke about dying. I liked your idea to loot the Order better."

He grinned. "You remembered that plan."

God, he was cocky. I pried our room key out of his hand and bounded upstairs, my muscles tight with unspent energy. He followed at a more leisurely pace than me, making the climb look effortless with his long legs.

"Why did we bypass the tearoom?" he asked. "And the delicious Turkish Delight?"

When I glanced back at him, his poker face would have been perfect without the wicked glint in his eyes. "Teatime? That's your top priority?"

He shrugged. "Aren't you hungry?"

"Not for Turkish Delight."

He stepped toward me as if magnetized. "Oh?"

"You know what I want," I murmured.

He backed me against the door, caging me in his arms. I ducked under his arm and twisted the key in the lock. When I shoved open the door, we both stumbled over the threshold. Darkness shrouded the room.

He found a switch on the wall and flicked it on.

"Electric lights," he mused. "How modern."

I smirked. "Maybe I can read in bed."

He captured me in a kiss. We tumbled onto the bed together. He grunted, a hoarse satisfied sound. The weight of his body held down mine. The clean, masculine scent of his sweat wound desire tighter in my belly.

I shoved him away. "Get the door," I panted.

He lunged and closed it. The click of the lock made me shiver. I sat on the edge of the bed, the back of my knees pressed into the mattress.

"Lie down," I said.

Smirking, Wendel tried to kiss me, but he let me push him onto the bed. When I straddled him, the bulge of his cock jutted between my thighs. His eyes darkened as he stared up at me, his pupils blown with lust.

"Still feel like teatime?" I asked.

He rocked his hips, his cock grinding against me. "Still feel like reading in bed?"

"Only if you have books with fucking in them."

"Damn, I don't."

"Shame."

"It's a shame I'm not fucking you already."

Desire rasped in his voice. He traced my neck with kisses while I unbuttoned his shirt. I fumbled with the last button-hole until he simply yanked the shirt over his head. The button pinged off the window.

"Be careful," I teased. "You're bankrupt."

"Almost. And don't you prefer me naked?"

I laughed. "Could you be any cockier?"

"Easily."

He slid off the bed and unbuckled his belt. A wholly wicked smirk curved his mouth. "Is this cocky enough for you?"

His hand stroked his length and dragged out a glistening hint of arousal. Watching him, my heartbeat pounded between my legs.

I smirked back at him. "No such thing as too much cock."

When he hooked his fingers into my trousers, I tilted my hips upward to help him undress me. I shivered in the cool air.

"Last time..." He cleared his throat. "It was dangerous."

"I know."

His eyes darkened. "It was also bliss."

"Yes, it was."

A muscle flexed as he tightened his jaw. "We should be more careful this time."

"Of course. But..."

"Ardis." He growled my name. "Don't tempt me." His rough voice made me shiver.

"God," I said, "I missed your voice. It's like honey and gravel."

He arched his eyebrows. "Is it now?"

"Much better than your terrible handwriting," I teased.

He snorted. "I don't need that particular talent."

"You are extremely talented, but don't let that go to your head."

"It's going somewhere else entirely."

He rolled a preventive over his cock. When he climbed over me on the bed, he kissed my neck, but went no further.

"Ride me," he commanded.

He hooked his arm under my shoulder and rolled us both. He landed flat on his back, my knees on either side of his hips. I looked down at him, greedy for the sight of his long, dark eyelashes and kiss-swollen lips.

"You're so gorgeous," I said.

He arched an eyebrow. "Gorgeous?"

"Everything about you."

He pressed into me, demanding entrance, until I sank lower and took all of him. It was a perfect fit. A delicious ache pulsed through my pussy. He sucked in his breath, his cock throbbing, his eyes smoky with desire.

While I rode him, he started thrusting into me. Sweat glittering on his skin, he set a relentless rhythm. When he slowed, I ground against him and moaned out my frustration. It was too much—it wasn't enough.

"Touch yourself," he said. "I like to watch."

My fingers rubbed my clit. I tightened the muscles in my thighs. Pleasure built and built until it resembled pain.

I teetered on the edge of ecstasy.

"Come for me," he said.

Bliss shuddered through me and turned me boneless. Gasping, I tilted back my head and rode out wave after wave of pleasure.

He groaned deep in his throat. "I'm tempted to come."

"Don't." I smiled at him through my tumbling hair. "I'm not done with you yet."

"Have mercy."

I pinned down his wrists. "You can't escape now."

"Escape?" He feigned innocence, but he twisted one of his hands free and caressed my nipple. "Perhaps I should."

I laughed. "Don't make me tie you to the bed."

"No."

He froze beneath me, every muscle in his body stiffening. The raw fear in his eyes hit me like a blow to the gut. Of course.

He had been chained to the wall in the coffin factory, tortured for God knew how long.

"Fuck. I forgot. I'm sorry."

He clenched his jaw. "I believe you."

He pulled out, his erection fading fast, and took care of the preventive. Shame scorched my face. God, I had ruined our night together. I bent over him and kissed him, my hair curtaining his face. He stayed tense before relaxing into the kiss. The ice in his eyes melted.

"Ardis." He sighed against my lips. "I wish I..."

When I leaned back, he closed his eyes. Maybe he couldn't bear to look at me. "Yes?"

"I wish I weren't so broken," he whispered.

My heart ached for him. "We're all broken, one way or another."

I lay by him on the bed and rested my head on his chest. He held very still. He must have been trying hard not to feel.

His ribs heaved in a sigh. "How did you do it?"

"Do what?"

"Leave America. Leave it all behind."

"Honestly? I'm not sure I did. I can't stop missing my mother. Sometimes I dream of San Francisco, but then I remember home isn't home anymore."

He swallowed hard. "Are you happy?"

I answered without hesitation. "You make me happy."

"Do I?"

"Without a doubt."

His words quieted. "I don't deserve you."

"That's not true. When I found you bleeding in the snow, I

never expected I would feel this way about you, but you quickly proved me wrong."

His mouth twitched. "You thought I was an abomination."

"I did."

"I can't blame you." He smiled.

I kissed his cheek. "Tonight, you don't have to go alone."

His eyes shuttered, his emotions hidden again. "I won't let the Grandmaster hurt you."

I cleared my throat. "Let me talk to him. Before you—"

"No."

"But he's my father."

His voice chilled. "It's dangerous to assume he would show you any empathy because you're his daughter. That bastard is heartless."

"I had only one chance to talk to him before."

He frowned. "Wasn't it enough when he broke into our hotel room in Vienna? Why on earth would you seek him out?"

"Because I don't want him to hurt you. There has to be a future where nobody dies."

"Somebody always has to die."

"I refuse to believe that."

Darkness shadowed his eyes. "I'm a necromancer. Death is inevitable. Inescapable."

Dread plummeted through my stomach like a boulder. "You don't think you're coming back, do you? It's why you spent all your inheritance. It's why you spent one more evening with me in the hotel."

"I never denied it."

I let out a shuddering sigh. "Wendel, no."

"The Grandmaster is ruthless. It's obvious that he wishes to punish me for my defiance, and he may take this to its ultimate conclusion." He closed his eyes for a moment. "I can't promise not to die."

"If you die, I'm going to kill you."

He laughed. "Tonight might be our last night together."

"We can't let this be our last night."

"Let's make it unforgettable."

Even now, he didn't believe he could escape. He could only steal fragments of a life that wasn't his. He kissed me, his hands tangling in my hair. He still hadn't come yet, and I wanted to bring him pleasure.

I hooked my legs behind his hips. "Take what you want from me."

He reached across the bed, then rolled on another preventive. He held his cock in his fist, toying with me, before he penetrated me in one thrust.

When he fucked me, he fucked me hard.

Every stroke was ruthless, setting a punishing pace. I clung to him, the muscles in his body flexing beneath my hands. His breathing became ragged.

He needed this. Needed me.

A guttural groan tore from his throat. His hips jerked forward, desperate to take me even deeper, before his tension shattered and he shuddered. He came so hard that every pulse of his cock was obvious.

"I love you," he whispered against my neck.

But I couldn't confess how I felt. He smoothed my hair from my face. His gentle touch unlocked more of my emotions. It hurt to be so vulnerable with him. I wasn't just letting his body into mine, but letting him into my heart.

I love you.

The words died in my throat. I couldn't say it. Not when I couldn't save him.

49

ightfall. Wendel didn't leave, as he had promised,
but lingered at the Grand Constantinople.

We ate dinner in the hotel restaurant. A delicious dinner, no doubt, though it tasted like nothing but ashes in my mouth. I sipped water to wet my parched throat. Wendel divided his food into ever smaller pieces. I wasn't sure he had eaten more than a bite.

I put down my glass. "I wasn't joking about running to Switzerland."

He shrugged, nudging a pea around his plate. "Oh?"

"How about France? We could seek asylum there. Enemy of my enemy, you know."

"Not France." He flattened the pea beneath his knife. "I hate speaking French."

"How do you feel about England?"

He ate the pea. "Indifferent."

"Let's go to England. If we survive. No, *when* we survive."

"This might be my last supper." His smile was fleeting. "Maybe they will make a painting out of it. *The Last Supper of the Necromancer* sounds a bit ludicrous, don't you think? Anyway, I doubt anyone will give a damn."

I glared at him. "This isn't funny."

He was quiet for a long time. The clink of silverware on plates scratched at my nerves.

"Say something," I said. "Please. Don't be silent after—"

"I don't want to lose you."

His confession startled me. "Me? Why?"

"I would rather die than let the Grandmaster hurt you."

"Wendel..." I didn't know what to say.

He flagged down the waiter. "Check, please?"

My stomach somersaulted. It was time. He paid for our dinner, with what might have been his last coins, then stood and pulled out my chair.

"You don't have to come with me," he said.

"No." I gripped his arm. "Hell no."

He pried my fingers from his arm. "Then let's go."

When Wendel walked from the restaurant, I followed at his heels. I was afraid that if I fell behind, he wouldn't wait for me to catch up. Together we strode through the twisting nocturnal streets of Constantinople.

"Where are we going?" I asked.

"The Galata Bridge."

"Why?"

"To find a boat."

The waters of the Bosporus glittered like a thousand silver

coins beneath the moonrise. The spire of the Maiden's Tower soared against the opposite bank. Not too far away, far too close, the Serpent's Tower loomed.

I felt sick. I tasted acid creeping from my stomach.

Fishermen lined the Galata Bridge, casting their lures into the rippling of reflected lights. Wendel surveyed them before he shouted in Turkish. One of the fishermen stepped forward. Wendel dropped coins into the man's hand. Gold coins, I noted, which seemed like a steep price to ferry us across to the Serpent's Tower.

"His boat is ours," Wendel said.

My eyes widened. "You bought the boat?"

"To come back."

Thank fuck he thought we would return.

The fisherman trotted down the Galata Bridge to the bank. A sleek little skiff bobbed in the water. I climbed in and clung to the sides of the boat. Wendel sat in the back, shoved off from the bank, and started rowing.

Waves slapped against the sides of the boat as we advanced on the Serpent's Tower. Lights glinted through the narrow windows of the fortress. Scrubby pine trees clung to the rocky island, the only cover besides boulders.

Almost there.

The bottom of the boat scraped along the gravel beach. Wendel jumped out and steadied the boat for me to disembark. I helped him drag the skiff onto the beach, and we hid it under the branches of a pine tree.

Moonlight shone on his pale face and highlighted the hard set of his jaw. "At the very top of the Serpent's Tower, we should find the Grandmaster."

"What's our strategy?"

The muscles in his neck tightened. "You want to talk with the Grandmaster?"

"Let me try."

"If he touches you, I will kill him."

His cold confidence shook me. "What about the assassins?"

He held out his hands as if weighing our options. "We kill anyone who tries to stop us. We have no other choice."

"I hate it when you're right."

He slipped his hand behind my neck, glanced into my eyes, and dragged me into a kiss. His necromancy knocked the breath out of me. Icy fire swirled over my skin and curled deep into the marrow of my bones.

I gasped. "What—?"

"Stay with me. No matter what happens."

"I will."

"Take my hand."

I twisted my fingers with his, feeling the strange sensation of his magic still tingling in my ribcage. When he drew his black dagger, Amarant's shadows cloaked us both. Silently, we strode toward the Serpent's Tower.

"All the doors will be locked," he muttered.

"What do we do?"

"He's our key." He pointed to a guard patrolling the fortress perimeter. "Stay here."

I dropped behind a boulder as the shadows faded from my skin. Wendel ran ahead, all but invisible, and disappeared into the darkness. The guard staggered, then straightened and continued his circuit around the tower. Moonlight caught him as he walked. Blood darkened the back of his cloak.

Damn, that was grimly efficient.

The dead man lingered at the foot of the fortress. He stopped by an arched door and rapped against the wood. Straining to hear, I caught some muttered Turkish on the wind. It might have been the dead man.

Light sliced the darkness as the door opened.

The dead man sidestepped. A shadow whisked past him. A strangled gasp preceded silence. I froze behind the boulder, my heartbeat thundering, and gripped the hilt of Chun Yi. Footsteps crunched the gravel.

"Ardis." It was Wendel.

His hand locked with mine. His fingers were smeared with the slick heat of blood. The shadows of his dagger clouded my vision, nearly suffocating.

"Ready?" he asked.

"Yes," I said, even though it was a lie.

We ran to the door and ducked into a small, bare room carved from stone. Kerosene lamplight flickered in the empty eyes of the two dead men waiting for us there.

Wendel clenched my hand so hard, I almost didn't realize he was shaking. Badly.

"You're hurting me," I whispered.

He released me. "Sorry."

"Where are we?"

"The western wing of the fortress." He jerked his chin toward a door on their right. "We head through that door, go down a corridor, and hit the bottom of the tower itself. Six flights of stairs to the top."

"How many assassins?" I asked.

"I don't know. Dozens?"

"Great." I stepped forward. "Let's find out."

He stopped me with a hand on my chest. "Allow me." When he snapped his fingers, the dead men flanked the door. "Locked?"

"Yes," one of the dead men said, his hollow voice startling me.

"Do you have the key?" Wendel asked.

"Yes."

"Then unlock it. Kill anyone you find." He glanced at me. "And keep her safe."

Undead bodyguards? That was unsettling.

The dead man who had spoken fumbled with a key, unlocked the door, and marched through with his companion.

"Wait." Wendel stopped me from following. A minute later, he flinched, his eyes distant. "My minions have company."

"How...?"

"I can feel it. Better help them out before they get beheaded."

He disappeared into the shadows. When I drew my sword, flames blazed down Chun Yi. I stepped through the doorway and into a fight. An assassin hacked at the neck of a dead man, his teeth bared, while the other dead man lunged with a clumsy sword blow. The assassin blocked him with his shield.

I thrust my sword into the assassin's chest.

He staggered, his eyes wide with shock, and I wrenched my

blade free. When I flicked my wrist, blood splattered on the wall. The assassin collapsed on the stones. Crimson pooled beneath his body as he choked, his dying breath a gurgling one. My sword burned, flames whispering of its thirst.

"Wendel?" I frowned. "This feels too easy. Like it's a trap."

"I don't care."

He stepped from the shadows. He crouched by the assassin, touched his wrist, and raised him from the dead. We ran down the corridor and reached the bottom of a spiral staircase. Footsteps pounded behind us.

"Reinforcements," Wendel said.

His undead men raised their scimitars and shambled down the corridor.

Wendel didn't wait for the fight. He hit the stairs running. I lowered my head and lunged after him. The clash of steel on steel echoed off the stone behind them. Hopefully his minions would buy us enough time.

Six flights to the top. Six stories of winding around and around until I was disoriented.

Footsteps chased us upstairs. Breathing hard, I stopped and whirled around. Assassins. Two of them, armed with scimitars and shields. I had no room to draw my sword, so I kicked one of them square in the chest.

The assassin staggered backward. I pressed my advantage and kicked him in the face. My heel hit his nose. His head snapped back as he flew down the stairs. The assassin standing below tumbled down with him. They collapsed at awkward angles on the steps, but they were still groaning. Not dead yet.

Wendel squeezed past me and swooped on the fallen assassins. He sliced open their throats with his dagger and let them bleed out. Crimson trickled down the stairs in rivulets. He waited only long enough to revive them with his necromancy. His minions staggered upright and waited for his command.

"Nobody gets past you alive," Wendel commanded. "And try not to lose your heads."

I shuddered at the icy disdain in his voice. Outside, beyond the windows, the wind carried the wingbeats and cawing of crows.

Wendel met my gaze. "Almost there."

His eyes blazed with conviction and certainty of the end. He started running again. I chased him higher and higher. My heartbeat thundered. At the top of the tower, we stopped outside a door and shared a glance.

"Talk to him," he whispered. "I will protect you. If he tries to hurt you..."

He didn't need to finish his thought. We both understood damn well what he meant.

Shadows crawled over his skin while he disappeared into darkness. I grabbed the door handle, the iron cold beneath my sweaty palm, before I yanked it open.

Candles flickered in lanterns. Plush Turkish rugs yielded beneath my boots. Across the room, a magnificent mahogany desk dominated the space beneath the windows.

His desk.

Thorsten Magnusson. The Grandmaster.

"You shouldn't be here, Ardis."

50

F ear poured through my veins and froze my blood to
ice, but I pretended to be brave.

"You asked me to join you," I said.

"Not like this." The Grandmaster's eyes looked dead in the
candlelight. "Not with the Prince of the Undying ready to stab
me in the back."

"I want you to let Wendel go."

The Grandmaster's mechanical laugh raised goosebumps
on my skin. "I had hoped you would help me. That you could
convince Wendel to return willingly and fulfill his destiny with
the Order of the Asphodel."

I clenched my hands, being careful to keep them away from
my sword. "His destiny?"

"To be my prodigy."

A shiver crawled down my spine. "You hurt him, ever since
he was just a boy, for years. I can't even imagine the cruelty he's

had to endure."

"Wendel considers cruelty an old friend. He slaughtered so many of my good men, I didn't even bother with assassins tonight. I hired some mercenaries as fodder to keep up appearances. No offense, Ardis."

Wendel crept from shadow to shadow, trapped by the pools of candlelight. The Grandmaster hadn't located him yet.

My stomach soured. "Those men didn't deserve to die."

"Pity." The Grandmaster lowered his gaze. His pen scratched across the paper on his desk. "Perhaps you shouldn't have killed them. I would have welcomed you both here with open arms, had you only asked."

"Welcomed? You mean tortured." I bared the long scars on my wrists, remembering my agony. "Your technomancer, Hieronymus, did this to me."

"Because you dared to be defiant." The Grandmaster dotted a sentence with a period. "Are you finished? This letter is of a time sensitive nature."

I challenged him with my stare. "A letter to who?"

"Whom."

I gritted my teeth. "Don't mock me."

Wendel spoke from the shadows. "He's telling the Russians about Project Lazarus. Betraying the Archmages of Vienna."

The Grandmaster put down his pen. "How far you have fallen. Wasting Amarant's magic to cower in the shadows and read over my shoulder."

He was trying to bait Wendel into attacking, wasn't he? I stalled for time.

"Why would you betray the archmages?" I asked.

"This isn't betrayal." The Grandmaster steepled his fingers. "War is good for business."

I snatched the letter from the desk. Before I could tear it in half, the Grandmaster caught me by the wrist and clenched my bones in an iron grip.

"Stop. Ruin this one, and I will have to start again."

"Don't touch her," Wendel said.

"Or what?" the Grandmaster said. "You will kill me? Aren't you tired of that threat?"

My knees wobbled, threatening to buckle under me, but I locked my legs. "Thorsten Magnusson, I wish I never found out you were my father."

He twisted my wrist. I gasped at the pain.

I spotted a silver paper knife. When he glanced away, I grabbed it and stabbed him. He blocked me with his arm, jerked back, and yanked the paper knife from his flesh. He wiped the blood on his sleeve.

"That was a mistake," he said.

I drew my sword and steeled my nerves.

I dodged his attack. His knife scraped down the length of my blade. He shoved my sword away, but I recognized this disarming move. When he reached for my sword's pommel with his free hand, I caught his wrist and twisted it aside. I didn't counterattack, too wary of his skill, and retreated instead.

Crouching, he slashed at me, his movements like lightning. I sidestepped and swung at his ribs. He was fast, but not fast enough. Chun Yi raked his ribs and blazed at the taste of blood. He touched his wound, little more than a scratch, and glanced at his red fingers. He arched his eyebrows and shook his head.

"Impressive," he said. "You show promise."

"Don't fucking try to father me," I replied.

The Grandmaster stabbed at me again.

Shadows rippled behind us. Wendel swooped from the darkness like an angel of death. The black dagger glinted in the candlelight an instant before he attacked. He aimed the dagger for his enemy's neck.

The Grandmaster blocked barehanded. He knocked Wendel's wrist aside and followed with a brutal elbow to the face. The shadows vanished from Wendel as he staggered back. He bared his bloodstained teeth.

"I'm warning you once," Wendel said. "Touch her again and you die."

"What does she mean to you?" asked the Grandmaster.

"I swore an undying vow to protect her."

"No." He tilted his head. "It's more than that, isn't it?"

My sword's thirst pounded like a deafening heartbeat in my ears. More. It wanted more. I would pay for my victory with blood.

I swung at the Grandmaster's legs, trying to hamstring him. When he danced back, I swung again to keep him on the defensive. He blocked my sword with his knife and hooked his foot behind mine. I crashed on the floor. The Grandmaster kicked me savagely in the ribs and wrenched my sword from my hand.

Winded, I curled on the floor and sucked in air. My eyes watered from the pain.

A feral snarl tore from Wendel's throat. "No."

He hurled a chair at a window. Shattered glass tinkled on the ground. Wind whirled inside the tower and all the candles in the lanterns spluttered out. Darkness flooded the room, brightened only by Chun Yi's burning.

The Grandmaster stood in the center of the room. He held the sword like a firebrand. "Why didn't you think of that sooner? Losing your touch?"

Wisely, Wendel kept quiet.

I crawled to my feet and clutched my aching ribs. Through the broken window, the sound of crows swelled. They flew against the moonlit clouds. Black birds swirled around the tower like ink circling a drain.

"I want my dagger back." The Grandmaster slid his foot forward. "It isn't worth as much to me as you, Wendel, but it will have to be my consolation prize."

I backed into a lantern. Brass. I tested its weight.

Too focused on Wendel, the Grandmaster missed the lantern arcing through the air. I hit him in the skull with the sickening gong of metal against bone. He staggered forward and drove the sword into the carpet to keep himself from falling. Triumph surged through me, and I hefted the lantern to smash him harder.

The Grandmaster whirled with blinding reflexes.

He dodged the lantern and twisted my wrist, hard enough that pain shot through my bones. I fell so he wouldn't break my arm. The Grandmaster hurled the lantern through a window, the glass chiming as it broke.

Wendel lunged to stab him in the back. The Grandmaster twisted, taking the blade in his shoulder instead, and dragged the dagger with him. With a sharp jerk, he yanked the weapon from Wendel's hand.

The Grandmaster had disarmed us both.

"Don't hurt her." Wendel reached out to me. He was shaking, his own blood turning his spit pink as he spoke. "Torture me, kill me, take me back for your sick games. I don't care what you do to me, just let her go."

"You betrayed me." The Grandmaster's eyes burned with fury. "I took you under my wing. Fed you, sheltered you, taught you, when your own family had abandoned you. Do you know who you were before me?"

Wendel's face twisted. "What?"

"Nothing. I shaped you into the Prince of the Undying."

"You think you saved me?" Wendel whispered.

"And yet you remain ungrateful."

Something shattered in Wendel's eyes.

He dove to the ground and rolled through the fragments of glass. He skidded under the sword, flipped to his feet, and yanked the black dagger from the Grandmaster's back. With a vicious grin, the Grandmaster counterattacked.

Wendel blocked the sword with his dagger. The Grandmaster feinted left, lunged right, and torqued Wendel's wrist.

They struggled for control of the dagger.

The blade sank into Wendel's heart.

Wendel staggered back, his lips parted, his hands finding the dagger between his ribs. He wrenched it out and stared at the bloody steel like he couldn't believe he had been mortally stabbed by his own blade.

Wendel coughed. "What—?"

He didn't seem to think he was dying.

51

I couldn't find the air to scream. I stood paralyzed.

The Grandmaster pried the black dagger from Wendel's fingers, then grabbed the lapels of his coat to keep him from falling. A river of blood poured from the wound between Wendel's ribs. Too much blood loss to survive.

The Grandmaster locked gazes with him. "Such a shame this is goodbye."

My paralysis shattered. "Wendel!"

Wendel looked into my eyes, his own so vivid with the clarity of pain that I didn't think I would ever forget them.

He tried to speak. I thought he said, "Ardis."

The Grandmaster dragged him to the broken window and threw him into the night.

I ran to the window and clung to the edge, the shattered glass cutting into my hands, the wind flinging my hair into my eyes.

I watched Wendel fall.

Six stories down, where he landed on the rocks below.

A wave curled onto the island and washed over Wendel. When it retreated, he was gone. Dragged into the dark water.

A scream tore from my throat and left it raw. "Wendel!"

The Grandmaster held my sword out to me. For a moment, I thought he was giving it back to me, but he dropped it out the window. Chun Yi plummeted down to the ground and clattered on the dark rocks.

My heartbeat sounded distant in my ears. My body belonged to someone else.

"Go," said the Grandmaster. "Return when you are ready, my daughter."

I ran downstairs, my feet flying. As I spiraled down the Serpent's Tower, I stumbled over the bodies of the mercenaries we had killed, the undead men that Wendel had commanded. They lay like discarded dolls, no longer controlled by necromancy. Outside the windows, there was the incessant cacophony of crows.

The crows. They would find Wendel.

I fled from the Serpent's Tower. No assassins or mercenaries stood in my way.

I ran faster, gasping for breath, and zigzagged along the island until I found a murder of crows perched at the edge of the water. Their hoarse cawing seesawed through the dank air. Crows gathered on the ground in a mass of black. They scattered into flight as I approached, and revealed a man on the rocks.

Wendel.

He was face down, one arm flung forward. I knelt beside him and grabbed his arm, grimacing at his sleeve soaked in blood. When I rolled him over, he stared past me at the sky, and his eyes reflected the stars.

He did not blink.

"Wendel?"

My voice sounded harsh in my ears. I wiped my bloody hand on my knee.

"No," I said. "You can't. You—you're a necromancer. You're the Prince of the Undying."

Our words from the first day we met echoed in my head.

"When a necromancer dies, does he die like a normal man?"

"God," he said, "I hope so."

My heart crumpled. His wish had been fulfilled.

I could barely find the strength to breathe. I couldn't look at him any longer, but I was terrified to look away. It was as if he might vanish, as if I might have never met him, as if I might have never fallen for him.

"Wendel," I sobbed. "I love you."

I hadn't said it until tonight, the only night it didn't matter.

I bent over him, my tears falling onto his face, and kissed him. His lips were cold against mine, but his skin still shivered with the icy fire of necromancy. Gasping, I jerked back and felt his neck for a pulse.

Wendel had no heartbeat.

But if he was dead, then why did his necromancy burn under my fingertips? Why was it growing stronger with my heartbeat? I shuddered at the intensity of magic. My fingers curled involuntarily around his neck.

A heartbeat thumped against my fingertips.

Wendel coughed, seawater spilling from his mouth. It jolted me into action. I grabbed his shoulder and rolled him onto his side. He coughed and coughed, his hands splayed on the rocks, until he sucked in a rattling breath. Then he coughed some more, even though his lungs had to be empty.

"Wendel?" I whispered.

I was afraid to touch him again. What had he become?

He turned his head. His face still looked as pale as death, but his green eyes glittered. "Ardis," he rasped. "I'm back."

"Are you—alive?"

He squinted. "Apparently."

He crawled to his hands and knees. He tried to stand, but he staggered and nearly fell. I caught his arm.

He certainly *felt* alive. Cold and wet, but alive.

"We need to run," he said, "before the Grandmaster realizes I'm not dead."

I glanced at the Serpent's Tower. "Oh, God. You're right."

Wendel's teeth had started chattering. He leaned heavily on me as we walked, his legs stiff, his arms shaking.

"How are you alive?" I asked.

"Necromancy."

My skin crawled. "Are you undead?"

"No."

I spotted the skiff where we had left it, hidden under the branches of a pine tree. I hurried to uncover the boat. The shadow of the Serpent's Tower still reached this far, and it was making me sick with fear.

"Almost free," I said, to convince myself more than anyone.

I dragged the skiff to the water and helped Wendel into the boat. I shoved off and climbed in after him. As I rowed from the island, a giddying tide of hope washed over me. I rowed farther and farther from the Serpent's Tower, until my arms burned, then let the skiff drift in the waters of the Bosporus.

"Ardis," Wendel said. "Thank you for saving me. Again."

I smiled, my eyes blurring. "Let's not make it a habit."

He returned my smile, then reached across the boat and clasped my hands. His skin didn't feel quite so icy, but he was shivering.

His gaze locked onto the Serpent's Tower. "He won."

My fingers tightened around his. "He hasn't defeated us. Not yet. The Grandmaster tops my list of people who need murdering."

"We can't go back." He searched my eyes. "It's too dangerous."

"The Grandmaster beat us this time, but he won't win twice."

His thumbs stroked my knuckles. "There's always Switzerland. Somewhere as far away from assassins and archmages as possible."

"You just want to walk away? After everything you have lost?"

"I can't risk losing you."

I shook my head in wonder and disbelief. "Wendel, I already lost you."

"I'm amazed that gamble worked."

"What gamble?"

"Lending you my necromancy."

"You—what?"

He bowed his head. "Before the Serpent's Tower, when I kissed you."

"I don't understand."

"Half of me thought I would be weakening myself for nothing, but half of me hoped that the stories were true."

My heartbeat skipped. "What stories?"

"When you asked me what happens to necromancers when they die, that afternoon on the train, I may have lied to you. I have read stories about necromancers, over the centuries, who cheated death."

My jaw dropped. "You knew?" I wasn't sure if I wanted to kiss him or smack him.

"Nearly all the necromancers died and stayed dead, though, because they never understood the secret."

"What secret?"

Sorrow twisted his smile. "Someone had to allow necromancy into their body and love the necromancer enough to bring them back."

"But what if you were wrong?"

"I figured that if you didn't love me, it wasn't worth coming back."

His words broke my heart. I kissed him, my hands cradling his face, and his tears streaked his cheeks. We held each other beneath the stars while the waves gently rocked us in this dark and unknown night.

We were together. We were alive.

"Of course I love you." I whispered my confession and kissed him again.

He smiled against my mouth. "I was right."

ACKNOWLEDGMENTS

- Asa Hurst, my long-suffering husband, for cooking endless dinners and answering endless questions.
- Chelsea Campbell, author and partner in crime, for hours of scheming over coffee.
- Regina Barber, for brainstorming story ideas when we were supposed to be studying Chinese and Calculus.
- Talya Garman, for sending emails full of exclamation marks and *Supernatural* GIFs.

Special thanks to these Kickstarter backers, who generously allowed me to steal their names in exchange for glory:

- Carol Swindaman
- Dean Vigoren
- Maili Weissman

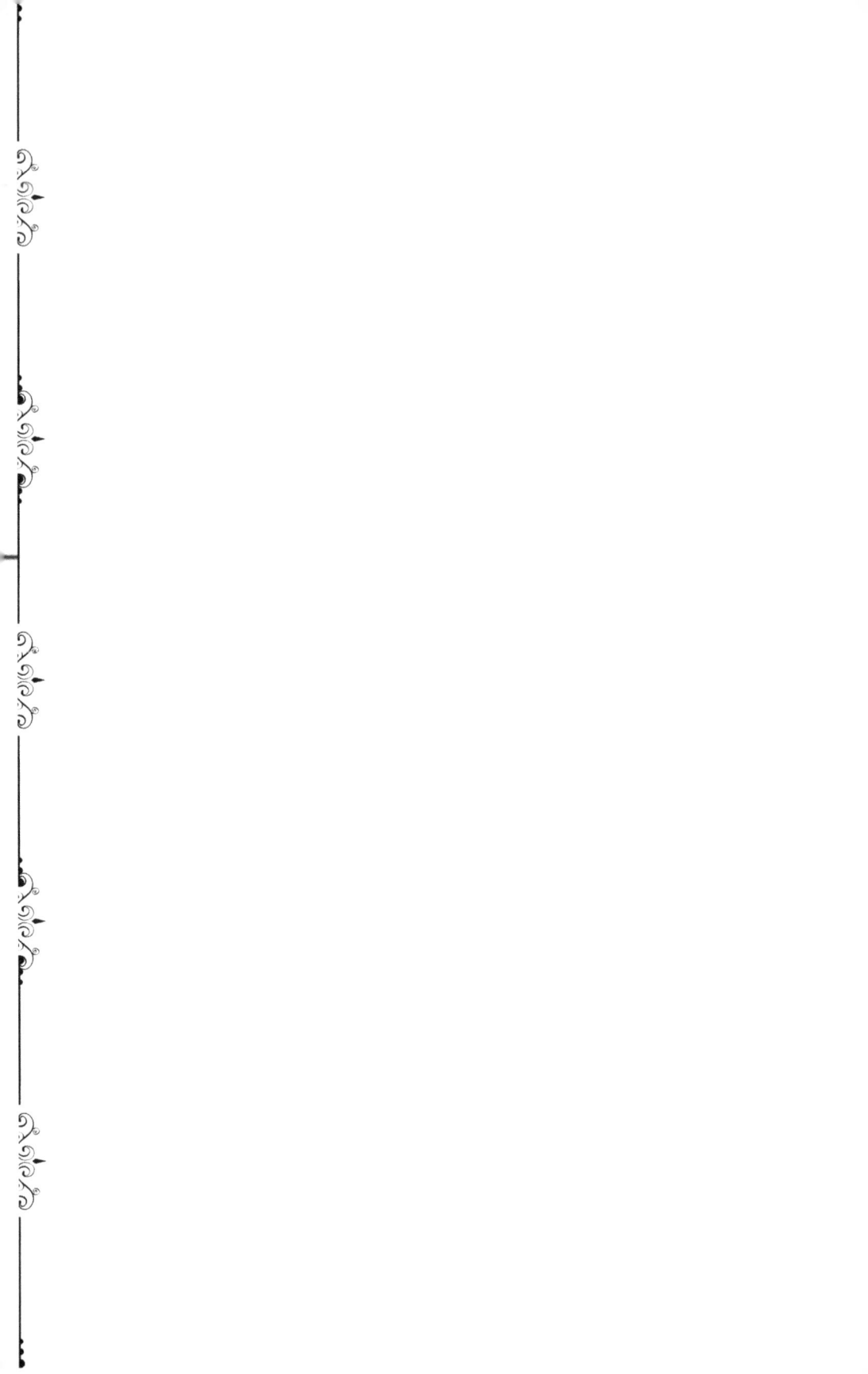

AUTHOR BIO

Karen Kincy writes books when she isn't writing code. She has a BA in Linguistics and Literature from The Evergreen State College, and an MS in Computational Linguistics from the University of Washington.

Find Karen online at:
    www.karenkincy.com
    www.facebook.com/KarenKincyAuthor
    www.twitter.com/karenkincy

More by Karen Kincy

FANTASY ROMANCE
Demonic Prince

YOUNG ADULT FANTASY
Dragon by Midnight

YOUNG ADULT PARANORMAL
Other
Foxfire
Bloodborn

Milton Keynes UK
Ingram Content Group UK Ltd.
UKHW010034300124
436936UK00017B/448/J

9 781737 925163